# NEITHER SAFE NOR SORRY

K. MCCRAE

K. MCCRAE BOOKS

First published 2020

Copyright © K. McCrae, 2020
All rights reserved

The moral right of the author has been asserted

ISBN: 978-1-8380322-1-0 (Paperback)
ISBN: 978-1-8380322-0-3 (eBook)

All characters and events in this publication are fictitious, and any resemblance to actual persons, living or dead, is purely coincidental.

# 1

'Who dat, Daddy?'

Nick Garrett faltered as he tried to fasten the safety belt of his son's car seat. He didn't need to turn and look. He could feel eyes boring into him as a dark blue metallic mass crept through his peripheral vision like a predatory beast. Making its presence known just enough to instil fear into its victim. A low rumble emanated from the car engine like an underlying growl. He thought he had managed to sneak away without being seen, but now he must focus on his son. He couldn't show any sign of panic to Chris.

'Oh, that's just someone from work,' Nick said. His voice as calm and playful as he could manage. The seat belt finally came together with a comforting clunk. 'Now, let's get home to Mummy,' he said and gave Chris a kiss on his forehead. 'Eww, you're all sweaty. You've had fun this afternoon, haven't you?'

Chris immediately began kicking his dangling legs with excitement. Words erupted from his mouth as though one long continuous word. Nick, too preoccupied to listen, answered with the occasional uh-huh in random places as he lurched into the driver's seat and started the engine. His effort to act casual only betrayed by his trembling hands. It was impossible to push out of his mind what he had seen only half hour ago.

He pulled away from the curb and watched in the rear-view mirror as the predatory car pulled out from its parking spot. He squinted at the main beam's reflection, dazzling him as they followed him around each corner, never out of sight.

Chris' excited babbling had faded into the background.

*Call the police as soon as I get home,* Nick thought. His heart thumping hard. *I can't risk a confrontation with Chris around. This must mean that—*

'Daddy, Daddy.'

Nick was jolted from his thoughts.

'Lef' my cake. I wan' cake.'

'We don't have time to get cake now,' Nick said impatiently.

'I wan' cake.' Chris began crying noisily. That tearless cry that occurs whenever a child doesn't get his own way.

'Shut up,' Nick shouted. Immediately he was furious with himself. He never spoke to Chris like that. Though also relieved that his sternness had worked. Chris suddenly went silent.

Nick manoeuvred his way through the dark country roads while a quiet whimper came from the back seat. Panic slowly rose in the ominous silence. His foot became heavy on the accelerator.

The streetlights' glow from the edge of town consoled him a little. The deserted roads of the quiet countryside that he had come to love, now only brought isolation. The familiar trees, fields and bushes flashed past unseen. The car's headlights only lighting the briefest of areas ahead before he raced into each with more blind faith than care. The headlights behind him edged closer until they seemed to disappear. They were now below his mirror's reflection.

Nick realised the car was no more than a couple of metres

away. Suddenly a roar came from behind and the car jolted hard.

'Shit,' Nick exclaimed before he could even try to stop the word escaping.

Chris' whimpering stopped for a moment. A brief eerie silence before his voice came again, but this time as a scream.

Nick pressed his foot down harder on the accelerator. 'We'll be home soon.'

He tried to sound reassuring through his sudden tears.

The second hit from behind was more forceful. Nick's sweaty, shaking hands lost control of the steering wheel and sheer panic set in. Chris' screams were the last thing he heard as the car juddered over the grassy bank at the side of the road. The line of large, sinister trees beyond the bank were the last thing he saw as they lit up briefly in front of him before the fatal impact.

Flames towered. First from the engine. Moments later came the explosion.

∼

**Eight Months Later**

'I need these typed up immediately and bring them through for signing as soon as you are done.'

Eleanor Garrett, who was used to Miss Osbourne's sharp demands, was already typing up a report that she had been given that morning, also needing to be done immediately. Motionless for a moment, her shoulders slightly hunched, she sat staring at the small pile of mini cassettes that had just been deposited on her desk. Such an old-fashioned method, but an effective one that worked well for them. She turned to gaze out the window at the dark, purple rain clouds that had been threatening all morning. Mother Nature creating a harsh contrast with the bright modern office, though notably attuned to Eleanor's heavy spirit.

*Everything is important, and everything needs to be done immediately,* Eleanor thought to herself. *What a shame I only have two hands, or maybe she hasn't noticed.*

Eleanor smiled slightly as she brought up an image of herself in her mind sitting at her desk with waving octopus tentacles. Shuffling papers to her left, flicking through files to her right, and of course, typing up the latest urgent document in front of her. Turning back to her desk the sight of the pile of mini cassettes brought her back to reality. She pushed them to one side, stretched her back and shoulders, and continued with the report.

Miss Osbourne had left the small office as fast as she had entered it leaving her eau de expensive perfume and air of self-importance trailing behind her. From the moment Eleanor had walked in the door that morning, before she had even had a chance to remove her coat and trainers, and put her heels on, Miss Osbourne had thrust a pile of documents into her hands.

'It's important,' she'd said. 'I need them ASAP.'

Eleanor's imagination immediately seized the opportunity and Miss Osbourne took on the characteristics of Minnie Mouse. She spoke high-pitched and child-like. Her tailored, navy skirt-suit and vivid orange blouse became a red and white polka-dot dress, complete with the full circle skirt. Large round black ears appeared from the top of her head.

'And don't forget Mr Saunders' report, I need it on my desk ASAP,' came Miss Osbourne's voice from her office doorway.

But it was Minnie Mouse Eleanor heard, *Hey, Mickey. Maybe all the children at home will be able to help us with this very important report. We don't want to let Mr Saunders down now, do we?*

Eleanor forced herself back into reality and settled down to work. Ten minutes after Miss Osbourne's latest interruption, she left her office and announced that she was leaving for her lunch. Eleanor knew it would be no more than thirty seconds until Gina and Marie passed her door for lunch too. Their laughter erupted through her door as they exited their office and strolled past. Gina's tight giggle, and Marie's over-enthusiastic exuberance. Although probably something irrelevant Eleanor always sensed their laughter was about her.

They didn't like her clothes. Her suits were deemed old-fashioned and bland. Whereas, Gina and Marie were constantly comparing their latest buys.

They didn't like her hair. Tied back in a ponytail. Smart and out of the way. Practical. Marie's hair was thick with dark brown, wavy locks. She had film-star looks and a Marilyn Monroe figure. Gina was more modern in her appearance. The antithesis of Marie with her short white hair, thick black eye make-up and thin boyish figure. An unmitigated mismatch as the two made their way, arm in arm, across the wide hallway toward the lift directly opposite Eleanor's office. Their hip-swaying walk, their figure-hugging - rather too revealing - outfits could have been considered glamorous. They clearly viewed themselves highly eligible, but Eleanor saw them as a female representation of Laurel and Hardy. She had to admit that Marie looked nothing like Oliver Hardy, but Gina sure made a good Stan Laurel being tall, skinny and with sticky up hair. Therefore, it was only logical that Marie must be Hardy.

However, there was a problem when it came to their shoes. They still wore their four-inch heels under the masculine suits that had been created in Eleanor's head, due to an overheard conversation one day.

'... seen her when she wears them with that navy-blue pencil skirt? It is just horrendous.'

Eleanor had been exiting the toilets and stopped with a jolt. The high-pitched exaggerated laughter of Marie came from outside in the hallway.

'They make her feet stick out like clown's shoes.' The clunk of the chocolate machine, which sat just outside in the hallway, could be heard over Gina's horror-stricken squeals.

'Surely, she could at least buy some new ones, they must be at least two, maybe even three years old,' said Marie with disgust.

'Maybe we should club together and buy her some new ones for her birthday.'

'Not likely,' replied Marie. 'I don't do this job to fund her lack of style, thank you very much. Her inadequacies are endless. You may start with her footwear, but then where does it end?'

Thoughts had started flying around Eleanor's head like a whirlwind as she realised her trainers were the source of their amusement. *I don't wear them for work. It's just for the journey. How can anyone wear those lethal weapons when rushing for the train?* She subconsciously reached for the beads of her bracelet, and the door closed quietly in front of her. Her breathing became shallow and laboured as she struggled for air. The energy drained from her body and she slumped against the wall. She twisted the smooth, solid beads of her bracelet between her fingers, but this did not stop the familiar knot appearing in her stomach. Her skin began to crawl as she became overwhelmed with the images that flashed in her mind.

She squeezed the beads harder.

An echo of two police officers standing at her front door, perpetually haunting her. Such sadness on their faces only reserved for the worst grief. She knew why they were there, just from that look. A hazy memory of her coffee mug as it slipped from her fingers and crashed to the floor, hitting the carpet only moments before she had joined it herself.

*The beads. Think about the beads.* Her fingers searched for the one bead that had somehow escaped the smoothing process in the factory. She squeezed so hard its sharp edges cut into her. She focused on the biting pain in her fingers. The pain of reality bringing her back to the here and now. A noiseless cry emanating from her throat.

Eleanor stumbled back to one of the basins and threw cold water over her face. She leant against the basin and waited for her legs to regain some strength. *When will it stop? Please stop.*

She had taken her time composing herself. No matter what she went through, she could not let the others see. They saw her fiddling with her bracelet, but that could be the same for anyone. Some play with their hair, others bite their nails, just another nervous habit. That in itself wouldn't be enough to make them suspect. A few more deep breaths and she could face the world again.

The hallway was quiet. Feeling stronger she marched down to Gina and Marie's office intent on explaining to them that heels were just too impractical. Surely, they would understand that. She stopped just short of their office door. A sickness rose in her stomach and her throat tightened. She grabbed hold of the sides of her skirt and tried to dry her perspiring hands. She couldn't go in. She just couldn't do it. She had lowered her head so far forward her chin almost touched her chest, and she had walked as fast as she could past their door into her own office. Ever since that moment Laurel and Hardy always wore four-inch heels.

~

Lunchtime, the most peaceful time of the day to get work done. Eleanor usually brought in a sandwich for her lunch and would often sit at her desk to eat while continuing with her work. No interruptions from Miss Osbourne or Gina and Marie. Besides, it kept her mind busy. A good thing as far as she was concerned.

Important clients were arriving this afternoon and so everything had to be done before they arrived, which meant immediately. When Mr Saunders and Mr Pearson arrived at three thirty the usual bustling about proceeded. Eleanor was ordered to make one black coffee and two teas with milk and, of course, for important clients such as Mr Saunders, biscuits to accompany their drinks were a must. Once Eleanor had delivered the tray to Miss Osbourne's office, she returned to her desk, keeping her mind occupied with house deeds, mortgage offers, and contracts.

Five o'clock arrived and the meeting in Miss Osbourne's office was still in full discussion. Eleanor knew it would be a while yet before Mr Saunders would be allowed to leave. His good-looks, successful business, and recent break-up of his marriage made him highly eligible in Miss Osbourne's eyes. Eleanor pushed her chair back from her desk and slipped her shoes off with her toes. A last glance out the window showed the afternoon's rain had stopped and the sky looked a little brighter. Gina and Marie were tottering around their office noisily, eager to leave and make their way to one of the local wine bars for the evening, as was their usual custom.

*Which one will it be tonight?* Eleanor thought. She watched as they walked past her door, paying particular attention to their four-inch heels. She looked down at her grubby, old trainers and smiled to herself. *Fashion, or comfort and practicality? There's just no competition.*

~

The trains were packed as usual for Eleanor's journey home. She was pushed and shoved as usual, and she had to stand for most of the journey, as usual. Then the rain started again just two minutes before she arrived at her station. Autumn was a troublesome season. It wasn't yet cold enough for her winter coat, but her thin, cotton summer coat did nothing to protect her from the heavier rains. By the time she had walked the eight minutes to reach home she was sodden. Her trainers squelched with every footstep and she envisaged herself as a large fish walking on her tail fins and sloshing her way up the driveway.

Before Eleanor reached her front door a woman in a pale-blue uniform appeared from behind it. She hurriedly beckoned Eleanor in holding open a small dark-green hand-towel. She immediately started fussing over Eleanor as though she were a young child.

'Come here, come here, lassie. You'll catch your death,' she said in a brusque Scottish accent.

'Thanks Aileen,' replied Eleanor. 'You're a star.'

'Aye, that I am. Now, get that coat off your back. It's wringing.'

Although Aileen was employed to look after Eleanor's mother, caring was more than just a job. In her late fifties, and, unfortunately, never able to have children of her own, Eleanor often felt that all the love and care she would have given her own child was now projected onto her and her mother.

'How has she been today?' Eleanor asked as she went through the daily ritual of hanging her coat on the hook, tucking her trainers under the stairs, and pulling out her hair-band and leaving it on the hall table. She rubbed her long, dark hair with the towel provided by Aileen, and they made their way to the lounge together.

'OK. No real change.' Aileen bent forwards toward the frail old woman sitting hunched in a tall upright armchair. Her expressionless face held eyes which were sunken and dark. Her hands looked almost skeletal as the skin dipped between the bones. The chair on which she sat looked as old as she was, with a faded pattern and holes in the threadbare fabric. 'Is there, Margaret? No change today.' Aileen's voice rose in volume when she turned her attention to the elderly woman.

Margaret's expression was vacant, but she clicked into reality for a moment and looked up when she heard her name. Her eyes lit up and widened at the sight of Eleanor. The muscles on her gaunt face stretched to achieve the smile that she reserved just for her daughter.

'Eleanor, it's so nice of you to come and see me,' she said cheerily.

'I live here now, remember, Mum?' Eleanor had crouched in front of her mother and gazed into the lost eyes.

'Yes, that's lovely dear. And what about Nick and Chris? Have they come too? You know how I like to see my grandson.'

'No, Mum. It's just you and me now, remember? They were killed in the car accident.' Eleanor couldn't help the catch in her voice.

'Oh, will they be here soon, then?'

'No, Mum. They haven't been here for eight months.'

Every day for the last four weeks Eleanor had had the same conversation, but it never seemed to get any easier. Tears started to roll down her cheeks. Pure adrenaline was the only thing that kept her going at the office. Most of the time she was able to shut out the real world, the memories. At home there was no such luxury. No deadlines to adhere to. No work to keep her mind focused. Only an elderly mother whose mind seemed as empty as Eleanor's heart.

'Eight months, one week and three days,' she said quietly to herself.

# 2

DARRYL WESTWOOD WALKED INTO THE PUB AND GLANCED around. His steps faltering from nervous anticipation. The old, dark wood-panelling surrounding the room soaked up most of what little light there was from each of the ornately coloured light fittings dotted around the room. It took a moment for his eyes to adjust. A few of the stools remained empty at the bar, but the rest of the pub was full of low murmured conversations in high-backed booths.

'Darryl, over here.'

Darryl saw his old friend, Dave Saunders, leaning his head out of the third booth along to the left. A familiar grin spread across his face. A sense of relief followed. He always could depend on Dave when reassurance by a trusted friend was the only solution to the problems of young adulthood. He regretted not keeping in touch.

'Get me a pint on your way.'

Darryl smiled to himself. Of course, alcohol had always been a major companion of that reassurance, and he should have known better than to head for the booth without visiting the bar first.

'Same as always?' Darryl called.

'As always,' came the reply from the booth.

'Pint of Carling and I'll have a pint of your local ale, please,' Darryl said to the barman, wishing he hadn't put his hands on the edge of the bar. The sticky wood left a residue on his fingers that he tried, unsuccessfully, to wipe down his jeans before putting his hand in his pocket for some cash. He paid the barman and carried the drinks over to the booth.

'You still drinking this shit?' Darryl said satirically as he put the glass of lager down on the table in front of Dave and sat opposite.

'As always,' Dave replied, and he drained the remnants of a pint already in his hand. 'And you're still trying out the local brew wherever you go, I see.'

'You can learn a lot about a place by their beer,' Darryl said. 'At least, that's my excuse.' He took a long draw of his beer and placed it on the table. 'Don't think much on your choice of pub, though.'

'What's wrong? Don't you like it?' Dave took an exaggerated breath of the stale air. 'It's all about the ambiance, my dear boy, you know that.'

'Yeah, well I wish that ambiance wasn't quite so tactile.' Darryl tried again to remove the sticky residue from his hands.

'I like the anonymity of the place. In other words, these days I like to hide.' Dave took a mouthful of his lager and sat back to take a look at the older Darryl. 'It's good to see you, mate. It's been what, nearly twenty years?'

'Something like that, and yet some things never change.'

Darryl was annoyed with himself for feeling just a tiny bit jealous that Dave hadn't lost any of his boyish, good looks. His red and black striped tie was pulled slightly loose at the neck. He looked comfortable in his smart suit. Darryl, on the other hand, felt old. Grey hairs were already glistening among the black.

'So, what you doing here?' Dave asked. 'Your call this morning was unexpected to say the least.'

'Going through a bit of a mid-life crisis and thought it would be good to look up my old college mate.'

'Last I heard you were married and settled down.'

'Married, yes. Children, yes, twins now at Uni. Settled down? My wife had other ideas.'

'Ah, there we go. I thought there'd be a woman involved. You never could handle the break-ups. Easy come, easy go, I say.'

Dave had always managed to move on with ease, without a thought to the girl he had left behind. Not an attribute Darryl admired, but sometimes envied.

'The divorce came through this morning,' Darryl continued. 'I guess that was the impetus for my call. A hankering for the good old days. You?'

'Waiting for my second divorce to come through as we speak,' said Dave, 'or should I say drink.'

Darryl took another long draw of his beer, draining his glass. 'Another?' he asked.

Dave laughed at him and shook his head. 'You're right, some things never change.'

'I haven't got drunk for years,' Darryl said. 'How sad is that? I've been too busy being sensible. Well, I think tonight's as good a night as any to pick up old habits.'

He rose and returned to the bar.

'Same again?' the barman asked.

'Just the ale, please.'

Darryl was careful not to put his hands on the bar this time. *There I go being sensible again,* he thought. *What's wrong with a bit of stickiness.* He tried to force himself to put his hands down on the bar. *It wouldn't have bothered you twenty years ago.* Thankfully his pint arrived saving him the prospect of more sticky residue, and he reached for the pint instead. *I guess I'm not twenty years younger anymore.* He paid and returned to the booth.

'What are you up to these days?' Dave asked.

'Not a lot. I've been working on a dig out of town for the last couple of years, but the funding ended and now I'm looking for something new, but in no rush. I need a break for a while.'

'If you're at a bit of a loose end I can offer you something.'

'No, thanks,' Darryl replied. 'I told you, I don't want a job, I want to get drunk. I'm done with being sensible.'

'Come on, you'd be doing me a big favour and it wouldn't take long. A couple of hours, that's all.'

Darryl looked at him suspiciously. 'What is it?' he asked.

'I've just bought a building here in Chartford Brooke and I want to renovate it.'

'But?'

'But there are some questions about its age and historical significance. It's right up your street. You always loved your buildings.'

'You're the architect, can't you do it?' Darryl asked.

'I was going to, I was even going to arrange a meeting for tomorrow with the local solicitors, Dolby and Patterson's. The office building is relatively new, the usual uninspiring clean lines trying to pass for minimalism, but the practice itself is decades old. They've got documents in their archives that should be in a museum. They'll probably have a copy of the earliest title deeds in their archives, but ...'

'But?'

'Miss Osbourne.'

Darryl noted a distinct tone of dread in Dave's voice. 'Miss Osbourne?' he repeated with particular emphasis on the Miss.

'Exactly. Miss Osbourne is on the lookout for a husband and neither of my marriages lasted half as long as yours.'

Darryl lifted his glass and made a toast, 'Here's to shitty marriages.'

'Never again,' Dave joined the toast and they drank with gusto till they both finished their pints. A familiar custom between the two from years ago. 'I swear Osbourne is determined to be my next victim,' Dave continued. 'And I've already been round there once today. I couldn't face her again tomorrow.'

'So, you want to throw me to the lions.'

'I guess you could put it like that. It will probably only be a couple of hours in the archives and then you're out,' Dave pleaded. 'Never to be seen again. Whereas I have a lot of business there.'

'Can't you try the County archives?' Darryl asked. He'd had no intention of getting involved in another job yet, big or small. He'd been looking forward to a break and had a need for quiet.

'They had a fire about a year ago and it's taking a long time for them to get themselves sorted. Please, mate. I've been holding interviews for researchers, but nobody suitable has come up, otherwise I'd get them to do it. Please. That place gives me the creeps.'

'Two hours?'

'Two hours, three tops.'

'OK. So, tell me what it is you want, but I'm only doing it as a favour.'

∼

Eleanor woke early the next day. The streetlights beamed through a gap in her bedroom curtains like a spotlight on the empty space beside her. She ran her hand gently over the smooth untouched pillow before thumping it with her fist. She climbed out of bed and got straight in the shower. An effort to block out the unwanted memories before they took hold.

She showered, dressed, ate breakfast, opened the curtains in her mother's room giving as cheery a, 'Good morning,' as she could manage, and the doorbell rang. It would be Aileen arriving for work, the same as any other day. Another day to drag herself through.

∼

Miss Osbourne was in more of a fluster than usual this morning.

'Mr Saunders will be dropping in this morning,' she said in her self-important manner. 'There's something particular that he'd like my help with. Shouldn't take too long, but you will need to hold my calls for half hour or so. I don't want to be interrupted. About eleven o'clock, OK?'

Miss Osbourne didn't wait for an answer. Eleanor often wondered why she bothered asking questions if she wasn't going to wait for the answer. She imagined herself getting up from her desk and following Miss Osbourne through to her office and simply replying, *No, that's not OK, or have you forgotten about the very important meeting you asked me to arrange for eleven o'clock? Or is it no longer as important as you had initially made it out to be?*'

But, of course, Eleanor turned back to her computer and continued typing. She completed the sentence Miss Osbourne had interrupted and then turned her attention to rearranging the very important meeting that was no longer so important. A quick phone call, a profuse amount of false apologies on Miss Osbourne's behalf, and it was rearranged for two o'clock instead.

At ten forty-five Miss Osbourne appeared at Eleanor's office door.

'Just enough time to grab a coffee before Mr Saunders arrives,' she stated. She turned and strolled along the main hallway to the small kitchen area with a confidence only known to those who believe they deserve only the best in everything.

'No, thank you, Miss Osbourne, I wouldn't like a coffee. Maybe I'll get one for myself later,' Eleanor replied to the empty space at the doorway. 'Oh, you weren't offering, my mistake.'

Eleanor often avoided the kitchen area at this time of day. All the comings and goings could be seen from the small kitchen placed centrally along the hallway and it was the one time everyone had an excuse for coming together. An unwritten rule had manifested regarding morning coffee gossip time. Between ten thirty and ten forty-five the staff from the other business on their floor, Samson's Digital World, indulged in their coffee gossip time. Ten forty-five to eleven o'clock, it was time for Dolby and Patterson's Solicitors to enjoy the respite. Staff between the offices would exchange polite smiles, but they never encroached on the other's morning coffee gossip times.

Gina and Marie had sashayed their way to the kitchen a couple of minutes earlier. Eleanor wasn't interested in the office gossip, and besides, whatever they had to say was probably about her.

A familiar ping sounded from the arrival of the lift across the hallway. Pete, the porter, walked out of the lift with a tall, dark-haired man behind him.

*That's not Mr Saunders,* Eleanor thought as they made their way toward her office. *That's going to upset her.*

This man's unshaven face was not the usual sight for a businessman, nor were the jeans, t-shirt, big brown work-boots, and weathered, brown leather jacket.

'Mr Westwood to see Miss Osbourne,' Pete announced.

'We were expecting Mr Saunders,' Eleanor said. 'Is he on his way?'

'No, I'm afraid he got caught up in a meeting and has asked me to come along in his stead. I hope that won't be a problem,' said Mr Westwood cheerily. 'Pleased to meet you.'

'Oh, I'm not Miss Osbourne. I'm just her secretary.' Eleanor flustered as she shook the hand he had proffered.

'Don't I know you from somewhere?' he asked still holding her hand.

'No, no, I don't think so.'

Eleanor pulled her hand away forcefully, trying to convince herself that he wasn't holding her hand any longer than necessary. It was just her imagination. Her fingers immediately found her bracelet and she started twisting the beads.

'I have, I'm sure I've seen you somewhere before. Never mind, it'll come back to me.'

His laid-back attitude jarred with Eleanor's sense of professionalism. Still clutching at her beads, she offered to show Mr Westwood through to Miss Osbourne's office.

'She'll be back in a moment. Can I get you a tea or coffee?'

'A coffee would be great, thanks. White, no sugar.'

Mr Westwood put his large satchel-type bag on the floor next to his chair and sat, Eleanor believed, a little too comfortably for office etiquette. One foot brought up on to the opposite knee, holding on to his ankle in a very relaxed pose.

Eleanor left hurriedly to make the coffee.

'Where's Mr Saunders?' snapped Miss Osbourne.

'Held up in a meeting,' Eleanor said as she tried to squeeze past to get in the kitchen.

With the culmination of Miss Osbourne, Gina, and Marie standing in the doorway, all trying to get a better view of the stranger, there wasn't a lot of space left for Eleanor. She managed to force her way through only to find the building caretaker restocking the shelves inside. The kitchen, though brightly lit with the same LED spotlights sunken into the ceiling as the rest of the offices, was never going to feel bright and airy. There was no window. The end wall was two cupboards wide, and the room was three cupboards long. The sense of confinement was difficult to escape, especially with the added continual ear-piercing lament from Miss Osbourne. It's only saving grace was the coffee it housed.

'So, who's that?' Miss Osbourne demanded.

'Mr Westwood, sent by Mr Saunders.'

'I was hoping to see Mr Saunders, not one of his minions.'

It was difficult to bear when Miss Osbourne spoke as though it was Eleanor's fault when things didn't go her way. Eleanor's shyness wouldn't allow her to argue her case and experience had taught her the only way she could console herself was by finding something else to focus on.

'Can I help you with that?' she asked the caretaker through gritted teeth.

He was having trouble trying to restock a large industrial-sized tin of coffee up on to the very top of one of the cupboards. He looked in his mid to late thirties, around the same age as Eleanor, but his shoulders were hunched in his long, white coat giving the impression that he was much older. She took the tin from him, probably a little too forcefully, and, being just an inch or so taller than him, was able to slide it on to the cupboard with a little more ease than he could.

'Thank you, Miss,' he smiled. 'You're very kind.'

'You're welcome,' she said. *It's nice to know someone appreciates what I do.* A sideways glance at Miss Osbourne revealed her to still be inspecting Mr Westwood through the windows strategically placed within certain office walls and doors.

'Well,' Miss Osbourne continued, 'he's not what I expected, but he's still rather handsome in a rugged sort of way.'

'A bit old don't you think?' Marie pitched in.

'Maybe for you youngsters. I'd say late thirties, forty at the most.'

'Like I said, old.'

'He'd look more at home on a building site,' joined in Gina with a giggle. 'Which is not necessarily a bad thing.'

'Now that I look at him, I must say, I certainly wouldn't say no.' Miss Osbourne walked off at a stride back to her office. The set of her shoulders made her intentions clear.

'I can't see what all the fuss is about. He's not your type at all,' Marie said.

Gina only giggled coyly.

'Oh really, Gina. There'll be nothing but trouble.'

'Maybe so, but it's fun.'

Gina and Marie soon left the kitchen doorway, coffees in hand, and made their way back to their office. The caretaker moved on to his next job toward the toilets with a mop and bucket, leaving Eleanor in peace.

She took some time for some long quiet breaths, while thinking to herself, *I'm glad he decided to restock the cupboards before cleaning the toilets,* and then made coffees for both herself and Mr Westwood.

She placed her own coffee on her desk and took Mr Westwood's through to him, still sitting very comfortably in Miss Osbourne's office.

'We're looking for a copy of some old title deeds to a house nearby, which we're hoping are in your archives,' Mr Westwood was explaining as Eleanor entered and placed his coffee on the desk in front of him.

'I could try the Council archives for these types of historical records, but Mr Saunders informs me they had a fire there last year, so I don't hold out much hope,' Mr Westwood continued without so much as a glance let alone a thank you to Eleanor.

At this point, Eleanor closed the door behind her.

'You're welcome,' she said with just a hint of sarcasm.

She returned to her desk and relaxed with her coffee while gazing out the window at the clear blue sky. *Some quiet time to get some work done,* she thought to herself. *He won't be out of there any time soon.*

# 3

An hour after Miss Osbourne had disappeared into her office with Mr Westwood Eleanor looked up from her computer at the ping of the lift. Pete appeared with one of their regular clients, Mr Watson. A short, stumpy, elderly looking man with thin metal-rimmed glasses perched on the end of his nose. There was something about his demeanour that gave the impression that he could have walked directly out of a Dickens novel. Eleanor immediately rose and greeted him at the door.

'Tea, Mr Watson?'

'Just the ticket, thank you, Eleanor,' he replied clutching his briefcase in front of him as though it contained the most precious of his family heirlooms.

'Miss Osbourne won't be long, please take a seat in my office and I'll get you your tea.'

∼

Darryl Westwood had decided thirty minutes ago that this meeting was over, but Miss Osbourne wasn't having any of it. No matter how many times he had tried to stay on the subject she seemed to turn it to some great deed she had done, or what a success she had become. She was currently telling him about how she and her two elder brothers had been brought up by their father to be hard-nosed business types.

'He always had a way of getting what he wanted, but there are times when a woman's touch is needed.'

*Here we go again,* Darryl thought to himself. *Dave what have you got me in to?* What she had said in itself wasn't too bad, but the flash of leg she had given really wasn't subtle. He had to admit she was an attractive woman. Her blond hair fell just above her shoulders accentuating her strong jaw line, and her large, blue eyes shone. But, after overhearing the conversation that had occurred in the kitchen when he'd first arrived, he was in no doubt. He needed to be on his guard. *This is the last thing I need or want.* His ex-wife's deceitfulness and the arguments that followed tore into his memory. If what Dave had said was true, Miss Osbourne wanting to ensnare him, she was certainly proving herself to be fickle. Or maybe Dave had got it wrong and she behaved this way with all men.

Darryl had agreed with Dave that they would make the meeting arrangements under Dave's name.

'They may put off seeing you if I say it's someone else,' Dave had told him. 'This way she'll make sure she fits you in. Any chance to get me in her clutches. Otherwise they may not see you till next week, and I could do with the information for the planning application soon. I've been putting this off for long enough.'

Darryl had to agree the tactic had worked, but he regretted agreeing to come in the first place, especially with this hangover. It had taken some time for his retinas to become used to the blinding white LED lights in the modern office block. The amount of glass used in place of solid walls left him feeling exposed. For an archaeologist, who had spent a large proportion of his time in trenches in the middle of wind-swept fields, he had never felt quite so vulnerable as he did now. Surely hangovers never used to be this bad.

'Well, thank you for your time, Miss Osbourne.' Darryl stood abruptly, eager to get out the door. 'I'll be back after lunch to get to work.'

He picked up his bag and stepped to the door, opening it before Miss Osbourne could say anything else. A man he hadn't seen earlier was sitting just inside the secretary's office, his briefcase held tightly on his lap.

'Mr Watson, you're here early,' Miss Osbourne stammered to the man. 'Go on through to my office. I'll just be a moment. Ah, is this Eleanor with your tea?'

Darryl stepped aside to allow Miss Osbourne's secretary to move past with her tray containing a modern interpretation of an old-fashioned china teapot, with cup and saucer to match. The sight of the three chocolate biscuits arranged on a small side plate churned his stomach.

'I'll take these straight through for you,' Eleanor said to Mr Watson, who sprung out of his seat and followed behind her.

'Thank you once again,' Darryl said turning back to shake Miss Osbourne's hand. After all, she may have been flirtatious, and maybe even annoying, but he didn't like to be rude.

'Cecilia, please,' she replied gently placing her fingertips on his hand with a limp wrist as though expecting him to kiss it.

Darryl took hold of her full hand and shook.

'I've worked hard to get where I am, Mr Westwood,' she said clearly trying to hide her disappointment, 'and though we are but a small part of this prestigious firm we are proud to be the holders of the main archives for all our practises. I will just say, however, that I'm afraid the archives are in a little disarray at the moment. We have quite recently taken on a new archivist and he is reorganising our current system. I'll be more than happy to give you my personal attention though.' Her tone made it clear the type of personal attention she had in mind.

'No need to trouble yourself,' Darryl said with a nervous laugh.

The thought of Miss Osbourne encroaching on him for the afternoon was more than he could bear. The last hour had been bad enough. The secretary came walking past them, returning to her desk. OK to look at but didn't make much of an effort. Her hair was tied back as simply as possible. Her make-up was minimal. More importantly, a wedding ring was set on her finger.

'I'll just borrow one of your minions,' he said, taking pleasure in using her word from earlier. A not-so-subtle hint that her conversation had been overheard. 'Eleanor, isn't it? I'm sure Eleanor will be able to help me. It'll only take a couple of hours, and then I'll be gone.'

'Eleanor? Well, actually Callum, our archivist, will probably be more than sufficient to help you,' Miss Osbourne stammered.

'No, no. I wouldn't want you worrying I couldn't get the job done. Eleanor can help me. I'm sure Mr Saunders will be more than grateful.' Darryl emphasised Dave's name with the hope that Miss Osbourne would remember that her original intentions had laid with him.

'Well, of course,' choked Miss Osbourne. 'Mr Saunders has been a tremendous asset to this company and I will help in whatever way I can in return.' She gave a small forced laugh.

Darryl couldn't turn quick enough to hide his mischievous smile. Walking to the lift he heard the gentle rhythm of trotting steps across the wooden floor behind him.

'Mr Westwood,' Miss Osbourne called.

*I will get out of here,* he thought as he put on a false smile before turning to face her.

'I'm sorry, but I feel it my duty to say something about Eleanor.'

*Yes, of course you do. What now?* 'Yes, Miss Osbourne. What is it?'

Miss Osbourne lowered her voice as she manoeuvred herself between him and the lift.

'Eleanor is in a very delicate situation right now. You may have noticed her wearing a ring, and I just want to confirm, well ... she's not available.'

'I'm not looking for someone who is available, Miss Osbourne, I just want to do my job.'

He reached behind her and jabbed at the button to call the lift.

'Of course, I don't mean ... What I'm trying to say is that she lost both her husband and her son in a car accident a few months ago. We were all incredibly shocked. Such an awful tragedy. Her husband worked here, and we took her on after. Tried to keep her busy, you understand. We've shown her as much kindness as we possibly can.'

*So, that's it,* Darryl thought. *You want to tell me again how wonderful you are.*

The lift doors opened behind her, and the caretaker struggled noisily to emerge. He was laden with boxes, cartons, bottles of spray, and dragging two mops behind him.

'In fact,' Miss Osbourne continued through gritted teeth, clearly annoyed by the interruption. 'I don't like to say it myself, but I believe we probably saved her from a complete breakdown.'

Darryl furtively watched the lift porter supposedly help the caretaker organise his load. Except, the porter was purposely placing items so precariously that it didn't take long for things to slip. Miss Osbourne, too, gave quick sideways glances. Her words began to sound more spiteful than sympathetic as her anger rose at the commotion.

'I couldn't possibly take all the credit, of course,' Miss Osbourne went on. 'But if I hadn't—' She suddenly turned on the porter. 'Pete, will you stop teasing the caretaker and get back to your job.'

He froze and coyly returned to the lift. In that moment Darryl saw the true nature of Miss Osbourne. For all the conceited prattle of her own self-importance, she obviously thought the caretaker so far beneath her she didn't even know his name. He was nothing more than an inconvenience to her flirtations. She turned back to Darryl.

'I'm just trying to say she's fragile,' Miss Osbourne spat out.

'I'll keep that in mind, thank you, Miss Osbourne.'

Darryl steered himself around her and entered the lift.

'Cecilia,' she reminded him, returning to her more gentle tone.

'I'll be back after lunch, Miss Osbourne,' he continued. He enjoyed ignoring her blatant flirtation. 'About one o'clock.'

The lift door closed between them as a loud crash came from behind Miss Osbourne. The caretaker had dropped the majority of his items.

∼

'You mean you actually eat here too,' said Darryl as he placed half a pint of shandy on the table and sat opposite Dave.

The dim lighting in the pub did nothing to help lessen the impact of the sight of the half-eaten burger and chips in front of Dave. Darryl's stomach churned much more so than at the glimpse of the three chocolate biscuits he had seen only a few minutes earlier. The hangover had finally shifted, but his stomach wasn't interested in improving any time soon.

'Gotta eat, why don't you get yourself something,' Dave said through a mouthful of food.

'No, thanks. I just thought I'd come and let you know how it went this morning.'

'Mmm, good.'

At least that's what Darryl thought Dave said. It was difficult to tell after another few chips had just entered the black hole of Dave's mouth.

'I quit,' Darryl said bluntly.

'Ha, ha, very funny. Come on, tell me, will she let you in the archives?'

'Yes, I'm going back at one o'clock, but I'm beginning to regret this already. What have you got me in to?'

'Yeah, yeah. It's nothing you haven't had to deal with before.'

'At least I managed to wangle it so that Osbourne won't be doing the job with me. Someone called Eleanor.'

'Ah,' said Dave in a way that told Darryl there was more to the story.

'What do you mean, ah?'

'A bit nuts that one, by all accounts,' Dave said tentatively.

'From what Osbourne said, losing both her husband and son in a car crash would be enough to send anyone nuts.'

'I suppose so.' Dave frowned as Darryl reached over and pinched one of his chips. 'He was the archivist there.'

'Who was?'

'Her husband.'

Darryl stopped halfway through his chip and stared at Dave.

'Her dead husband was the archivist at those offices?' he asked, not quite believing what he was hearing.

'U-huh.'

'And this afternoon I'm going to be taking her to those archives.'

'U-huh.'

Dave seemed to be finding the whole situation more entertaining than Darryl liked.

'Oh, shit.' Darryl threw the half-eaten chip back on Dave's plate, which took the grin off Dave's face. 'Still, nuts I can deal with, at least she won't be hitting on me.'

Dave laughed. 'It's good to see you again, mate.'

'You're getting the better deal out of this friendship right now; I can tell you.'

Darryl sat back and stared at his shandy while his stomach swirled with unease. Was it the food or the thought of Miss Osbourne?

'What is the deal with Osbourne?' Darryl went on. 'She did nothing but boast about how great she is.'

'There is a story that she only got the job by default because the other applicant didn't show up. I reckon she's trying to convince herself, as well as everyone else, that it's not true. Continuously,' Dave added with a drawl. He wiped his mouth with his paper napkin and threw it on top of his plate. Pushing his plate toward Darryl he said, 'You can finish that off if you like.'

All that was left on the plate was what Darryl could only assume constituted a salad garnish; two bits of lettuce and a slice of tomato. It still made him nauseous.

'I didn't ask you last night. Who is it you're hiding from in here? Must be someone pretty bad.' Darryl shifted uncomfortably on his seat. The thin padding he was sat on did nothing to help disguise the hard wooden seat.

'Used to be the second wife, she would never have set foot in a place like this. But I quite like it now. It's friendly. It's not trying to pretend to be something it's not. It's just a good old-fashioned pub with sticky floors and loo's that stink.'

'And hard, uncomfortable seats.'

'And hard, uncomfortable seats. Homely.'

'Remind me never to visit your home.'

'No, I don't mean it's like my home. More like how a home

would be if you didn't feel like you had to clean it just for the benefit of visitors.' Dave finished his pint. 'Up for another session tonight?'

'No,' Darryl replied thinking Dave sounded far too enthusiastic for how much he had also drunk the night before. 'I haven't been able to eat all day. I'll see you for a quick one after work to let you know what I find this afternoon, but then I need some sleep.'

'No, you just need more practice. Too many years of marriage can do that to you. I'll see you back in here, then.'

Darryl gave a small nod in reply as Dave got up and left the table. His half a shandy was calling to him, but even that was turning his stomach and he pushed it away untouched.

~

Eleanor felt sick. She sat facing the lift doors dreading their announcement of Mr Westwood's arrival at one o'clock. For the last hour, every ping had made her jump as staff came and went for lunch, or clients arrived for lunchtime appointments. Miss Osbourne had explained to Eleanor that she would be helping Mr Westwood in the archives for the afternoon. She then quickly disappeared into her office for her meeting with Mr Watson, and there she stayed. She hadn't specified what they would be doing, or maybe she had but Eleanor's auditory canals ceased working the moment the archives were mentioned. Or in particular, needing to spend time in the archives.

She had managed to avoid them since she had started working there. The new archivist, Callum, was always kind to her when he came up to the offices, but they would always be her Nick's archives. He had been highly protective over the organisation and working standards of the rooms. Eleanor had often teased him that she felt as though the archives meant more to him than she did. And, if anyone could get geeky over a filing system, it was Nick.

Immediately after the accident Eleanor had felt the dull ache of disbelief. The expectation of Nick and Chris walking into the room. Hoping to see their faces; longing to hear their breath. But they never did walk into the room. The life she had longed to see and hear had gone.

A week later she had moved in with her mother and she had managed to smother that ache. Kept herself busy with someone else to care for. Now, with the prospect of going down to the archives, just the thought of that same expectation, that same hope, brought a knot to her stomach. It slowly tightened minute by minute the closer it came to that moment when she would need to face the truth. Nick wasn't there and wouldn't ever be there again.

Today, avoiding the archives was no longer possible. The best she could hope for was to at least delay it as much as possible. The lift arrived exactly at one o'clock, and Eleanor was out of her chair as soon as Mr Westwood appeared.

'Coffee, Mr Westwood?' she asked across the hallway.

'No, we'll get straight on,' he replied bluntly.

Eleanor was ready to disappear into the kitchen. She hadn't expected him to say no. Mr Westwood pulled over one of the chairs intended for waiting clients and dropped his huge leather satchel on her desk. Eleanor slowly returned to her seat.

'Let me show you what we're looking for,' Mr Westwood continued.

He reached inside his bag and pulled out a file containing, among other things, a stack of photographs. The top of which was of an old building Eleanor recognised.

'This is Thornewick Manor,' Mr Westwood said as he passed her the top photograph. 'It's just up the road from here. Do you know it?' He sat back in his too-comfortable-for-an-office posture and waited.

Eleanor, stunned, nodded. Her normal delaying tactic usually worked. Now her throat began to tighten as though trapped in a noose.

'I don't know anything about it,' she stammered, 'but I walk past it on my way here every day.'

'We believe you may have some early deeds here in your archives, or maybe copies of,' Mr Westwood explained. 'Probably not for the original building but there may be plans or something from over the next hundred years or so that may be of some use. If we can find those I could be out of here by the end of this afternoon and you can get back to typing and making tea.'

Until that moment everything Mr Westwood had said had drifted aimlessly over her. But, now, Eleanor was furious. *Typing and making tea. Is that what you think I do all day?* Her forced smile suddenly dropped, but Mr Westwood didn't seem to notice.

'This is the full address,' she could hear him saying as he passed her a piece of paper with writing on it.

She stared at it blankly.

'Hopefully it won't be too much trouble to find if it's there,' he continued.

*Find it yourself,* she wanted to scream back at him. *You come in here with your laid-back attitude, expecting people to drop everything at a snap of your fingers and do your bidding. Well, I'm sorry to tell you, that that is not going to happen. If you want something, get up and get it yourself.* She forced the smile back on her face.

'I'll show you the way,' is what she actually said.

She handed the address back to Mr Westwood and they made their way to the lift.

'We need to go down to the basement for the archives, and

speak to Callum,' Eleanor said as she pressed the button to call the lift.

'Hold the lift,' came a call from behind.

Gina was tottering along on her heels in a skirt too tight for any more than her usual hip swaying swagger. She conveniently stumbled with a flourish as she reached the lift, tripping just enough for Mr Westwood to catch her. Pure contrivance.

'Oh my, you are strong,' said Gina, and held out her hand. 'Gina,' she stated.

Mr Westwood said nothing, but he didn't have much choice but to shake her hand. She made certain of that.

'Rough hands too. You're no conveyancer,' Gina said as the lift doors opened and the three of them walked in.

'No, I'm an archaeologist,' Mr Westwood replied flatly.

Eleanor was distracted for a moment. She was always amused by the sparkle in Pete's eyes that appeared when Gina was around. He always seemed to grow two inches taller. His smart, dark-blue uniform jacket pulled tight at the buttons as he drew his shoulders back and his chest expanded. His hand subconsciously smoothed his hair as he grinned at her. His pock-marked face gave him the appearance of an adolescent who had only just left school and scarred by teenage acne, and there was a certain naivety about him. But Eleanor knew he was older than he looked from conversations with Nick, her husband. She remembered with a jolt why she was there. Their visit to the archives.

'Basement, please,' Eleanor said kindly to Pete inside the lift.

Pete had become good friends with Nick, visiting him often in the archives. And consequently, when Eleanor began working there Pete had always been nice to her. Though not as nice as he was to Gina.

'Good morning, Gina,' said Pete. 'I missed you at reception this morning, how are you?'

Gina gave Pete the briefest of glances with the mildest of smiles and returned her focus back to Mr Westwood.

'There's a coincidence, I'm going to the basement too.'

Gina had somehow managed to arrange herself at the back of the lift, next to Mr Westwood. The lift wasn't particularly large, but neither was it small. Not small enough to warrant Gina standing quite so close to Mr Westwood.

'So,' she continued. 'An archaeologist. What does an archaeologist want in our archives?'

'Just doing a bit of research for Dave— Mr Saunders,' he corrected himself.

'Dave? First name terms. That doesn't sound like the Mr Saunders we know, does it, Eleanor?'

Eleanor didn't answer, but she knew Gina didn't expect her to. She was aware of the conversation behind her, but her thoughts had returned back to the archives. She had become preoccupied with watching the numbers blink above the doors as the lift sank through the building. The moment the red light encircling the number one had turned dark Eleanor's stomach jolted with the lift's movement down toward the basement. The letter G in the adjacent circle lit up for a moment, and then blinked off. Her stomach jolted again, though this time it didn't come from the movement of the lift. Her knees began to give a little and she reached for her bracelet. Feeling nauseous, she leant against the chrome bar that ran around the lift walls. Only faintly aware of talking still going on around her, though now the words had become barely identifiable sounds to her.

'... college together, ... friends,' said a man's voice.

'... anything I can do ... Eleanor's not ... happy to join you ... quite cosy.'

The circle surrounding the letter B seemed, to Eleanor, to light up brightest of all, and the doors opened in front of her. A numbness took over her body.

'... we'll be fine ... I'll be gone ...,' Eleanor vaguely heard.
'Shame.'

The three of them stepped out into a small brightly lit corridor. Eleanor couldn't remember putting one foot in front of the other, but somehow, she had been swept along by Gina and Mr Westwood.

'Oops,' said Gina. 'It wasn't the basement I needed ...' She stepped back inside the lift. 'Remember, ... if you want me,' she sighed as the doors closed.

Eleanor was left in the silence of the basement hallway, and the chaos of her mind.

# 4

Darryl was grateful for the silence. In the basement there was no Gina, no traffic noise, not even the background murmur of voices persistently present within a town. Only a slight electrical hum that seemed to emanate from the walls. He was standing in a stark corridor with four doors leading off it, two on each side. In contrast to the offices upstairs, there were no windows in the dividing walls or doors. Only blank, white walls punctuated by heavy, solid fire doors.

Eleanor hadn't moved since stepping out of the lift. She looked pale and a slight shade of yellow. Her breaths were shallow, and her eyes were darting from side to side. Darryl was concerned that she was either about to faint or throw up, or possibly both.

'Are you OK?' he asked, but she didn't seem to hear him. 'Eleanor? Are you OK? I'm sorry, I shouldn't have brought you down here to help me with this. We'll go back.'

He reached for the lift button.

'No,' she said quickly and quietly. She seemed to be gasping for breath. 'It's been over eight months since ... There was an accident although I'm sure Miss Osbourne told you what happened. She likes to do that.'

She made a strange breathy sound that Darryl could only assume was supposed to be a laugh, but it came out more like a terrified sigh.

'It's about time I was able to come down here,' she continued. 'You'd think I'd be over it after eight months, wouldn't you?'

She was playing with the beads of her bracelet the same way she had played with them when Darryl had first arrived that morning. A nervous habit, he assumed, though strange that a woman would choose to be wearing a bracelet with beads so obviously made of cheap plastic.

'Why don't you go back upstairs. I'm sure Callum will be more than able to help.'

Eleanor shook her head. Her breaths were now deeper and more measured. 'I'll be fine,' she stammered. 'I really must apologise.'

A door opened to the left causing Eleanor to jump.

'Eleanor, it's so nice to see you down here.'

A tall, slender man in a well-tailored suit stepped out. He was well groomed, as though he had this moment stepped out of the salon. Eleanor smiled at him but didn't remove her hand from her bracelet.

'What are you here for? Can I help?' he asked.

He was soft spoken and attentive toward Eleanor, but Darryl decided to take over. Maybe it would help to give Eleanor some time to adjust, time to get some colour back in her cheeks. He had put the address for Thornewick Manor in his pocket, which he now pulled out.

'Are you Callum? I'm looking for the title deeds to this address. Specifically, I'm looking for the size of the original building, so anything you may have on it could be of some help.'

'Thornewick Manor? We can have a look. I will just warn you that I'm afraid you may consider it a bit of a mess down here at the moment. It will look to you like there are files everywhere.' Callum gave a small, friendly laugh. 'But there is a method here.'

'That's OK,' Eleanor said quietly. 'I know the organising system very well.'

'Well, that's just it,' said Callum. His large, brown eyes full of pity. 'The organising system has changed. I find my method much easier and more efficient, but I am still in the process of reorganising it. A few of the older files have already been moved, which will probably include this one.'

Darryl noticed that the shadow of colour that had returned to Eleanor's face had drained again.

'It didn't need changing,' she whispered.

'I'm sorry, Eleanor. Times move on and that system was outdated. Please, let me help you find what you need.' Callum led them down the corridor and entered the second door on the right. 'Under the new system it should be in room four,' he said.

Darryl and Eleanor followed him into a large, dark room. Callum flicked on a switch and four long strip-lights flickered into existence. One for each of the four aisles in the room.

'Now, if I'm right, it should be ...' he walked around some box files that were piled knee-high on the floor, examining the hand drawn charts stuck on the ends of the aisles, 'down this one. Now, as I said, I am still in the middle of reorganising. If it hasn't been moved yet it could be back in room two. I'll make a start in there, if you like.'

The phone started to ring back down the corridor. Callum placed a hand gently on Eleanor's arm.

'Are you OK if I leave you to it? I'd better go get that call,' Callum continued.

'Of course, go ahead,' Eleanor replied politely.

Darryl clambered over a pile of loose papers and headed

down the aisle Callum had indicated. He pulled out a box full of files and dropped it on the floor. They both started coughing from the dust that plumed into the air as the box hit the smooth concrete floor.

'This place doesn't look organised to me at all,' said Eleanor. 'Nick would never have let it get to this state.'

'Nick was your husband?'

Eleanor nodded.

Darryl had never seen an archive in such a state of confusion before, but he couldn't tell Eleanor that. He continued searching through various files, boxes and indexes. As far as he was concerned, the quicker he got this job done the better.

'Like he said, he's still in the middle of organising it. Of course, it's going to be a bit chaotic until it's sorted.' Darryl tried to sound reassuring.

He reached through to the back of a shelf to get to a file that had slipped and was now wedged between the shelf and the steel backing.

'But there was nothing wrong with the way it was. More efficient? Nobody ever accused Nick's system of being inefficient.'

Darryl could see that Eleanor's colour was now returning rapidly, but with anger. *Great,* he thought. *Now I'm going to have to deal with an emotionally wound up widow too.* He stopped looking through the files and gently took hold of her wrists.

'Eleanor,' he said softly. 'I'm sure this isn't how Nick would have kept the archives, but Nick is no longer here. You have to accept that somebody else is doing the job now, and things need to be done their way.'

Eleanor was rigid, her eyes wide. She suddenly pulled her arms away forcefully, reminding Darryl of the same reaction at their first meeting. The simple act of shaking hands. She was clearly uncomfortable with physical contact. 'Do you want to go back upstairs?' he continued.

'No,' she said firmly. 'I'm sorry, Mr Westwood. I was being very unprofessional, and it won't happen again.'

Darryl turned back to the boxes and files. 'It wasn't unprofessional,' he said, trying to hide the awkwardness of the situation. 'I think the people here care for you, and have been protecting you, and rightly so. Just maybe for too long.'

'I ... I ...'

She was now trembling, and he was concerned that he may have offended her. He had no wish to distress her further and thought it best to change the subject.

'You know, I'm sure I've seen you before,' he said as he pulled down another box file from a shelf and opened it. He scanned the contents list written on the inside.

'Have you been to these offices before?' Eleanor stammered.

'No.'

'Did you have children at Greenacre primary before eight months ago?'

'Both my kids have just started Uni, so no.'

'Then, I don't think you can have, Mr Westwood.'

'It'll come to me. It might just take some time, but it'll come. And it's Darryl, please. I can't stand Mr Westwood.'

He closed the box file lid and another plume of dust filled the air.

∼

'We found nothing,' Darryl said disappointedly. He sipped at his pint determined not to drink too much tonight. 'Four hours of breathing in dust, and nothing.'

'What do you mean nothing?' Dave frowned, finally showing an inkling of age. 'They've got to have something there.'

'Have you ever been down to those archives?'

'Yeah. Nick was a good bloke. Maybe a little obsessive about a bunch of files, but—'

Darryl gave a derisory laugh. 'You wouldn't know it now. The place is in such a mess it could take a week to find the light switch.'

'I haven't been down there for ... probably over a year. Who's the new archivist?'

'A guy called Callum.'

Dave shook his head. It wasn't a name he recognised.

'Don't get me wrong, he seems like an alright guy, just shit at his job. Eleanor wasn't too happy about it either.'

'I bet. How did that go?' Dave's mischievous smile returned. 'I thought the whole idea is to save the damsel in distress, not take her down to the depths of her worst nightmare.'

'A bit shaky to start with, but I handled it with my usual care and consideration.'

Dave laughed so loudly others in the bar turned to look at him.

'Sorry, mate. Tell me again, what were the grounds for your divorce?'

'*She* had the affair, not me.'

'Darryl, you're such an arse.'

'I know. That's one of my more lovable traits.' Darryl said in a derisory tone. 'I see why the place gives you the creeps though, and not just the women. I swear that porter was giving me shifty looks. He's a bit on the devious side. The police seem to think so, too.'

'The police?' asked Dave. 'What did they want with him?'

'I don't know, unless playing practical jokes on your workmates is now against the law.' Darryl smiled at the memory of the porter furtively knocking boxes over that the caretaker had just stacked from a delivery. 'I assume they were both police. The one doing the talking was in plain clothes, but he had that particular stance of someone who enjoys their authority. They pulled him over to one side as we were leaving.'

'*We* were leaving?' Dave asked suspiciously.

'I wanted to take another look at Thornewick Manor and Eleanor walks past it on her way to the train station, so we walked together.'

'Don't.' Dave shook his head.

'Don't what?'

'We shared rooms for three years at college. I know you, Darryl. Just don't.'

'I have no idea what you're talking about.' Darryl took another sip of his beer and searched to change the subject. His mind on Eleanor, he remembered the attentiveness Callum had shown toward her. 'That archivist is a bit of a smarmy git though, too,' Darryl added passively.

'So,' Dave sighed. 'What are we going to do now, try the County archives? They may have got themselves sorted by now, but I really don't hold out much hope.'

'Not just yet. Callum did offer to keep looking for a while longer. I'll pop back in the morning to see if he's found anything. I can always take a look at the area for you, see what I can find out. There's only so much I can tell from the photographs you gave me, and it was already dark when I looked this afternoon.'

'Really be appreciated, mate. I have to say I'm impressed you're willing to go back into the lion's den.'

'So you should be. You didn't tell me about Gina. Jesus!'

'I thought you'd like to find that one out for yourself. Osbourne and Gina seem to love competing against each other. They are the only ones I have trouble with. Everywhere else is really quite normal. Besides, I didn't think you'd do the job if I gave you all the details. And let's face it, there are no words to describe Gina.'

*Who does this man think he is? How dare he come here and treat her that way. Thankfully she has me to look out for her, and God knows I'll do whatever I need to do to make her happy.*

~

Wednesday morning was stifled with a dark mood and a short temper. There was no reason why, not that Eleanor could understand. On the train people were standing just that bit closer. The doors were taking just that bit longer to close, making the train late. What little air there was lay thick from the heating, seemingly stuck on full making it harder to breathe. It was enough to make anyone short tempered, but Eleanor knew her bad mood was with her as soon as she had woken. Silly little accidents and misplaced paraphernalia had filled her morning.

Yesterday had been a blow. Spending so long in the one place she had tried her hardest to avoid had taken its toll. After the failure of finding anything of any relevance to Thornewick Manor in the archives, the thought of spending more time down there again today weighed heavily on her. The familiar silence of the rooms, the distinctive musty smell of the older documents, all brought the presence of Nick to her senses. Those times when she would meet him for lunch. Walking into the ordered quiet of his office. Seeing him look up from his desk as she entered, and his entire face lit up with a smile. A precious moment, she realised now, that she had always taken for granted.

To be back there, in those rooms, every sound could have been his movement, every shadow could have been his semblance. Maybe she was angry at having to go back there again this morning. Although, if she was truthful with herself, it was Nick she was angry with. If he hadn't died in the first place, then she wouldn't be in this position of having to go down there. All logic told her that this thought was irrational and even ridiculous, but it wasn't logic that ruled her brain anymore, it was emotions. This emotion hurt and made her angry, even if it was at Nick.

Harassed, she hurried along in the cold. The train had arrived fifteen minutes late and she had to rush to get to work on time. Her hope of speaking with Pete before going up to her office was slipping away. She wanted to know why the police were there yesterday. She hadn't been able to stop at the time. She didn't trust herself to stay calm and she didn't want to risk another outburst in front of Darryl. But surely, they couldn't have been there because of Nick and Chris' accident. It had all been dealt with months ago. But then why?

'Eleanor,' a voice called from behind her. Darryl jogged alongside. 'Didn't you hear me?'

'Obviously not,' she snapped back. She suddenly realised what she had said. 'I ... I'm so sorry. I didn't have a good night. I ... I ...' She floundered for an excuse and failed. She put her head down and hurried on, leaving Darryl behind.

'It's OK. Don't worry.' Darryl ran to catch up with her again. 'It was a bit of a stupid question, I guess,' he continued in his cheery manner. '... heard me the first time ... would have stopped. Well, I hope you ... not that onerous ..., am I?'

Eleanor's thoughts had wandered back to the archives again, the unorganised piles of documents left lying around, and the plumes of dust they would have to endure. Nick would have been horrified to have seen it in such a state. She wondered if Miss Osbourne knew as she had professed herself so proud of them yesterday. Eleanor couldn't see anything to be proud of and immediately brought up the image of Miss Osbourne as Minnie Mouse, dashing round the archives with a large colourful feather duster. She even added Laurel and Hardy fighting over a mop and bucket just for fun.

'... you're supposed to say, "No, of course not. ... pleasure working with you,"' Darryl continued.

'Ow,' Eleanor snapped at Darryl as they rushed along the street. Her arm stinging from his pinch. 'What was that for?'

'Just making sure you're still here.'

Eleanor realised she had drifted off while he was talking to her and apologised again.

'Never mind,' he smiled back. 'Is it OK if I walk in with you?'

'Of course. Is there a problem?' She decided she had better try and focus on what was going on around her. That thing called reality she so disliked.

'Let's just say I'd feel safer.'

Eleanor felt a smile come to her lips, but she wouldn't let it stay for long.

'I remembered you walked this way, so I've been waiting for you,' Darryl continued.

'Waiting?'

'Actually, I've been sat in Kath's Cafe for the last hour.'

'Where?'

'It's a cafe you walk past every day,' Darryl said incredulously.

Eleanor shook her head. It wasn't one she knew of, but then she usually had her head down, only focusing on the two square foot immediately in front of her that she was about to step into.

'I wasn't sure what time you started, anyway, so I got here early and waited,' Darryl went on.

'Are we all that bad?'

'Not all, just a select few, but that's enough.'

*Just as well you did wait*, Eleanor thought. *With Miss Osbourne usually starting at eight o'clock she would have had you all to herself. She would certainly have been pleased about that.* Eleanor noticed that Darryl was still wearing the same well-worn leather jacket as yesterday, though with a blue, woollen jumper underneath. The jeans could have been the same too, but the boots had changed to trainers. Her own trainers peeped out from beneath her trousers. *He gets to keep his trainers on all day. I wonder what Miss Osbourne would say if I asked if I could do that.*

The image of Minnie Mouse sprang into her head again. *'Oh no, Eleanor. I don't think that would be at all acceptable. Do you boys and girls?'*

Another pinch on her arm and Eleanor looked round at Darryl, scowling.

'Where were you?' Darryl asked with a laugh.

'Here, of course.'

'No, you weren't. Only in body, your mind was elsewhere. You seem to live in a dream. Is real life so hard to face?'

A lump immediately came to her throat. Eight months had healed nothing. She was only learning to live with it. To get through day by day. The true answer was yes. Yes, real life is too hard to face, but she wasn't going to tell him that.

'Don't be ridiculous,' she snapped at him.

They turned into the main street and were now fighting their way among the many other workers, all scrambling to arrive for the nine o'clock deadline. Most of the time they drifted along on the tide with the majority of people going toward the town. Only every now and again the odd person fought against the current and held back the flow.

By the time they were approaching The Birds Building Eleanor's anger was beginning to subside, and guilt crept in for the way she had spoken to Darryl.

'Can you explain why an archaeologist is doing this job?' she asked politely, hoping he would forgive her without her having to apologise again. 'Aren't you supposed to be digging holes?'

'It is still part of archaeology, but admittedly not my usual area. I've always loved buildings and when Dave— Mr Saunders was looking for someone to research this property he gave me the job. And, they're called trenches.'

They had arrived at the offices and Pete was already prepared, holding the door open for them to walk straight through.

'Morning, Pete,' said Eleanor trying to catch his attention and move slightly away from the doors. 'May I ask, why were the police here yesterday? It was nothing to do with—

'No, no,' Pete calmed her quickly. He could obviously tell what had been going on in her mind. 'They were asking about Doug. Apparently, he's not been home either. He seems to have gone missing.'

'Missing? I didn't realise it was anything as sinister as that. I hope he's alright.' The familiar knot in Eleanor's stomach was tightening.

'I'm sure he'll turn up in a couple of days with an almighty hangover.' Pete laughed outwardly, but his concern for his friend, Doug, was plain to see. His outwardly cheery demeanour couldn't hide his anxiety. He fidgeted rigidly as though he'd just received bad news.

'They wanted to have a look in the personnel files, and I sent them to Miss Osbourne, but I'm sure Miss High-and-Mighty will pass the job down to you this morning.'

'Oh no. The personnel files are precious. She won't let *anyone* near them.'

Eleanor smiled at the memory of the last time she had tried to find some information from the personnel files. Miss Osbourne had been out at lunch. She had almost sacked Eleanor on the spot through rage when she had returned early because of a sudden downpour. Later she came and apologised, giving the excuse of wet feet for her anger. According to Miss

Osbourne, there is a lot she can deal with, but wet feet is not one of them.

As Eleanor and Darryl walked across the expansive entrance hall to the lift Darryl asked, 'What was that about? Who's Doug?'

'Doug was a porter here. There are usually four porters. One left about a month ago, and Doug just didn't turn up for work the other day, or so we thought. So, we're down to two at the moment. They never seem to stay very long. It can't be the most interesting of jobs I suppose.'

Eleanor heard Darryl snigger quietly to himself and looked at him curiously.

'Sorry,' he said. 'Pete the porter.'

'Yes, very funny.' Eleanor didn't laugh at his childish sense of humour.

On entering the lift Eleanor recognised two others. Both from Samson's Digital World and she smiled politely as courtesy dictated. A strained smile was all she could manage, preoccupied with other thoughts. Surely there couldn't be a connection. *Nick and Chris' death was an accident, nothing more,* she berated herself

## 5

Darryl jittered nervously. He had been hoping they'd be able to slip in and out of the office quietly before certain people realised they were there, but he should have known better. *She's back in the world of cuckoos and lollipops again,* he thought frustratedly. He was sure Eleanor was purposefully taking her time as she meticulously hung her coat on a hook on the wall behind her office door, placed her handbag beneath her desk, changed from her trainers to her heels, and finally disappeared out the door again, making her way toward the kitchen.

'We don't need coffee,' Darryl implored. 'I thought we could just get straight on.'

'It's not for us. It's become part of the morning routine to make coffee for Miss Osbourne when I arrive.'

Darryl quietly seethed.

A moment later Miss Osbourne strolled out of her office and into Eleanor's. She perched herself on the edge of the desk. The tight, short skirt made certain that Darryl didn't miss any leg.

'Back again, I see, Mr Westwood. Is your quarry proving itself elusive?

Darryl smiled to himself. He was used to elusive, but even

when he was knee deep in mud there was still some kind of method.

'You were quite right about your archives not being organised at the moment. Personally, I think that may be a bit of an understatement,' Darryl replied.

'Our new archivist came highly recommended from his last employer, though the solitude of the archives may mean it will take a while till he's got the place just as he wants. Such a huge undertaking can't be rushed. Maybe it's something I could look into with you.'

'That's not needed, thank you, Miss Osbourne. We'll be trying again this morning, hopefully we'll have better luck this time. I hope you can spare Eleanor a while longer yet. I'm sure Mr Saunders would be very grateful.'

'Of course, anything for Mr Saunders. May I ask, is there a reason why you purposefully refuse to call me Cecilia?' she asked.

Darryl let out a small laugh. Subtlety was obviously not her strong point, and neither was the gracious acceptance of a well-intentioned hint.

'I like to keep an air of professionalism between work colleagues,' he replied, furtively glancing for Eleanor and hoping she would return soon.

'You know, depending on your success today, I could always celebrate or console over a drink tonight. Then we wouldn't be work colleagues and there would be no need for professionalism.'

'I'm afraid I have plans tonight,' Darryl said relieved to see Eleanor walking back toward the office, coffee mug in hand.

He let her reach the doorway before he blocked her entry, hoping she would realise he was keen to leave.

'Your coffee, Miss Osbourne.' Eleanor stammered from the doorway.

'Thank you.' Miss Osbourne reached across and took the coffee mug from Eleanor. 'What would I do without you?'

'I understand the police wanted some information from the personnel files.'

'Yes, that's right, but I can do that little job.'

'I'm sure it won't take a moment if you'd like me to—'

'No, no. You carry on. You're obviously very busy.' Miss Osbourne waved her hand as though shooing Eleanor out the door.

Darryl was surprised. Maybe Miss Osbourne had got the hint at last.

'OK.' Eleanor turned to Darry and asked, 'Shall we go straight down to the archives, then, Darryl?'

Miss Osbourne's mug slipped in her fingers at the apparent un-professionalism Darryl was sharing with Eleanor.

'Yes, we've got a lot to do,' he replied quickly. This was not a conversation he wanted to get in to and he joined Miss Osbourne in hurrying Eleanor out the door.

Eleanor, having no space, turned on the spot to walk out the door and suddenly disappeared from view. Darryl, impatient to exit the office, almost fell on top of her.

'Oh, Miss. Are you alright? We wouldn't want you to get hurt.' The caretaker was outside the doorway with the floor polisher.

'I think it's just my leg,' she said as she lifted her trouser leg to inspect the damage.

She had tripped over the large, bulky machine. The lever on the side had scraped up the front of her shin and she had landed on the floor.

'Not to worry. I'm sure I'll live to dance another day. I need to learn to watch where I'm going,' she said apologetically.

Something clicked in Darryl's mind when he heard this, but he couldn't quite make the connection. The sight of Gina making her way down the corridor arm in arm with a dark-haired, hourglass-figured beauty soon distracted his thoughts. *Not another one.*

'Mr Westwood,' Gina called to him.

He grabbed Eleanor's arm and pulled her up from the floor in desperation.

'Shall we go? We've got a lot of work to get through today,' he said to her through a forced smile.

'Mr Westwood,' Gina called again.

'We're in a bit of a rush,' he called back as he walked quickly over to the lift, dragging a limping Eleanor with him. 'Can it wait? Lots to do.'

He jabbed at the lift button several times with impatience.

'It's just a quickie, if you pardon my meaning,' Gina said coyly, reaching him at the lift. Doors not yet opened. 'I've noticed you're not wearing a ring. You're not married?'

'Divorced,' he said bluntly. 'Have you noticed the grey hairs, too?'

Gina giggled gently, as though not quite understanding the relevance.

'Oh dear, does it worry you? You could always dye the grey ones.'

Darryl was relieved to hear the lift arrive and the doors open behind him. He backed inside as quickly as he could. Eleanor following him, quietly.

'I like to keep them, thank you. They are a constant reminder of what *not* to do.'

Gina's face dropped, and the lift doors closed.

'You need more men working here,' Darryl snarled.

A small cough came from the side of the lift. Pete was standing there.

'The basement is it, *sir*?'

When they reached the archives, Callum was already on his feet and waiting for them.

'Good morning, I hope you had a good night, Eleanor.'

There was something more than kindness to Callum's greeting. *Even for a smarmy git*, Darryl thought.

'Thank you, Callum. How did you get on yesterday after we left?'

'I was here till eight o'clock but couldn't find a thing regarding that property.'

'Well, thanks for all your help,' Darryl interrupted. After all it was him that wanted the information. 'I guess it's a trip to the Council archives, then, to see if they have anything. Let's hope something survived the fire.'

'That's OK,' said Callum, finally addressing Darryl. 'That's what I thought too. I used to work there, before the fire, and I know the archivist. I'll go down and have a chat with them. It'll be much quicker that way. You could be there all day, whereas I'll probably be back by lunchtime.'

'Are you sure?' asked Eleanor.

'Absolutely, I'll grab my jacket and go now. I was only waiting for you to arrive to let you know I was going.'

Darryl smiled to himself as he realised what that *something more* was to Callum's greeting. The way he gave Eleanor his full attention when he spoke to her. The manner in which he gently touched her arm. *No wonder he's being so helpful,* he thought.

'It'll be a great excuse to catch up with them down there anyway,' continued Callum. 'I'll need to lock up though while I'm not here, so, if you've got anything else to be getting on with you can go back upstairs—'

Darryl didn't let him finish that sentence. 'Not likely. Come on,' he said to Eleanor. 'We're going out.'

He grabbed Eleanor's elbow and dragged her toward the lift, before suddenly stopping.

'On second thoughts,' he said, 'we'll take the stairs. That Pete sends shivers up my spine.'

'Nick never used to lock the archives. I didn't even know it had a lock,' said Eleanor.

'Things change,' Darryl replied, pulling her up the stairs.

'Where are we going?' she asked.

'To dig some trenches.'

'In these shoes?'

∼

The last of Eleanor's dark mood lifted as they left the building and walked back out into the fresh air. She should have returned to her office as there was still other work for her to be doing, but she was so relieved at not spending more time in the archives, that the cool air was too inviting to turn down. The sun had risen a little further and had warmed the chilly autumn morning. She breathed deeply. Her shoulders relaxed as she exhaled the worries of the morning.

The street seemed almost empty now that most people had disappeared into their offices or places of work.

'This place is so full of history, it's great,' said Darryl.

His head turned from side to side, trying to take in as much as he could.

'I guess the buildings are quite old,' replied Eleanor.

Darryl stopped in the street and stared at her.

'Old? Have you actually ever looked at them? I know there are these modern offices like the one you work in, and the abysmal modern shop fronts, but look up. Look at the architecture around the modern facades. That's the problem with everyone these days. They walk around with their heads down and all that beautiful architecture is simply missed.'

Eleanor looked across the street and at the building directly opposite. The shoe shop on the ground floor was light and bright, in keeping with all the other shops along the main street. LED lights blazed inside showing off the shoes on stainless steel racks strategically placed around the shop floor. The shop front was practically nothing but glass. Large featureless windows inside a thin framework. The door simply a replica of the window. The large expanse of glass made sure that there was nothing to distract the onlooker's eye from the shoes on display. Directly above the wall-sized windows was the brightly coloured shop name, *Come to Heel*. Eleanor knew the shop, though didn't venture inside often. But, as Darryl had instructed, she looked up. On the first floor the two windows were smaller. Still large but not filling an entire wall. A decorative shelf above the windows stuck out about six inches, suitable for nothing but a resting place for the town pigeons. Ornate scrolls embellished the sides, and for the first time Eleanor realised how beautiful they were. Their only purpose seemed to be as an ornamental border, just like a picture frame. But they framed something as mundane as windows, making them not so mundane after all. The shop next door, a tea-room, had large dark wooden beams running through it like a framework. Again, the ground floor facade was practically nothing but glass, while upstairs the beams were in-filled with white panels. Eleanor knew the street well, but the large glass windows baring the wares of the shops behind them was all she had ever really seen. Of course, she had noticed how one building was different to another, but she had never really *seen* them. Never taken note of the ornate decorations added to the buildings or within the brickwork itself.

'Do you see how different they all are? All from a different period in history.' Darryl pointed to a row of buildings a short way down the street. 'This row is Victorian, between about a hundred and twenty and a hundred and eighty years old, whereas this one,' Darryl pointed to a large building converted into a restaurant in the other direction, 'is from the Georgian period, going back two to three hundred years. And this one ...'

Darryl started to stride out, excitement in his footsteps. He walked about thirty metres and turned right. Eleanor was having trouble keeping up and as she turned the corner Darryl was already standing facing the building they were researching. He had crossed the road for a better view of the large structure in front of him.

'Such a beautiful building,' he breathed. 'And this one, this one is about six hundred and fifty to seven hundred years old.'

This was Thornewick Manor. This was where Eleanor had left him yesterday when she had continued for the train. She wasn't interested to stop then, but now she took the time to focus on it.

'It's certainly different from the others, but how can you tell it's that old just by looking at it?' she asked.

'Practice. But also, this is our first trench.'

Eleanor was beginning to have her doubts about this man now. So, OK, he may know a bit about buildings, but no matter how much he managed to charm the ladies at the office, nobody was going to let him dig a hole in the middle of this building. Darryl must have realised her doubts as he started to try and explain.

'Look at the windows,' he said, 'and please don't say they're old.'

Eleanor bit her lip and let him continue.

'You see how there are four panes with a central mullion that leads up. The trefoil heads at the top of the two top panes date these windows from the first half of the fourteenth century. This is the time when people were beginning to show off their fortune, their success. Their home was a statement as to how wealthy they were.'

Eleanor could see the windows were different from any of the others in the high street, but that still didn't explain where he wanted to dig his trench.

'So, where do you plan on digging your hole?' she asked slightly worried.

'Archaeology isn't just about finding out what's in the ground. It's finding out about history. This *is* the hole— trench,' he corrected. 'I don't need to physically dig, I can look at the windows, at the doors, at the stonework, and so many other things, and they will all reveal the history behind it. The material that was available to use at that time, tools of that time, and of course, the fashion of that time.'

'OK, I can see that,' Eleanor said, relieved. 'But how does that help? Can all these different things tell you the size of the original building?'

'No, which is why I'm hoping to find a plan, either of the entire original building, or maybe extensions built on over the years. We just don't know how big it was. This section you can see here is all we have to go on.'

'Maybe this was it. Maybe it wasn't any bigger. What makes you think it could have been?'

'I'll show you,' said Darryl excitedly.

Thornewick Manor was the only house on that side of the street before the next turning right, and about thirty-five metres in length. They turned down the side of the building and Darryl stopped at the entrance to a car port that had been built on the back of the building, sometime within the last twenty years or so.

'Look at that door,' he said indicating a door half-way down the side of the car port leading into the back of the Manor.

'It's definitely a door,' Eleanor replied wondering what was so remarkable about it.

'Look at the stonework around the frame. That's the kind of stonework that would be used for an internal door.'

'But it's external.'

'Which suggests?'

'Which suggests it was originally an internal door and the building came out further this way,' Eleanor said realising the significance.

'You've got it. Not hard really, you just need to know what to look for. Come on. Our second trench, and the reason why we're doing all this, is this way.'

They carried on walking past the car port, past an overgrown paved courtyard, and continued until they reached another building. This one was much smaller, maybe ten metres in length. Though, as far as Eleanor could tell, it had the same brickwork and windows. The same grandeur though run down and clearly unused for many years.

'This looks like it could be part of the same building to me,' said Eleanor convinced she was about to be chastised for saying the wrong thing again.

'Exactly,' Darryl said to her surprise. 'Our second trench reveals a building of about the same age. We need to find out whether it was once part of Thornewick Manor. The door we found back there in trench one could mean that it was, and the structure between the two has been destroyed or fallen away over time. Or the manor was extended, and this section was only built to look like the main structure. Or it may be that it is, and always has been, a completely separate building. Dave is applying for planning permission to turn this into a residence, but needs an archaeological evaluation done before anything can go ahead.'

'Which is where you come in.'

'Which is where I come in. If we can find the title deeds or any other documents from its early history, there will probably be a map or plan of the entire original structure and that's the job done.'

'And that's it?'

'That's it. Well, my part anyway. He can deal with the rest of it, that's all he wants from me. On the other hand, if we can't find a plan, we'll need to dig a third trench.'

'Where?'

'I haven't worked that out yet.'

~

Darryl and Eleanor spent the morning walking around the town. Every now and again Darryl would stop to inspect a gable wall, a chimney, or a particularly decorative moulding. He only lived just under an hour from Chartford Brooke, but hardly ever came here. He was always either working away, or simply travelled to a closer town for convenience sake.

'I understand you like the architecture, but why are we wandering around the town? I do have other work to do,' Eleanor said wearily.

'It's not about wandering around enjoying the architecture,' Darryl replied. Though secretly, for him, a major aspect of their wanderings was about exactly that. That and staying out of the office. 'We're doing research for anything from the same time period that may help give an idea of how the area at the time was laid out. Stop a moment and look around you.'

They stopped in the middle of the pavement, much to the annoyance of the man talking on his mobile and walking too close behind them. Eleanor apologised even though it was him that wasn't watching where he was going and had walked into her.

'See what I mean,' said Darryl annoyed. 'Walking around with their heads down and missing it all.' He turned his focus back to Eleanor. 'Now, look around and tell me what you see.'

'Buildings,' she said bluntly. 'And I'm sure you can tell me about each and every one of them.'

'I could, but there's no point,' he replied. 'Because each and every one of these buildings wasn't here when Thornewick Manor was built.'

'What was here?'

'Probably gardens and fields, farmland mostly. So, now imagine this entire area as open fields, going on for miles, with Thornewick Manor standing proudly in the middle of it all.'

Eleanor turned slowly, gazing all around her. Darryl loved occasions like this. That moment when someone began to understand the reality of what the place would have been like, and what would have been going on here, so many years ago. He watched as she continued to turn, a misty glaze over her eyes.

'Isn't that Callum?' Eleanor suddenly said as her gaze fell on a cafe. 'In there, having coffee.'

Callum was sat at the back of a brightly lit cafe fully absorbed in what he was reading. For Darryl, the moment was lost.

'Surely he's entitled to a quick coffee break?' he said disappointedly.

'What's he reading? Maybe he's already got something from the archives. Let's go in and see?'

'No, we don't want to disturb him. You know archivists, they never stop reading.' Darryl suddenly realised how his flippant remark may mean more to Eleanor than he had intended. He continued quickly. 'He won't have anything yet; he's probably reading a newspaper. It's more than likely that they've sent him for a coffee while they sort out what he needs. That's how these places often work. It'll take all morning at least.'

Thankfully, Eleanor believed his excuses. If Callum had already finished at the County archives it would have meant getting back to work in a stuffy office, instead of being outside in the fresh air. And so, they carried on with their so-called research. In truth, Darryl didn't understand why Callum would have been in the cafe instead of the archives either.

# 6

Darryl insisted on getting lunch while they were out, even if it was only eleven thirty. By the time they ordered, and the food had arrived, it would be closer to twelve, anyway, he told Eleanor. And it would give Callum more time to complete his search. The longer he could drag this out the better.

They enjoyed a pub lunch sitting at a table outside, overlooking one end of the park. The bright sunshine was blissful. Thankfully, the winter hadn't yet taken full hold of the autumn sun and it still held some warmth from the summer. Darryl sat back and closed his eyes, savouring the sun's gentle rays as they warmed his face. He couldn't remember the last time he had sat quietly, had a nice meal, and just took pleasure in being there, in that moment. The last three years had been nothing but arguments. A constant rant from his ex, Rachel. Here, the only noise was a soft rumble of traffic, the gentle murmur of conversations from the other patrons, and the joyful yells and screams of young children playing at a nearby playground.

A dark cloud moved across the sun revealing the true chilliness of the day. Darryl opened his eyes and saw Eleanor watching the playground silently. No expression on her face. No joy from watching the happy children. No torment from losing her own child. Only a blank silence. He couldn't imagine how it must feel to lose a child, and the agony she must be going through every waking moment. He thought briefly of his own children, Kathy and Alex. He had helped them move to their university lodgings only a few weeks ago. Their first year of so-called freedom. More often than not they drove him crazy, but he would never want to be without them. The thought of losing them made his heart ache. It was too much to bear.

'Shall we go?' he said brightly, hoping to distract Eleanor's attention away from the mothers with their children, and distract himself from such morbid thoughts.

'Yes,' she said. 'Let's hope Callum is back by now.' A catch in her voice. Barely audible but there.

She stood ready to leave. She tried to furtively wipe away a tear that had appeared as she blinked, but Darryl saw. He was glad to see his distraction seemed to work, for now at least.

∞

When they returned to The Birds Building Darryl was pleased to see that a different porter held the door for them. Pleased to avoid a repeat of the uncomfortable silence and the accusing glares he had received earlier from Pete.

'No Pete,' Darryl remarked.

'They swap about,' Eleanor said. 'Meet Sidney.'

'Hi, Sidney,' Darryl said happily.

Sidney was a large, bald man who looked as though he would be more comfortable in a boxing ring than in the smart, tight uniform that stretched over his muscles. He nodded in reply without removing the frown from his face.

If Sidney was on the door, Darryl deduced that Pete was more than likely in the lift. He gently guided Eleanor toward the stairs and they made their way to the basement. Eleanor tapped on Callum's office door and walked straight in. He was reading at his desk and was startled by their arrival.

'Did you manage to find anything, Callum?' she asked.

'Yes, I did.' He quickly got up from his cluttered desk and came to greet her. 'I left them on your desk only five minutes ago. I didn't expect you to come all the way down here again. There's not much there, I'm afraid, for a whole morning's work. An old watercolour print, and a couple of diaries, well, copies of. I'm afraid the originals are too precious to be taken out of the archives, but they do have copies that they loan out and these may be of some help.'

'Still no deeds or plans?' Darryl asked.

'No, I'm afraid not.' Callum turned again to Eleanor. 'Is there anything else I can help with?'

'We'll let you know,' Eleanor replied. 'Thank you for your help this morning though.'

'You're more than welcome.' He gently placed a hand on her arm. 'When you're done just bring them back and I'll return them. It'll be easier that way.'

Darryl sniggered behind Eleanor's back. He could only hope that Eleanor hadn't seen. He noted that she didn't flinch at Callum's touch, but neither did she encourage it.

'We'll go and see what you did manage to find,' she said. 'Thank you, again.'

Callum stayed close to Eleanor as she left his office and he gently closed the door behind them. Distracted, Darryl had already pressed the lift button before realising what he was doing. He tried not to look straight at Eleanor, but she could still see.

'What are you smirking at?' she said as the lift doors opened, and they walked in. 'Hi, Pete. First floor, please.'

'He likes you,' Darryl whispered loudly in her ear.'

'He's just being kind.'

'Of course, he is. You carry on believing that. Did you notice how he immediately got up to greet you when we went in the room? And how he held your arm as he spoke to you?'

'Stop it. Imagine what it must be like for him, knowing that he's taken my husband's job. That's an awful position for him to be in.'

'Yes, absolutely,' Darryl replied with mock seriousness. Outwardly Darryl was still smirking, but secretly he was wondering if she was ever going to let anybody back into her life.

A chance glance at Pete revealed no effort to hide his scowl. Darryl was glad when he could escape the lift, though he still felt on edge as he and Eleanor walked across the hallway to her office.

'Don't worry,' Eleanor said. 'Miss Osbourne, Gina, and Marie are probably still out at lunch.'

His hesitation must have shown. He only half-smiled a reply as reassurance didn't come easy.

A small pile of items were neatly placed in the centre of Eleanor's desk. She picked up the top folder and quickly flicked through it.

Darryl had never had trouble with claustrophobia before, but he was certainly struggling with a closed-in feeling now. 'There's not a lot of space in your office, is there?'

'That's because it's a cupboard,' Eleanor replied as a matter-of-fact, and continued looking to see what else had been left on her desk.

Darryl was wondering if she had actually said what he thought she'd said.

'A what?'

'A cupboard. Each floor is built to exactly the same dimensions,' she explained as though Darryl was stupid. 'Directly below is the caretaker's cupboard, directly above is a stationery cupboard.'

'And, that's why it's so small.'

'I'm very fond of my office, thank you very much. But there is a conference room available if you would be happier.'

This was an idea Darryl approved of. The further he could remove himself from the vicinity of Eleanor's office, the better.

'Follow me.' Eleanor collected together the three items from the County archives and led Darryl a short way down the hall.

The conference room was as bright, spacious and boring as any of the other offices he had seen. It had one advantage though. The frosted windows in both the door and internal wall adjacent to the hallway gave both light and, more importantly, privacy. The room was larger than Miss Osbourne's office with one large central table, surrounded by ten chairs. Ten black, uncomfortable-looking chairs. The only sign of personality in the room was an over-sized painting of randomly placed, different sized, red squares, but even this had an air of industry about it. The view from the large window caught Darryl's eye. The rear of Dave's recently acquired building was about fifteen metres from the back of The Birds Building. It looked even more run down from the back than it did from the street. The garden area was more of a wasteland with trees and climbers taking over like some furtive predator. He was glad that Dave wanted to bring the house back to life and he knew the job would be done sympathetically. It had always been something he had wanted to do himself, but Rachel liked the convenience of more modern properties and so that's what they had. Seeing Dave's building, looking so forlorn but full of potential, only served to add to his resentment of being manipulated over the years, and never able to fulfil that ambition. *Focus on the job,* Darryl told himself and turned his attention back to the conference room.

Eleanor had spread the items on the table. The print of the

watercolour painting, which was dated 1793 on the back, showed the main frontage of the house. Darryl was drawn to the detailing of the distinctive style of the window frames. Four on either side; two on the ground floor and two on the first, just as they had seen this morning. The stonework around the central door was a little grander than Darryl remembered, but artists always had their own interpretations. Either side of the house was a tall, widespread tree. Unfortunately, the sides of the building were obscured by their delicately painted summer foliage, so there was no telling how far back the building stretched. A track led up to the front of the house, flanked by two grand entrance pillars, and swept round to the left and out of sight behind the foliage of one of the trees. In the distance a little way to the right of the Manor stood a smaller building, which Darryl was certain looked like a chapel.

'I didn't see anything this morning that looked like it might have been a chapel from this period,' he said.

Eleanor held up the picture and turned in the room as though viewing the front of the building in situ.

'If Thornewick Manor faces this way, then the chapel would be somewhere over there.' She waved her right hand in the air in a generalised direction. 'There is a ruin over that way,' she said thoughtfully. 'On the other side of the street and through the park. I can't remember much about it but there's definitely something there, and I think it would be in about the same position as it is in this picture.'

'Great. Sounds like you've just found us trench three.' Darryl's spirit rose at the thought of another excuse to get outside.

'What about these?' Eleanor asked. She picked up one of the two plastic files full of A4 colour photocopies, which even included copies of the tattered binding and deep red leather jackets.

'How much information will we be able to get from diaries?'

'Diaries can be a great source.' Darryl had to admit to himself that he was excited about the diaries as they revealed the day to day life during that time in history. 'For what we need now, though, I'm not sure how helpful they'll be. We'll need to read through them. One for you and one for me,' he said picking up the other plastic file.

They sat round one end of the table and started reading in silence.

∽

Both diaries were written by the same hand. It seemed to be the Lady of the Manor. The flamboyant script was hard going for Eleanor, but Darryl seemed to be making great progress. Written in first person, it was soon evident that there was no reference to her name. Eleanor suggested the name Lady Rose.

'A very appropriate choice for the Lady of Thornewick Manor,' Darryl said.

The descriptions of the daily routines, the occasional problematic servant, and her children's antics were interesting, but there was nothing about the Manor itself beyond the simple mention of a particular room relevant to the circumstance Lady Rose was describing.

After a couple of hours Eleanor needed coffee. She slipped her shoes back on and went through to the kitchen. Unfortunately, Gina and Marie entered the kitchen just as she was leaving carrying the two mugs of coffee. They took great delight in noting that she and Darryl were working in the conference room.

'Don't keep him all to yourself,' she heard Gina call after her.

Eleanor's steps faltered momentarily as she approached the

conference room door. She closed her eyes and imagined Laurel and Hardy in their four-inch heels fighting over a biscuit tin.

'Don't keep them all to yourself,' Laurel was whimpering to Hardy.

When Eleanor opened her eyes again Darryl was holding the door open for her, eyebrows raised.

'What was all that about?' he asked.

'Don't worry about them, they're just the local comedy double act,' Eleanor said placing the coffees on the table. 'Did you find anything of interest in your diary?'

'No, not really. Well, no, that's not true. Lady Rose gives some great detail about everyday life, especially things like the treatment of the servants, and how children were expected to behave. There's a lot of interesting stuff in here, but nothing that's going to help me now. How about yours?'

'Same, but I've still got a way to go.'

'I think this watercolour is going to be our best bet. Maybe we should go and have a look at those ruins you were talking about. Could we make a copy of this here instead of taking the archives' copy out with us?'

'I'll tell you what. You finish Lady Rose's second diary and I'll get this photocopied, but after my coffee.'

'Fair enough,' Darryl replied. He lounged back in his chair with his coffee, put his feet up on the table, and continued reading from Eleanor's diary copy.

*Someone needs to learn some manners,* Eleanor frowned. *That is no way to behave in an office.* A short while later Eleanor had finished her coffee, copied the watercolour print, and returned to the conference room.

'I'm almost done here,' Darryl said as she entered the room, 'and then we can give these back to your *friend* in the archives.'

Eleanor saw him smiling to himself. An inexplicable rage emerged.

'He is not my friend,' Eleanor said. The effort to keep calm made her hands shake.

'Sure, whatever you say,' he said not looking up.

Eleanor began to feel the knot in her stomach begin to tighten. How could this man, a man who didn't even know her, be so arrogant as to even consider that she would look upon anyone in that way?

'I do not appreciate your lewd comments and I think you should keep them to yourself. He is not my friend and certainly not in that manner,' Eleanor said, calm and measured. Inside she was burning.

'OK, there's nothing wrong with it,' he said casually, still not looking up from the diary. 'There's nothing wrong with someone taking a liking to you.'

Eleanor's hand reached for her bracelet and she rolled the beads between her fingers. Her temper rising further inside her.

'Let's face it, it's going to happen sometime,' he continued.

'How dare you,' she strained through her teeth.

Darryl finally looked up. He seemed to be stunned into silence for a moment.

'I'm sorry,' he said gently. 'I won't say any more. Let's just carry on with this last diary and see if we have anything of use.'

Eleanor couldn't move. She was afraid that her knees would give way completely if she tried. Her heart was pounding hard. It felt as though it had swollen leaving no room for her lungs to breathe. She was barely aware of Darryl still talking, something about the diaries, but her focus was on her beads. They twisted and spun in her fingers, becoming clammy like her hands. She clung to their familiarity to get her through this moment. The faces of the two officers on her doorstep came into view. Their solemn faces, their eyes full of pity—

Suddenly, the image vanished as the conference room door

burst open behind her, shocking Eleanor back to reality. Stunned in the moment.

'Anything we can help with?' asked Gina from the doorway.

'No, thank you,' said Darryl, with only a glance from the diary.

'Did Eleanor offer you a biscuit to go with your coffee?' she continued.

'I said, I'm fine,' he said more firmly.

'Eleanor, how about you?' she persisted.

Eleanor just shook her head. The blood had run from her face and she was glad she had her back to the door.

'We're both fine,' Darryl said more firmly still.

A large audible sigh came from Gina over the closing of the door as it gently brushed the hard wood floor. Gina's voice drifted in before the click of the door latch. 'She's still fiddling about with those stupid plastic beads.'

'I know, they're horrendous,' came Marie's voice. 'But with her fashion sense what else would you expect.'

Eleanor was still silent, for now she was just numb.

'Why do you put up with that?' Darryl asked.

*Because it's just me,* Eleanor thought, but she said nothing.

'How often do you have to put up with their nasty remarks?' Darryl continued through Eleanor's silence.

Eleanor's anger rose again abruptly. Anger from being left alone; anger of the world still turning while her world withered away in silence.

'You've got to stand up for yourself, Eleanor. You've just shown me you have it inside you.'

'Shut up,' she screamed. 'Who do you think you are walking in here making demands. How dare you judge me. I didn't ask to do this job with you. You asked for me, so damn well stop criticising me and just let me get on with it.'

Eleanor headed for the door. She needed air, but Darryl got to his feet fast and grabbed her wrist as she made for the handle.

'I'm sorry, I'm so, so sorry.' His voice almost a whisper. 'Come and sit down.'

But Eleanor didn't want to hear it. She yanked her wrist out of his hand and watched as the beads from her bracelet flew from her wrist and fell to the floor. Eleanor retched from pain for the slightest of moments, and then ran. She didn't wait for the lift, she headed straight for the stairs.

'Eleanor, Eleanor,' Darryl called after her, but she wasn't going to stop.

She could hear him following her down the stairs. She forced her way past a client entering the building. The door only half open. Darryl's footsteps weren't far behind her. She suddenly found herself surrounded by people. The tears in her eyes made a haze of nothing but rudimentary shapes and colours. She didn't know where she was going, she just knew she had to get away from here. Away from the memories; away from the guilt of carrying on with this futile life.

People swarmed around her, jostling her from one side to another. The noise of the traffic was no more than a din. The world was closing in. Everything around her was disjointed. A baby crying loudly; a large vehicle next to her blocking her way; amplified music coming from somewhere nearby; Darryl's voice, closer now. She had to get away.

∽

Darryl could see Eleanor running toward the road. Luckily, she was slowed by the amount of people waiting at the crossing. *Dave was right*, he thought. *She is nuts.* But he couldn't help but feel responsible for her running out. He was only a few metres away from her now. Her face contorted with confusion as she twisted and turned in amongst the people, but still struggling through. A mother with a buggy moved to the side. A space opened. Darryl moved around the couple holding hands in front of him and moved himself in front of Eleanor. An effort to try and stop her from running into the road.

'Eleanor, Eleanor stop,' he called. He was almost there and reached out.

∼

Eleanor was overwhelmed. By people, by noise, by grief. She pushed her way through the crowd. She had to escape. A hand appeared on her shoulder. But then something was wrong. There was a jab in her ribs. No, not a jab. A push. She was pushed toward the road. As she fell, she felt the resistance of another body. This someone broke her fall, but, like a domino, they fell in her stead.

Tyres screeched. A thud of a person hitting the bonnet of a car. Another thud as that person hit the ground. Screams seemed to be coming from all directions and Eleanor's eyes began to come back into focus.

A couple of metres in front of her, Darryl was lying in the road.

# 7

Eleanor tried to scream but the lump in her throat was solid. Sick rushed to her throat at the sight of Darryl lying motionless in the road. She wanted to go to him, but her legs wouldn't move. People were everywhere, darting all around her. Well-meaning people trying to help, parents moving their children away, others just curious. Eleanor felt a hand on her arm. Callum was there beside her.

'Come back inside,' he said. 'There's nothing we can do here.'

'It's my fault. I have to help,' Eleanor muttered.

'Come back inside.'

'I won't,' Eleanor said, stronger now that she had found her voice. 'I have to help him. Darryl, Darryl,' she called, fighting Callum to let her go.

'Eleanor, no.'

Callum's grip became tighter as he tried to pull her away.

'Let go of me. I have to help.'

A cacophony of sirens came closer. The crowd was growing as morbid fascination took over. Eleanor found herself being pushed against the front of the dark-green van that was parked at the side of the road. Another pair of hands took hold of her. It was Pete. She couldn't fight anymore as weakness consumed her. *It's all my fault. Not again.* How could she let another death happen because of her. Her legs would no longer hold her. She fell, only saved from the ground by Callum and Pete's grasp.

They managed to support Eleanor back to the foyer of The Birds. The caretaker brought her a chair from the porter's room, and she collapsed into it. She stared blankly at the commotion outside, unable to move, unable to understand what had happened. The ambulance arrived. Police too, trying to move onlookers back. After a few moments two ambulance crew rose from behind the crowd carrying a stretcher. A limp and lifeless body was carried into the back of the ambulance and out of sight. The sirens blared as the ambulance left. *Does that mean he is still alive? They wouldn't need sirens if he was already d—* she couldn't bring herself to even think it.

Miss Osbourne, Gina and Marie were slowly walking back to the office building. Eleanor managed to stagger to her feet as they approached the doors.

'Is he still alive?' Eleanor asked.

'No thanks to you,' snapped Gina.

'He's going to be fine,' said Miss Osbourne reassuringly. 'The car that hit him was already slowing down for the lights at the crossing. They are just taking him to the hospital as a precaution. Accidents are always occurring at that crossing.'

A memory came back to Eleanor.

'Somebody pushed me,' she said, shivering from the cold, or was it the shock?

'Yes, of course they did,' Gina sneered. 'It's all about you, isn't it? Someone pushed you and yet it was Mr Westwood that ended up in the road. You seemed pretty upset with him, are you sure it wasn't you that did the pushing?'

'Don't listen to her,' Miss Osbourne interjected quickly. 'I'm sure it was nothing but an accident. Do you want to talk about what happened?'

Eleanor, stunned by Gina's outburst, shook her head. Miss Osbourne just wanted details for the kitchen gossip. Her sympathy wasn't out of kindness toward her.

'I don't know ... I don't know what happened.'

'Why don't you go get your things and take the rest of the day off? There's only an hour or so to go anyway and there's no point you staying here,' Miss Osbourne said gently.

Pete kindly offered to help Eleanor return upstairs to get her things. She changed from her heels to her trainers and retrieved her bag and coat from her office. The door to the conference room was half open. Darryl's jacket was still hanging over the back of his chair. *He's going to be fine,* she told herself. *That's what Miss Osbourne said.*

She was still shivering but turned down all help of getting home. There was something comforting about the normality of getting the train. She started the walk to the station, but when she reached Thornewick Manor she changed her mind. She needed to explain to Darryl what had happened, and why she was so upset about her bracelet. She needed to apologise. She needed to make sure for herself that he was going to be alright.

The hospital was a forty-minute walk away and the fresh air and exercise helped to clear Eleanor's mind. Dark rain clouds had moved in during the afternoon and now covered the sky bringing on the night early, but the rain held off, for now.

She rang Aileen on the way to explain there had been an accident at work and she was going to be home late. She didn't want to give details. An accident, nothing more. Aileen, as Eleanor knew she would, told her she would stay as long as needed. Aileen was always happy to stay in the spare room during those times Eleanor had needed to work late. Having no family of her own at home, they had often joked about her moving in.

When Eleanor arrived at the hospital's main reception the man at the desk pointed her in the right direction. She followed the blue line painted on the floor as instructed and stopped outside the ward. She could see Darryl through the window in the door to his room. She didn't know what she'd expected to see, but she didn't expect this.

Darryl was sat on the edge of the hospital bed. He was fully dressed and looked as though he was ready to leave. He was deep in conversation with two smartly dressed men, their backs toward her. His brow was furrowed as he listened intently. By chance he glanced up and saw Eleanor watching him through the glass in the door. The look of concern on his face didn't disappear. He just stared at her.

*He blames me and so he should.* She slowly moved toward the door and opened it.

'Please remember what we said, Mr Westwood,' the older of the two men said as he handed Darryl a business card.

Eleanor jolted when she saw the local police logo on the card. *The police again?*

'Hopefully it was all very innocent and just an unfortunate accident,' the man continued, 'but I felt I must make you aware of our concerns.'

'Yes, thank you. I'll certainly keep it in mind.'

'Take care of yourself. Remember, give us a call if you need to.'

The two men left the room with only a nod of acknowledgement toward Eleanor. Then there was nothing but silence.

Eleanor didn't know where to start. She had been churning over what she wanted to say all the way to the hospital, but now, nothing came to her. She thought Darryl looked as uncomfortable with the situation as she felt.

'Are you alright?' she finally managed to say.

Darryl only nodded in reply.

'I ... I came to apologise, and explain to you—'

'There's no need to explain anything. I was—'

'Why were the police here?' she interrupted. 'What were they making you aware of?'

Darryl didn't reply.

'I'm sorry, it's none of my business. I came to explain about my bracelet.'

Her fingers moved automatically to find it, but they only found an empty wrist. She hated the silence, and more to fill it with some kind of noise than anything else, she kept talking.

'I know it was plastic and cheap, but my son gave it to me for my birthday three weeks before ... before ...'

'It's fine. You don't need to—'

'He'd used his own pocket money to buy the beads,' she interrupted again. Nervousness had kept her going and now she had started she was unable to stop. 'He'd saved up and then made it for me. I wore it to keep him close. I found it comforting to have something so special from him close to me ... and now ... and now I have nothing left. Nothing but a pain in my heart that hurts so much I feel I can hardly breathe.'

Darryl stepped off the bed and held her while she sobbed. She couldn't hold it in any longer. The pain, the anger, the guilt, all came flooding out in her tears. She had come to the hospital to apologise and explain herself. Instead she had lost control and crumbled. It was easier to keep her emotions hidden while at work. It had become a habit. Being professional, she called it. This man was a relative stranger who she knew she would never see again in a few days time. It somehow made it easier to crack. She had nothing to prove to him.

She hadn't spoken aloud of this to anyone for nearly eight months. Everyone rallied round with their sympathies and condolences for the first two or three weeks, but life was expected to carry on as normal. But it wasn't normal and never would be normal again.

After a few minutes a doctor entered the room carrying a large, flat, brown file. The results of Darryl's x-rays. Eleanor's tears had begun to lessen, and the sound of the door opening jolted her back to the world of conformity. Without a word, Darryl gently led her to the chair next to the bed and turned back to the doctor.

'You're all clear, Mr Westwood. You will ache for a few days and I'm sure there'll be some very colourful bruises but keep up with the painkillers we've prescribed for you over the next few days and you'll be fine. That was quite a bump to the head though, so please watch out for any signs of concussion. Other than that, you're free to go. You're very lucky, that could have been a very nasty accident.'

The doctor left quietly, with as much diplomacy as he had shown when entering and discovering their moment of comfort.

Eleanor looked up suddenly. That word – accident – again.

'It wasn't an accident.'

'What? Don't be silly. Everyone's pushing and shoving at those road crossings—'

'No. Someone pushed me. I swear it. Someone pushed me, which caused me to knock into you.'

Darryl's look of concern reappeared as he listened. The one she had seen when she had first arrived.

'Come on,' he said. 'I need to tell you something, but let's get out of here first.'

~

Darryl and Eleanor left the hospital and started to walk slowly back toward town. The news he had been given was not going to be easy to convey to Eleanor. She had already proved herself to be emotionally unsteady. This information may be more than she could cope with, but she had a right to know.

'Those two men are detectives.' His voice calm and measured. 'They think there may be a possibility that the accident wasn't ... an accident.'

Darryl saw the haste in Eleanor's reaction as she turned to face him. He continued quickly, not giving her the opportunity to interrupt. 'I dismissed it because nobody would go to the trouble of killing me, not even my ex. She's already taken everything she possibly could from me. And, after all, if what you say is true, then it was you that was pushed, not me.'

'So, someone might be trying to kill me?'

'No.' The inference was unintentional and he quickly tried to appease her. 'I mean I don't think it's likely that someone is trying to kill me, you, or anybody. It was just an accident.'

'What would make them think that anyway?' Eleanor asked.

Darryl took a deep breath. He took his time, choosing his words carefully.

'Apparently, there have been a few deaths and disappearances all around, or to do with, The Birds Building. They have nothing conclusive but—'

'But that means— Nick. Are you saying Nick was murdered?'

'No ... I don't know. Like I said, they have nothing conclusive, but in the last eighteen months or so there has also been the disappearance of a porter, and a job applicant was later found dead. Then this happens to me and apparently I fit the profile.'

Eleanor had turned white. Darryl failed to convince himself that it was the change of streetlights from their orange glow to the newer white lights as they drew closer to the main street and market square.

'I don't understand. If Nick was murdered why haven't they

said anything to me before? I was his wife, surely I should have been told.'

'Because individually they looked like accidents, nothing suspicious about them at all. But when put together they all centre around that building.'

'Why would anyone want to kill Nick? He was well liked. He did a good job. He was a good man. Why Nick? And why my boy?'

Eleanor was close to hysterics. Darryl led her to a bench in the market square. The streets were virtually empty again now, before the evening mass of people.

'Listen to me, Eleanor. It was an accident. Me and Nick, both accidents. The police look for conspiracy theories in everything. I guess it's part of their job to look for connections where there are none.'

Eleanor's confusion was written all over her face. Darryl didn't want to leave her so vulnerable. She needed time. Time for everything to sink in. Instead they sat quietly and listened to some buskers playing in the square. A keyboard player and a violinist playing a John Williams film soundtrack. Immediately recognisable without being able to pinpoint which film.

Darryl hadn't realised the significance of her bracelet. He had assumed her playing with it was nothing more than a nervous habit. And now, after giving her this news, he felt responsible for her present state.

'Do you want to tell me what happened?' Darryl asked.

Eleanor looked at him silently.

'You don't have to, just if you want to. I thought you may want to talk ...'

'There's not much to tell really,' she answered as a whisper. 'All I know is that Nick left work as usual at the end of the day. He stopped off on his way home, as we had arranged, to pick up Christopher, our son, from a friend's house. He'd had a play date with one of his school friends. A few miles later he drove into a tree. There were no witnesses. The car was already in flames by the time anyone reached them. There was nothing left after the fire had been put out, hardly even the shell of the car, let alone anything else. There was nothing to suggest it was anything more than an accident. What more is there to say?'

'How did you end up working at Dolby and Patterson's?'

'I used to be a primary school teacher, before Chris came along. I couldn't go back to that. Not after ...'

'I understand,' Darryl said, not wanting to distress Eleanor further.

He knew there was nothing he could say that would help, and so they sat quietly once more listening to the buskers. They had moved on to a different soundtrack but with the same recognisable style.

After a few minutes, Eleanor asked, 'Weren't you supposed to be going out tonight? Must be quite a hot date for you to have turned Miss Osbourne down,' she joked.

Darryl was glad that Eleanor had managed to think about something other than Nick and Chris. Surely, it was a sign that the quiet time they had spent together had given her the chance to absorb the information. He hoped rather than believed this to be true. He had forgotten about his evening out.

'Don't laugh at me,' he said shyly. 'I go dancing.'

'Even better. A hot date down the nightclub.'

'Nightclub? I haven't been to a nightclub in nearly twenty years.' Darryl shook his head. His evening out wasn't something he usually mentioned to anyone. But he felt his hesitation only made Eleanor all the more curious. 'No, ballroom dancing.'

Eleanor's face suddenly fell, and Darryl realised it at the same time.

'That's where I've seen you before,' he said. 'I started going a couple of years ago, and you were there with ...'

'With Nick,' Eleanor continued.

'I'm sorry, bringing it all up again,' he said.

'Don't be, they were happy times. That was our one night together a week, when we went to those classes.'

'Maybe that was where I failed. We should have gone earlier on in the marriage rather than trying to save it at the end.'

'Does your wife still go?' Eleanor asked.

'Ex,' Darryl corrected. 'No, turned out I'm too "techniquey" for her.'

'You're what?'

'"Techniquey."' Darryl spoke the word clearly. Pronouncing every syllable. 'She never did have the greatest grasp of the English language. It meant I cared too much about technique and getting it right, rather than just "twirling around and having a bit of fun," her words again.'

'But it's more fun if you can do it right.'

'Exactly, but she didn't get it. To be honest, I don't think anything would have helped by that point. The marriage was over.'

'I'm sorry to hear that.'

'Don't be. It's freeing in a way. I no longer have to try and earn enough to keep her in the manner in which she would like to be accustomed, which, let's face it, as an archaeologist I was never going to do.' Darryl had never spoken so pragmatically about his marriage break-up. His head cleared with every word and he finally accepted it was over. 'It's time to move on,' he continued. 'And besides, I found out I enjoy dancing. It wasn't a complete waste of time.'

Eleanor smiled and for the first time in a long time found that she liked it. She had never thought about it before, but the feeling of a smile, a smile from pleasure not obligation, and without guilt, was a lovely thing. She felt her shoulders relax and the tension in her back drift away.

'I suppose I should really be getting home,' Eleanor said, suddenly feeling embarrassed.

'Will you wait just a moment. I'd like to give the buskers something. They're good, aren't they?'

Darryl walked over to the buskers, pulling some change from one of his pockets, and spoke a few quick words to them. Eleanor thought about all the people who must pass them by every day without a word of thanks, or even an acknowledgement of them being there.

The tune they were playing ended and they began to play a new one. Eleanor recognised the familiar three beat rhythm of a waltz. Darryl came back to Eleanor and held out his hand.

'May I have this dance?' he asked.

'No,' said Eleanor. Her cheeks reddening at the thought of dancing in the town square while people ambled past.

'I am missing my class because of you.'

Eleanor only shook her head. She stayed firmly on the bench, even to the point of subconsciously hooking her hands around one of the bench's slats, either side of her.

'I'm not going anywhere until I get my dance. You pushed me under a car today, I think it's the least you can do.'

Eleanor took a deep breath and finally gave in. They were already attracting some funny looks by those not yet fully absorbed in their quest for a fun night out. She took his hand and stood. She allowed Darryl to lead her a few steps closer to the centre of the vast, exposed square. Darryl put his arm around her, resting just above her waist, and waited. Troubled by the gentle pressure of his hand on her back, Eleanor hesitantly placed her hand lightly on his shoulder, slightly to the left. As she corrected her posture for the dance, she savoured the stretch in her back and neck. From the first step the warmth of joy she used to feel came back to her. Though Eleanor's nerves were fading, Darryl seemed to have no inhibitions at all and moved in large sweeping steps as they swung across the paving slabs together. Eleanor had loved those classes. It had always felt like a kind of magic to her. The music began and two people moved as one. Gliding across the floor with no other thoughts than her and Nick. Putting all her trust in his hands to lead them around the floor. If she closed her eyes, she could almost imagine she was back in those classes. It had been a long time since she had felt this, what seemed to her, a strange kind of ethereal joy. Not just a fleeting smile, but the true deep-down pleasure she used to get from the graceful motion created by two people and a lilting rhythm. Tears began to run down her cheeks. Inevitably, with the joy came the guilt. She was dancing in another man's arms.

# 8

Once their dance had come to an end, Darryl had insisted on driving Eleanor home. She could tell he was trying to make conversation as they travelled along in his old Land Rover. He spoke about the last time he had visited that suburb of the town. Something to do with looking at a second-hand car only a couple of months before he'd decided on the Land Rover they were in now. He spoke about how the heating took so long to work and how he wished he had his jacket. Eleanor remembered the last time she had seen it, hanging on the back of his chair in the conference room. It seemed like such a long time ago and so much had happened since, but it was only a matter of hours.

Whether his conversation was out of nervous embarrassment or if dancing a waltz in the middle of the town square was a normal, everyday occurrence for him, she didn't know. She wasn't even sure how she felt at this moment. Embarrassed, certainly, but mainly confused. She had never expected to feel the pleasure she used to feel from dancing. *It was just a silly dance, woman*, she scorned herself. *Life does still hold some pleasures, no matter what you may think.* And, then there was the possibility of Nick and Chris being murdered. She still wasn't sure whether that would ever sink in.

Eleanor remained silent for most of the journey. She couldn't seem to find the right words to say, other than giving directions to her house. Darryl was currently giving his opinion on the seventies housing estate he was driving through, but for Eleanor silence was easier. Silence among Darryl's monologue, and the rattles that came from his old Land Rover. A Land Rover that, to Eleanor, felt reminiscent of riding in an old tin can.

By the time Darryl pulled up in front of Eleanor's house the rain that had been threatening all evening was now in full force.

'Wait there,' he said as he got out the car. The rear door opened. A moment later it closed, and Darryl was at Eleanor's door with a large umbrella. She ducked under the umbrella, and they ran up the drive together.

The front door opened as they arrived, 'You're always coming home wet, lassie,' Aileen said as she greeted them at the door. 'Och, and with a fellow this time too.'

Eleanor and Darryl stepped in out of the rain.

'We're just working together at the moment,' Eleanor said quickly as she removed her coat and trainers. She could feel her cheeks begin to burn.

'Is that right? At half past eight in the evening?'

'There was a bit of an accident,' Darryl interjected. He shook his umbrella out the door and left it standing in the porch. 'Nothing to worry about. I just wanted to make sure she got home safe. I'm Darryl.'

He wiped his damp hand down his jeans before holding it out to shake Aileen's.

'Aileen, pleased to meet you.'

Aileen shook his hand awkwardly as though it was an alien action to her. Eleanor wondered how long it had been since she had shaken someone's hand. Aileen was more of a hugging person.

'How's Mum?' Eleanor asked, wanting to change the subject.

'Not been too good a day today, I'm afraid. She had another fall this evening, not that long ago. Aye, I've only recently finished patching her up and got her back to her chair. She's in the lounge. You go on through, hen.'

Eleanor removed her hair band and her hair fell comfortably around her shoulders. She walked through to the lounge aware of Darryl following behind. Her mother looked up as she walked in the room. Something was wrong. The smile she had gotten used to when she returned from work didn't appear on her mother's lips today. Her eyes stared coldly.

'Have you come to get the ... the ... oh, what is it? ... The milk,' she suddenly seemed to remember.

'No,' Eleanor laughed nervously. 'Why would I want milk?'

'What do you want then?'

Eleanor's heart stopped for a moment. The harshness in her mother's tone brought the familiar lump to her throat.

'I live here. It's me, Eleanor.'

'Eleanor? I don't know any Eleanor.' Margaret spoke quietly, thinking to herself. 'Eleanor, Eleanor, Ellie ... Nellie? I know a Nellie. Are you Nellie? Nellie Fitzpatrick from down the way? My eyes aren't as good as they used to be.'

'No,' she replied. 'I'm Eleanor, your daughter.'

'Eleanor, my daughter?' The look of confusion on her face said it all.

Tears welled in Eleanor's eyes. Her hands clenched so tight her nails dug into her palms. 'I moved in a few months ago. After Nick and Chris— after the accident. You remember, Mum. Please remember.'

The look of bewilderment on Margaret's face didn't change.

'What about you, young man?' Margaret had seen Darryl watching from the doorway. 'Are you here for the milk?'

'No, I'm afraid not. I'm Darryl,' he replied. 'I'm a friend of Eleanor's.'

'Friend?'

'We've been out dancing.' Darryl took a seat on the sofa, next to Margaret's armchair.

'Oh, I see.' Margaret smiled. 'That type of friend.'

'No, I don't—'

'When my husband and I,' interrupted Margaret, 'were ... were ... oh, what's the word? Courting. When we were courting, we used to go dancing every Friday and Saturday night.'

'I bet you were good.'

'Good?' Margaret sat up proudly. 'Town champions for three years running. Or was it four?'

'Maybe I should take you dancing next time.'

'I'll give you a run for your money.'

Darryl laughed, 'I bet you could.'

'Darryl, did you say? I'm Margaret, though you can call me Maggie. If you need any dancing tips you just come and ask me, you hear that?'

'Absolutely.'

Eleanor felt sick to her stomach. She knew this would happen one day, but it didn't make it any easier. She watched the easy-going conversation between her mother and Darryl. Her mother had seemed to come alive with the conversation. From Darryl's laid-back attitude Eleanor guessed he couldn't have understood what was going on. The way they were talking it was as though there was nothing wrong with her at all, and yet this morning she was quiet and still, spending most of her waking hours asleep. Eleanor's stomach began to churn.

'Och, hen. I wish I could have warned you, but there had been no sign of this.' Aileen took a step toward Eleanor, comforting hands outstretched. 'There was nothing to say, to say—'

Eleanor pushed her way through the doorway. She just made it to the downstairs cloakroom before she threw up. Aileen followed her through and comforted her like she was her own daughter. Only silence between them. There was nothing Aileen could say that would make this any easier.

After a few minutes Eleanor felt safe enough to move from the toilet to the basin, and she rinsed her face. The cool water helped bring her focus back to Aileen and the lateness of the evening. 'Thank you again for staying. I swear you look after me as much as Mum. I'm sure you'll want to be getting home.'

'Och, don't be daft. I'm not leaving you here like this, hen. This is not an easy thing to go through.'

'Thank you, I'll be fine now. It was a shock initially, but I'll be fine.'

'Well, at least you have some company.' Aileen nodded toward the lounge where they could still hear voices chatting. 'But I'll be here bright and early in the morning.'

Aileen left the small cloakroom leaving Eleanor in peace. *Space to breathe, that's all I need,* she tried to convince herself.

A few minutes later, when Eleanor left the cloakroom, she could hear Aileen and Darryl's voices coming from the kitchen. She glanced through the lounge door as she walked past and saw that her mother was sleeping in her chair. Her head slumped forward on her chest, gently snoring. When Eleanor entered the kitchen both Aileen and Darryl turned to look at her. She immediately had that uncomfortable feeling from being the subject of an unheard conversation.

Aileen was wearing her long, padded coat, her handbag already over her shoulder, and she was ready to leave. She turned back to Darryl, 'Take care of the wee lass for me.'

Darryl smiled in reply. A sad looking smile that was only enough to say he'll try. 'Nice to meet you, Aileen.'

'You too.' Aileen moved toward Eleanor and kissed her on the forehead. 'I'll be back in the morning,' she said gently. 'Dancing eh? I thought you were going to the hospital.' She winked at Eleanor and quickly left before Eleanor had the chance to explain.

Eleanor briefly thought of the pleasure she had felt from her waltz. It was no more than half hour ago, and yet it seemed like much longer. Her thoughts soon turned back to her mother and her illness, like a punishment.

'Would you like me to stay a while?' Darryl asked quietly, breaking the silence between them. 'Not for anything in particular,' he added quickly. 'I can see you're upset and, as you heard, I've been given instructions to look after you.'

'She knew who I was this morning,' Eleanor replied in a daze. 'Now I'm a stranger to her.' Eleanor felt the need to explain what probably seemed like an over-reaction to someone who didn't understand the situation.

'Aileen explained. You may be a stranger to her, but she is still your mother. She will still respond to your smile, to your love. She will remember things about her life, just things from long ago.'

'From before I existed, it would seem. I don't think I've heard her chatting away like that for years. I didn't even know she used to go dancing with Dad.'

'Have you ever asked her?'

Eleanor shook her head.

'What do you talk about?' Darryl asked.

'We don't really. I come home and ...' Eleanor couldn't remember the last time she'd tried to talk with her mother. Not a proper conversation. She felt ashamed to admit the truth, but it was like she had given up. The normal everyday things were so hard for her mother to remember, or to remember the words she needed. Or, she would just fall asleep half-way through a sentence. Eleanor had simply stopped trying. That was even before this last month when it all changed again. She didn't want to explain to Darryl how she'd had to have the same conversation every day about losing Nick and Chris. The evening was always quiet after a conversation like that. 'We don't,' she simply said.

'Talk to her. Ask her questions about when she was younger. There will still be times when she does remember you, but it will get worse.'

'How come you're so knowledgeable on the subject?' Eleanor said curiously.

'My father had dementia a few years ago. I could easily recognise the signs.'

'I'm sorry. It's not easy is it? You seemed very at ease talking with her in there.'

'I had some great talks toward the end of my father's life. You wouldn't believe some of the things he got up to when he was younger. Things he probably wouldn't actually tell his son, if he had known I was his son.'

The two of them laughed together.

'I bet that's the first time you've laughed in eight months,' Darryl said.

'Of course not. You make me sound like a misery.'

'I mean a real laugh. A laugh because you're happy, not a forced laugh to show the world how strong you are or how well you're coping.'

Loneliness swept over Eleanor in the silence that followed, but it always came with a handful of guilt. Why was this man being so good to her?

'Thank you for your kindness, but I'll be fine now. I'll see you in the office tomorrow.' She spoke as pragmatically as she could. She had shown too much weakness already.

'OK,' he replied. 'I don't mind staying a while if you want me to.'

'It's really not necessary,' Eleanor said, conscious of the fact that she was reverting to the so-called strong Eleanor that Darryl could obviously see through. 'I have things I need to get on with. Getting Mum to bed and such like.'

'Maybe tomorrow we can dig a few more holes.'

Eleanor wouldn't let herself smile at the reference to holes. An uncomfortable silence fell on the kitchen. After a moment's pause Darryl turned and left. As Eleanor heard the front door quietly close behind him her knees finally gave way and she fell to the floor. The tears followed soon after.

∼

'I was beginning to think you weren't coming tonight, mate.'

Dave was almost at the bottom of his glass of Carling when Darryl arrived at the pub, although he knew it wouldn't have been Dave's first. Either way, a replacement was always in order and Darryl obliged.

'Tried ringing your mobile but it was off,' Dave went on.

'Sorry, been a bit tied up.'

'You got lucky tonight?' Dave's cockeyed smile an indication of being up to no good.

Darryl picked up what was left of a cardboard coaster from the table and threw it at him with a flick of his wrist, reminiscent of their college days as students together.

'Oh, Darryl, no.' Dave shook his head. 'I know that look. Don't do it.'

'Do what?'

'I told you not to do it. Eleanor.'

Darryl didn't reply. He looked deeply into his glass, or as deeply as he could into the short tumbler of orange juice.

'You always were a sucker for a hard luck story. This is how you were always getting yourself into trouble at college.'

'I think what she's going through is a bit more than a hard luck story. How can anybody not feel sorry for her? And that's all it is. I just feel sorry for her, I'm not interested in getting tangled in more lies and deceit. But—'

'But,' repeated Dave. 'There's always a but.'

Darryl wondered how to phrase his words without receiving the inevitable contemptuous judgement from Dave.

'She had a particularly bad day today, so I took her home tonight.'

'There's a surprise.' Dave rolled his eyes. 'There's no point trying to convince me. I know you too well.'

Darryl ignored him. 'Did you know she lives with her mum?'

'I think I heard she moved in with her mum soon after the crash.'

'Sounds about right. It looked like an old person's home.' Darryl remembered the house had looked as though it hadn't been decorated since it was built in the seventies. The brown wallpaper covered in tiny faded flowers, the carpet a slightly darker shade of brown than the wallpaper. 'It smelt like an old person's home.'

'A bit of extra support for her I suppose,' Dave said.

'I don't think the support was for Eleanor. Did you know her mum has dementia?'

'No, shit. I didn't. Well, OK, so it's not like she lost her luggage on the way back from holiday, but still. Think about what you're doing.'

'Don't worry. She's so wrapped up in her own little world she's not going to *let* anything happen, even if I tried.'

'Which you're not going to do,' Dave said hastily.

'Which I'm not going to do. I told you, I'm not interested.'

'Good, she doesn't need fucking up any more than she already is. Just finish the job and get out, mate.'

Both men disappeared into their own thoughts for a moment. Darryl wondering about Dave's advice. Finish the job and get out. It was probably the most sensible advice Dave had ever given him. Dave, obviously reminiscing about the good old college days.

'Do you remember that one, Sarah or Susie, I think it was? Told you her dog had just been put down,' Dave said with an ironic smile. 'She was only out clubbing to drown her sorrows.'

'Yeah, I remember. She never even had a dog,' Darryl said, resigned to the fact that he was about to have Dave rub his nose in all the bad choices he had made during their time as flat mates.

'And there was that one who told you she'd lost her front door key and she was going to have to stay out all night—'

'And sleep on the streets,' Darryl continued.

'And then you found the key in her shoe the next morning. No wonder she couldn't find it in her bag.'

'Yeah, that was Rachel. That's the one I married.'

Dave laughed loudly.

'Now she's on at me to meet her tomorrow,' Darryl continued, 'probably just so she can hassle me some more about getting the house on the market.'

'Oh shit,' Dave said through his laughter.

'Shit nothing. I can't help it if I'm thoughtful and caring. It makes me kind-hearted,' Darryl said with more than a hint of sarcasm.

'It makes you gullible,' Dave blurted.

'OK, so I may have met a few manipulative bitches along the way, but there's always hope.'

'For Eleanor maybe, 'cause I'm sorry to tell you, mate, you've no hope.'

Unfortunately, Darryl believed him. 'What the hell am I doing?' he implored, and drained his measly glass of juice.

'More to the point, what the hell are you drinking?'

'Orange juice, I'm on medication.'

'You bloody well need it, mate.'

Memories of Dave's teasing, his laughter, his well-intentioned, though sometimes hurtful, remarks rose from Darryl's subconscious. The consumption of alcohol had always helped to laugh them off during their college days. But now, Darryl wasn't so keen on laughing them off.

'I was hit by a car today, thank you for your concern,' Darryl went on.

'Shit, what happened?'

'Eleanor pushed me into the road.'

Dave could not speak for a full twenty minutes. His laughter rang round the pub like persistent church bells on a Sunday morning, and just as annoying for those that weren't part of the occasion.

# 9

Darryl had every intention of getting to work for nine o'clock the following morning. Unfortunately, when his alarm rang at seven as usual, and he reached out to hit the off button, his body had other ideas. Every muscle had seized overnight and seemed to be screaming at him. Even the effort of trying to roll out of bed was agony. He tried again, gritting his teeth from the pain. This time he managed to reach across to the bedside table, switch off his alarm, and grab the painkillers given to him at the hospital. He swallowed them dry. There was some water left in the glass on his bedside table from when he had taken last night's dose, but he couldn't bring himself to sit up. Even the act of breathing felt like torture.

He spent the next twenty minutes lying flat on his back regretting his decision to help out his old mate with this job. Surely no job, or mate for that matter, was worth this. As he laid waiting for the painkillers to kick in, he began to think about all the evidence they had so far, or rather lack of. He couldn't believe that there was nothing in the archives of one of, if not the, oldest solicitors in town. The print of the watercolour painting, which was interesting and would be great if he could find the chapel depicted in it, was of no real help for what he needed now. The diaries were much the same. Interesting, but unhelpful. It was while he was thinking about the diaries that an idea came to him. This spurred his decision to try and move again. The painkillers weren't working yet but at least he was prepared this time, and determined. He forced himself to roll over and perched himself on the edge of his bed. He reached for his glass of water. The effort of tensing his muscles just to hold it felt like a thousand needles being driven into his arm, but he forced himself to drink until the glass was drained. After a couple more minutes of agonising gasps, he fell backwards on to his bed.

'Oh, shit!'

Consequently, the morning routine took longer than normal.

~

Three hours later Darryl called into a small florist's en route to the office.

'I'd like a rose, please,' he said to the teenage girl behind the counter.

Lying on his bed that morning he'd had an idea of how he may be able to cheer Eleanor a little. A bunch of flowers would have been too much. He didn't want it to come across as anything other than a friendly gesture. The girl stood up from her chair with that internal indignation teenagers often display and immediately reached for a red rose.

'No,' Darryl interrupted quickly. 'Better make it a white one.'

The girl shrugged her shoulders and pulled out a beautiful white rose just emerging from its bud.

'Don't worry about wrapping it,' he said.

He didn't want it to seem like he'd made too much of an effort, just a simple rose to hopefully put a smile on Eleanor's face, even if only for a short while.

Eleanor's morning at home had been a busy one. There was nothing more than the usual things that needed to be done, but she had managed to find things to keep herself occupied. Anything that had meant she was able to stay out of her mother's company. She knew it was nothing but selfishness, but still it hurt that her mother hadn't recognised her. Today she was glad to be going to work, getting out of the house, leaving it all behind.

Once she reached Chartford Brooke and left the train station she found herself subconsciously watching for Darryl. She glanced in every cafe window and behind each corner. *Maybe he'll be brave enough to walk into the office on his own today.*

After depositing her things in her office and making Miss Osbourne's morning coffee, Eleanor returned to the conference room and began reading the final section of the second diary. Nine thirty came and there was still no Darryl. *Maybe I should call the hospital. Maybe he was hurt more than they first thought. That doctor did mention a knock to his head.* She shook herself back to the present, told herself to stop being ridiculous, and she returned her focus to the diary.

She stared blankly at the pages. The words of Lady Rose refused to sink in. The large and empty conference room felt cold. Darryl's jacket still hung on the back of his chair, a constant reminder of his absence. She took the diary back to her office and tried again within her own comfortable four walls.

*Did I upset him? Maybe I offended him.* She started running through the events of last night. *After all, he was only trying to help.*

Ten o'clock came and went, and Eleanor was starting to feel annoyed. *We still have a job to do, he can't just disappear.* Her thoughts lingered on her final word as she stared past the pages of the diary. *Isn't that what the police had said was happening to people around this office block?* Her heart beat faster, the knot in her stomach tightened. *Disappearances and deaths.* As these thoughts hurtled through her head a single white rose appeared on the desk in front of her. She looked up with a jolt, shaken from her imaginings. A huge grin spread across Darryl's face as though he was up to some mischief. So preoccupied with her thoughts, Eleanor hadn't heard the lift arrive or see him walk across the hallway.

'Now, don't go getting the wrong idea,' he said. 'I was careful not to get a red one. I could say it's a rose for Lady Rose, but the truth is I thought we'd try a tango next time.'

Eleanor couldn't help herself and smiled. Relief swept through her.

'A tango? What's this?' Miss Osbourne had appeared at the doorway.

'We had a bit of a waltz last night,' Darryl said with no hint of the reservation he'd shown last night. In fact, he seemed to take pleasure in breaking this news to Miss Osbourne, while Eleanor, herself, began to flounder with embarrassment.

'So that was your plan for last night, was it?' Miss Osbourne asked.

'Not exactly, but she had a bad day yesterday and I thought she might need cheering up.'

'A rose too. It must be serious.'

'You can't do a tango without a rose, everyone knows that.'

Darryl sneaked a wink at Eleanor. Feeling awkward she couldn't help but chuckle at Darryl's audacity.

'She wasn't the only one who had a bad day yesterday.' Miss Osbourne was clearly riled and struggled to keep her composure. 'I'm surprised to see you here this morning. How are you?'

'I don't think there's a single muscle in my body that's not in pain,' Darryl said in his usual cheery manner. He turned back to

Eleanor thoughtfully, 'Actually, we may have to postpone that tango if it's OK with you.'

'I had no intentions of ...' Eleanor stammered before allowing the sentence to drift off.

'Sorry, Miss.' The caretaker had strayed into the office behind Darryl.

'How many times have I told you not to come into the offices during working hours?' snapped Miss Osbourne. Her annoyance finally breaking through. Unfortunately for the caretaker, it was aimed at him.

The caretaker bowed slightly in shame and moved toward Eleanor. He held out his hands.

'Sorry, Miss. I picked these up for you yesterday. Such a shame,' he said quietly. In his hands were all the loose beads from her bracelet. 'I'm afraid some of them got stuck under the door and are ruined.'

'Thank you,' Eleanor said as she watched the beads drop from his hands and land in hers.

'Such a pretty bracelet to go with your pretty face, just like a flower.'

The warmth of the last few moments had suddenly gone out of her and all her memories came flooding back.

'Thank you, you're very kind,' she said quietly. She smiled to the caretaker but it was her usual sad smile. The one forced to her lips that didn't reach her eyes.

The caretaker bowed his head to Eleanor and then again to Miss Osbourne, and quietly left the room.

Eleanor's shoulders sank. The small of her back curved into the back of her chair as she folded into a stoop. Her face muscles seemed to wither with each second.

'Well, I'm late in this morning,' Darryl said cheerily. 'I think we'd better get straight on. Eleanor, shall we go over to the conference room?'

His bright, energetic voice shook her from her stupor, and she stood, dazed but back in the present moment. She watched, almost as though through a fog, as Darryl turned to leave the office. She looked down at the beads in her hand. Several were mangled into unrecognisable masses. She forced herself to think of the here and now. She had a job to do. Her beads went in her top drawer. There was no time to think about them now.

'Yoo-hoo,' came Gina's voice from down the hall.

Darryl had only just stepped into the hallway. He looked back again at Eleanor.

'Maybe we'll check in with Callum first,' he said through gritted teeth.

Eleanor could see the pleading in his eyes. He turned back to the hallway and made his way toward the lift. The sight of him hobbling across the hallway with his aching limbs brought a slight smile back to Eleanor's face.

Darryl reached the lift and jabbed the button several times impatiently.

'Sorry ladies, in a rush,' he said to Gina as she came nearer, Marie sauntered behind.

Eleanor hurried to reach the lift, concerned that Darryl would leave without her, but then she double backed to retrieve the diary. The doors to the lift were already opening, but she had a suspicion that Darryl may appreciate having the diary to hand and not needing to return anytime soon.

'Pete, so nice to see you,' Eleanor heard Darryl say behind her, a little too enthusiastically. She guessed he was probably welcome for any distraction that would stop him having to talk to Gina.

'Good morning, Mr Westwood. How are you today? No broken bones, I hope.' The polite words were there but not the civility to go with them.

Eleanor was now on her way back toward the lift.

'Eleanor,' Miss Osbourne called across the hallway waving the rose in the air for everyone to see. 'You've forgotten your rose.' Her tone couldn't have been more humiliating if she'd tried.

Eleanor turned again and made back for the rose, head down, hiding her flushing cheeks.

'Thank you,' Darryl called back. 'She'll pick it up later.'

Eleanor stopped and looked back at Darryl. The image of her as the ball in a game of table tennis, pinging backwards and forwards, appeared in her mind. She forced herself to stop and headed back toward the lift again. Darryl was now holding the door open for her, which he clearly felt uneasy with.

'A rose?' said Gina. Her head bobbing between the rose, Eleanor and Darryl.

'You can't do a tango without a rose,' replied Darryl matter-of-factly.

'You like to dance, Mr Westwood? I love dancing.' Gina swayed her hips about to imaginary music.

'Oh good, you're here,' Darryl said as Eleanor rushed into the lift.

She turned and noticed Miss Osbourne talking quietly to the caretaker. *That's always her way,* Eleanor thought. *Apologise after the fact. It's easier than thinking before she speaks. He was only being helpful.*

Darryl, meanwhile, seemed to be trying his best to ignore Gina's writhing. 'Basement please,' he said as he reached across in front of Pete and pressed the button himself. 'Sorry,' he called through the closing doors. 'Busy day.'

Gina stopped her dance attempt abruptly and made no effort to hide her disappointment. Marie stood behind her, frowning at the pantomime of the situation. But it seemed to be Pete who was most annoyed. From the tight expression on his face he wasn't overjoyed about somebody else pushing his buttons.

'You like upsetting people, do you?' he asked infuriated.

Darryl was clearly taken aback. 'Of course not, but they're ...' Darryl looked as though he was struggling to find words that wouldn't make the situation worse.

'They're what? They're not people? Not at your level of education? They don't move in the same social circles as you and so are not worthy?'

'Pete,' said Eleanor stunned. 'Remember your manners, remember your job.'

'My job?' His slightly pink face had gone a deep red.

'No, it's OK Eleanor. He's right. I'm sorry, I was rude, and I will make sure I apologise to them both— all ... later. And, I apologise to you now. I'll never press your buttons again.'

This didn't seem to calm Pete down. Eleanor was sure that Darryl was as glad as she was when the lift doors opened, and they could leave the small enclosed compartment.

∼

'Is that usual?' Darryl asked once the lift doors had closed behind them. He was glad to see that the colour had returned to Eleanor's cheeks. He couldn't have helped but notice the way Eleanor's face had turned ashen, and her body seemed to implode as she had received her son's beads.

'Not at all, I've never seen him react like that.'

'Let's hope I don't step on anybody else's toes this morning. I might find myself being pushed under a faster moving car.'

Darryl noticed that Eleanor didn't find this attempt at humour funny from the distasteful glance she gave him.

Eleanor opened the door to Callum's office. Callum was absorbed in the paperwork he was studying at an over-sized wooden desk in the centre of the room. Every inch of the surface was scattered with papers, files, notebooks, pens, and every piece of stationery possible.

To say he jumped when Eleanor spoke would be an understatement. He quickly rose to his feet and came to greet her. Taking her hand, they stood just inside the room.

From the doorway Darryl observed the darkness of the room. Floor to ceiling shelves were on all but one wall, the one with the door, and these looked just as chaotic as the rest of the archives. Piles of boxes and files were scattered around the floor with no semblance of order. The only light in the room came from a desk lamp that shone a spotlight with a circumference of about eighteen inches. Darryl wasn't surprised at Callum's decision to read from the lamp rather than the bright LED striplights. *I think I'd rather sit in the dark if my office was in this state too.*

'Eleanor, how are you?' Callum said, holding her hand gently. 'I'm so sorry to hear what happened.'

'It was me that went under the car,' Darryl remarked.

'To be honest, Mr Westwood, it sounded like you deserved it.'

'What?' Darryl was beginning to wonder if the police were right after all. First Pete, now Callum.

'Do you know how precious that bracelet was to Eleanor?'

'It's very kind of you, Callum,' Eleanor interrupted. 'But it was all one big accident.'

Darryl decided it would probably be better if he stayed quiet and let Eleanor do the talking.

'We just came down to see if anything has turned up yet?' she continued.

'Yes,' Callum said with excitement. 'I found them last thing yesterday. I was determined to find something for you.'

'That's great, can we see them?'

'Well, actually no. I'm afraid some of the pieces are too old and fragile for me to let you handle them. Especially when some hands are clumsier than others,' he added, directed at Darryl.

Darryl felt ready to hit someone soon, and Callum looked like a good target right now.

Callum turned his attention back to Eleanor, 'I'm in the process of copying them for you, and then you can look through them at your leisure.'

'We're running out of time.' Darryl said abruptly.

Eleanor looked at him questioningly.

'I spoke with Dave— Mr Saunders last night,' he continued. 'This was only supposed to take two or three hours and he wants it all wrapped up by the end of tomorrow.'

The truth was Darryl had been thinking about what Dave had actually said. *Finish the job and get out.* He knew it made sense. And, even though he personally felt that Callum was a smarmy git, he clearly liked Eleanor, no matter what she said. And, given time, he thought she would probably begin to like Callum.

'That's a bit short notice, don't you think, Mr Westwood?' Callum turned on him in Eleanor's defence.

'I'm just repeating what the boss said.' Darryl didn't want to get into an argument, he just wanted to get out.

'Don't worry, Eleanor. I'll have everything copied and ready for you straight after lunch. How's that?'

Darryl knew Callum was making a point of ignoring him.

'I don't know how helpful it will be though,' Callum continued. 'It's plans of the original building you're after, isn't it, or as close to it as possible? So far I haven't seen anything like that.'

'We'll be grateful for whatever you do have,' she said. 'We'll come back after lunch.'

'No, don't worry. I'll bring them up to you. No need for you to keep troubling yourself with coming all the way down here.' He smiled at her while leading her by the hand, which he had held since she had entered, out into the corridor.

'Are you finished with those pieces from the County archives yet? Callum asked.

'Not yet, but it shouldn't be too long,' Eleanor replied.

'Don't forget, just pass them back to me when you're done, and I'll run them back for you.'

Darryl watched their gentle conversation. *They would be well suited. When she's ready.*

'Thank you. We're working in the conference room now, so if you could put the new bits you've found in there, we'd appreciate it,' Eleanor said, and Callum closed the office door behind them.

Darryl didn't want to face going back upstairs. 'How do you feel about digging trench three?' he asked. 'It's probably not going to help us with Dave's building, but it would be interesting to see.'

'And you don't want to go back upstairs to the offices,' Eleanor said.

'And I don't want to go back up to the offices.'

As they reached the lift, they turned to each other and both asked, 'stairs?'

Darryl stopped as they reached the bottom of the stairs. 'We could do with the watercolour copy. Could you go up and get it and I'll meet you outside?'

'Sure, I'll go up in the lift. Just do me a favour and mind the road.'

Darryl made a false laugh and turned back to the stairs as Eleanor made her way back to the lift. He groaned as his aching limbs tried to ascend the stairs.

*Dave, you're going to pay for this.*

## 10

Eleanor found Darryl waiting outside The Birds main entrance.

'OK, for trench three you need to show me where these ruins are,' he said excitedly.

'This way.' Eleanor nodded to the left. 'But I'm warning you, there's not much there.'

The park was on the other side of the road, but Eleanor wanted to avoid the crossing directly outside the offices, and so she led Darryl further down the road. She was already wondering if she had made a mistake not changing into her trainers while she was upstairs, but at least Darryl wasn't able to walk too fast, which helped.

'If I remember correctly,' Eleanor said, 'it was just a couple of walls covered in ivy in a small cornered section of the park.'

'The same park where we had lunch yesterday?' Darryl asked.

'Yes, but a bit further down.'

As they entered the park Eleanor could hear the children playing in the playground they had sat near yesterday. She had struggled then with her memories of Chris playing in that very playground, and she knew that today would be no easier. She walked straight past determined not to give it a second glance.

Over to their right was a woodland area. The trees were beginning to lose their green, and the reds and oranges were emerging. Their foliage hid any sign of buildings behind them and framed the edge of the park giving the impression they could have gone on forever. The woodland walks were a favourite with Chris. The feeling of freedom for Eleanor meant she could imagine they were miles from anywhere. Chris would run between the trees and stopped with a wide-eyed look of surprise whenever he had seen a squirrel, no matter how many times he saw one. Another place for her to avoid.

They passed an ornamental garden with tightly clipped low box hedges creating a maze-like pattern. This then opened out onto a large paved area where children were running in and out of water jets shooting up from the ground. During the summer season this area swarmed with children, now there were only a few stubborn ones that wouldn't let the autumn ruin their fun just yet. She marched straight past. She hadn't realised just how many memories she would have to try and prevent seeping into her consciousness in such a short walk.

'Can we slow down a bit,' Darryl asked. 'You seem to have picked up speed and I'm having trouble keeping up.'

'Sorry,' Eleanor replied. She hadn't realised that she had unconsciously begun to walk at a faster pace past the playing children. She tried not to let Darryl see her smile at him hobbling along, but it didn't work.

'The painkillers they've given me don't seem to be nearly as good as the ones they gave me in the hospital.'

'Are you sure you should be doing this today?' she asked, concerned he may be over-doing things. If Mr Saunders was any kind of friend, he would let Darryl off such a strict deadline.

'The job needs doing. It shouldn't take too much longer. Just slow it down a little and I'll be fine.'

They soon arrived at a patio area tucked away in one corner. The raised beds were full of colourful flowers, even in the autumn. The boundary corner was made up of two uneven stone walls. Four metres at its highest and leading down jaggedly to around two metres. They had been taller in the past, but time had taken its toll. As Eleanor had said, the walls were now covered in ivy, and Darryl excitedly started to push some of it aside and ran his hands over the stones. Every now and again he would flinch from pain as he stretched a little too far. An alleyway led behind one of the walls and back toward the town. This side was kept mainly clear of the ivy and Darryl could see the details more easily. The lay of the stonework, the mortar used, the marks on the stones from the instruments used to cut them. Eleanor smiled at Darryl's enthusiasm as he tried to explain these different aspects to her. But then a frown came to his face.

'What's wrong?' she asked. 'Is it not from the same time period?'

'Yes, yes, it is, but ... look at this arch,' he said running his hand along some smoother stones that made an edge.

'That's an arch?' she questioned.

'Well, the beginnings of one. There's only about two and half metres left of it here, but you can tell it would have carried on up into an arch.'

'OK, what about it? Chapels have arches.'

'Yes, they do, but the trajectory of this one makes me think that it's too big for a chapel, unless the chapel itself was a lot bigger than the one in the painting.'

'What do you think it might be, then?'

'To me, that looks more the size for a gatehouse. The arch

would need to be big enough for a coach to come through, but then that makes no sense from the painting's point of view.'

'So, the conclusion for trench three is?'

'More questions than answers unfortunately. Is there anything else like this around here?'

'Not that I know of, but to be honest it's not something I tend to look for. I only knew about this because I had to tell Chris off for climbing on it once when we had a surprise birthday picnic here for Nick.'

Darryl disappeared down the alleyway again, examining the wall closely. In the quiet the memory of Nick's birthday picnic forced its way to the forefront of Eleanor's mind. Chris would not sit still. She had chased him around the flower beds several times, before she'd finally lost her temper when she'd caught him trying to climb the ruin wall. But then she remembered Chris' laughter when he was sat on Nick's shoulders, and Nick had galloped along like a horse. There was nothing more infectious than Chris' laugh. She looked up toward the cold blue sky, trying to stop the tears from breaking through.

'Eleanor? Eleanor, are you OK?' Darryl had returned from his exploration.

Eleanor forced herself back to the present and nodded.

'Come on,' Darryl said quietly. 'The more I look at this, the more I'm convinced it's not a chapel. Let's see if we can find another trench.'

∼

Eleanor couldn't help but feel disappointed that the ruin in the park wasn't part of the chapel after all. It also meant that they spent the next two hours walking around the park and through the streets inspecting anything that may be of interest, which, of course, for Darryl was most of the town. They were now in a different part of the town to where they had been yesterday. Here Darryl particularly wanted to explore the small alleyways and Eleanor started to enjoy learning more about the town she had lived near for so many years, but never really knew. The only aspect she didn't enjoy was the cobbles. Most of the town had modern roads and pavements. But a few, especially the alleyways that Darryl seemed so fond of, had the original cobbles under foot. Here she tried her best to walk on her toes, not wanting to risk a heel sliding on one of the well-worn stones and ending up with a twisted ankle, or worse, sitting on the ground, humiliated by a fall.

Several times they stopped to take another look at the painting, trying to judge the distance between Thornewick Manor and the chapel. How far back and how far out to the right-hand side.

'Of course, it is only a painting,' said Darryl when they stopped in a cafe for some lunch.

Eleanor had ordered a chicken salad sandwich, while Darryl had asked for the crispy bacon baguette. And, two coffees.

'What do you mean, only a painting?' Eleanor asked.

'It's not like a photograph, where the objects are fixed in place. Being a painting, they could have painted the chapel anywhere, wherever it was aesthetically pleasing to the painter's eye. It's probably not to scale at all. "The factual elements of the scene are open to interpretation," as my old tutor would say.'

'Why have we been wandering around for the past two hours, then?' Eleanor asked. Her feet were aching, and her shoes had been pinching her toes for at least the last hour. 'Is there really any point to this?'

'Of course, there's a point. Look at what we've found.'

'A dilapidated wall covered in ivy and cobwebs,' Eleanor said flatly.

'Yes, but a dilapidated wall that I don't believe was a chapel but a gatehouse.'

'So?'

'So, there's no gatehouse in the painting. Nor was a gatehouse mentioned in the diaries, but the chapel was. Well, the gatehouse wasn't mentioned in mine anyway. Was it in yours?'

'No, I don't think so. Not that I can remember. Maybe you're just wrong.'

Darryl almost dropped what was left of his bacon baguette onto his plate and stared at her, eyebrows raised.

'I just mean it could be a case of mistaken identity,' she quickly continued. 'The gatehouse was never mentioned in either of the diaries because there wasn't one. And the chapel just happened to have had bigger arches than you would have expected a chapel of that time to have.'

Darryl wasn't looking convinced, so she went on.

'Surely, new discoveries are found that change the way you people think of these places. Let's face it, there's not a lot of actual science in this, is there? From what you've told me this morning, there's a lot of theorising going on, and not much fact-based evidence. I'm just saying you may be, not so much wrong, just mistaken.'

'I will concede that there is some theorising, but you'd be surprised how much science is involved these days. And, OK, I may be mistaken, but I've been doing this a long time and I'm certain that the ruin in the park is not a chapel.'

'So, where does that leave us?' Eleanor was now not only disappointed but deflated too.

Darryl picked up his bacon baguette and asked, 'Do you like jigsaw puzzles?' before he took a big bite.

'Not a big fan, no. I always felt very frustrated when somebody lost the pieces and I'd end up spending hours trying to do a jigsaw with holes in.'

'Those holes that got you frustrated are the same as what we're trying to find in our trenches.'

'You do know that makes no sense, don't you?'

Darryl began to show his frustration.

'We're looking for evidence, the missing jigsaw pieces, to complete the picture and tell us what was going on here. We may never get a complete picture, but it's the searching that's the fun bit.'

'Under sofas, between cushions, behind radiators—'

'In a park on a beautiful, sunny morning,' Darryl continued.

'In high heels,' Eleanor finished with a sigh. 'Everyone was surprised when you first arrived in jeans and t-shirt. We're all used to businessmen in suits. I see that a suit would get a little ruined in the trenches.'

'It's true, I don't do suits.' Darryl smiled. 'Mainly though because I'm lazy and suits are too high maintenance. Besides, this morning has had another use. It's kept us out of the office for a few hours.'

'Great, tell my feet that.' Eleanor slipped off her shoes and wiggled her toes.

'It's all about the research,' Darryl said. 'You've got to do your research.'

As they finished their lunch Eleanor found she was able to relax. There were no expectations put on her, no urgent something-or-other that needed typing. No dinner needing cooking, no washing needing doing, and the many other mundane things that everyday life required. She was, for the first time in a long time, just enjoying the stillness of a quiet moment. She had spent the last eight months avoiding these times as they would often let the memories seep through. There was a time when she was grateful to be so busy. But not today, not right now.

Eleanor insisted on paying as Darryl had paid for yesterday's lunch, and she got up from the table to leave. When Darryl tried to stand his muscles had tightened again from sitting in one place for over an hour. He tried to smile an apology to the elderly couple sat at the next table, after swearing at the pain. Eleanor laughed quietly to herself and quickly left the cafe to wait outside, embarrassed by his outburst.

They walked slowly back to the office. It took a while for Darryl to stretch his muscles out again, but by the time they reached The Birds he was back to his normal hobbling. Insisting on taking extra painkillers before they left the cafe probably helped too. It was now gone two o'clock and Eleanor couldn't wait to get back in the office, slip her shoes off, and feel the air between her toes. She stopped at the crossing outside the office, but Darryl seemed preoccupied and kept on walking up the street. It seemed something had caught his eye. A little further on from the crossing was the large Georgian building that had been converted into a restaurant that Darryl had pointed out to Eleanor only yesterday. The front area was paved, with tables and chairs under large, navy parasols. Either side of the paved area were two large stone pillars about five or six metres apart.

'Eleanor, do you have the painting?' Darryl called.

Eleanor took the rolled-up picture from her bag and gave it to a very excited Darryl.

'These pillars don't match the style of the Georgian building. I think I've just found trench four. Look.' Darryl showed Eleanor the picture. 'These are the entrance pillars in the painting.'

'But they can't be, they're in the wrong place. They're supposed to be at the front of the building.'

'What if the original building stretched down this road, and this side *was* the front. A lot can happen over that amount of time. Just like at the opposite side of the building. Do you remember the external internal door in the car port? The original frontage may have disappeared for some reason, and over the years the side elevation is all that's left. That's what's wrong with the doorway.'

Darryl had clearly realised something that had been bothering him. Eleanor was left confused.

'A different doorway, or the same one?'

'Come, I'll show you.'

Darryl grabbed her hand and dragged her further up the road and around the corner till they were facing the front entrance of Thornewick Manor again. His excitement seemed to be over-ruling his pain receptors.

'It was niggling at me, but I just took it as an example of artistic licence. The stones around the main entrance are smaller than we would expect on a building of this stature. It's a good entrance, don't get me wrong, but not a great entrance. That's because it's a side door, and not the main threshold. And look at the painting. It's the same style stonework, but in the painting the stones are much larger, much grander.'

'So, you're saying that the whole picture needs to be turned ninety degrees? We're no longer facing this way, with a chapel to the right somewhere over there …' Eleanor indicated the direction of the ruin in the park.

'But we're turning and,' Darryl grabbed Eleanor's hand again and pulled her all the way back till they were standing facing The Birds entrance, 'the chapel would be to the right and back over there. That would make complete sense to have a gatehouse in the park. The horses would arrive through the gatehouse, sweep round through the entrance pillars and pull up by the main door. And, in the painting the gatehouse wouldn't be seen from the artist's viewpoint.'

'Let me get this straight. You are theorising,' Eleanor said with a sideways glance at Darryl, 'that the original front of Thornewick Manor was actually down this road?'

Darryl grinned at her and nodded. 'But I have two pillars as evidence, your honour.'

Eleanor laughed. 'Does that help with your building at the back? Mr Saunders' building?'

'Yes and no. From the picture we can't see how far the side elevations go back, but we now know that the left-hand flank goes back for some way.' Darryl spoke quickly, finding it hard to contain his excitement. 'In fact, I'd say the front layout is probably identical to the side to have caused so much confusion. Otherwise it wouldn't have had everyone believing that the side was the front for so many years.'

Eleanor's head was now whirling as she tried to keep up.

'Now, it's not necessarily so,' continued Darryl, 'that the right-hand flank is the same, but if it is, then that would mean that Dave's building *is* part of the original Manor.'

'Does that mean we go back on the paper trail?'

Darryl nodded enthusiastically. 'Let's hope Callum's brought us something good.'

When they entered The Birds Eleanor's feet were aching more than ever, but even so she felt like she could have run up the stairs three at a time. She tried to show a little decorum, however, and waited patiently for the lift. Pete had already opened the entrance door for them, so they knew the lift would be safe.

As Eleanor and Darryl entered the conference room, once again, Eleanor's heart sank. Callum had already left the promised paperwork on the table. In fact, he'd left a large crate full of documents that had overflowed. The top wedge of sheets had slipped off and spread themselves in a fan across the table.

'There's rather a lot here,' Eleanor said. She had her doubts as to whether they would be able to get through the entire crate load before the end of tomorrow.

'There often is with old places. All the paperwork from over the years, sometimes hundreds of years as is the case here. I have to admit, the guy did well getting this lot copied in one morning.'

'Maybe he's gone up a little in your estimation?' Eleanor smirked. She swept together the loose pages and dropped them on the table with a loud thump. 'There's not too long before the end of the day. I guess we'd better get started.'

She sat with her bundle of papers, while Darryl pulled out a wedge of his own from the top of the pile in the crate. Eleanor looked forward to an afternoon of quiet reading and heavy sighs. *At least I don't need to wear my shoes,* and she wriggled her toes under the table.

## 11

EARLY ON DARRYL HAD DECIDED HE DIDN'T WANT A REPEAT OF lunchtime's misery. Every ten minutes or so he got up and paced round the room, keeping his muscles moving and the painkillers topped up. As the afternoon went on Eleanor could sense Darryl's frustration increase. The first few times he got up his gentle pacing motion was no more than a stroll. As they worked their way further through the pile of documents his pacing became faster and more harassed.

Every now and again Darryl would ask, 'Anything yet?'

'Nothing,' Eleanor would reply.

She wanted to ask him, *How's your jigsaw looking? Not so much fun now, is it?* But she decided against this. He seemed agitated enough as it was.

It was almost five o'clock when Darryl's pocket chimed. A text on his mobile.

'I've got to go,' he said, reading the text.

They were barely half-way through the crate of paperwork.

'I don't mind staying for a bit,' said Eleanor.

'You don't need to do that. It can wait till tomorrow.'

'I often stay late; I like it when it's quiet.' Eleanor was happy to have an excuse to stay away from home a while longer. 'I can get another batch done in a couple more hours, then there will be less for the morning. You did say Mr Saunders wants this tomorrow.'

'Yeah, I know, but ... I'm supposed to be seeing someone tonight, but I'll give them a call and cancel—'

'Don't be silly, it's not a problem. Go and enjoy yourself. All I need is coffee.'

'Thanks Eleanor. I'll see you in the morning.'

Darryl left for the lift as Eleanor went to make coffee. Behind her Eleanor heard the ding of the lift arriving and then, 'Hi Pete,' came Darryl's voice. Eleanor knew him well enough by now to know the cheerfulness in his voice came from facetiousness and not pleasure. She couldn't help but smile at the awkward silence that was probably now going on in the lift.

'Oh, we've just missed the lift,' she heard Gina's voice.

'Shall we take the stairs?' from Marie.

Only a laugh came in reply.

Eleanor turned into the kitchen and headed for the coffee as she heard, 'Which bar are you going to, ladies? May I join you?'

*Miss Osbourne too, in the same lift. Good job Darryl left when he did. All three of them in the one lift, he would never have got out alive.* She laughed to herself at the thought of Darryl being accosted by Laurel, Hardy and Minnie Mouse, with Pete standing as referee. Maybe if she hadn't been daydreaming, she wouldn't have jumped quite so hard as she did when the caretaker said goodnight to her through the doorway. Coffee granules covered the floor.

'Oh, I'm sorry, Miss. I didn't mean to make you jump,' he said apologetically. 'Let me clear that up for you.'

'No, no, it's fine. I can do it. I made the mess. You get off home and have a nice evening.'

He had already changed from his blue caretaker's overcoat to a long, black mac. A black, woollen hat covered his blond, hair. A confusion of voices seemed to appear from nowhere as a group of people walked behind him. The staff from Samson's Digital World's offices, all with their coats on too. They were chatting tiredly after a day's work, though not too tired for a quick visit to the pub. The noise disappeared again after they had passed the kitchen doorway. The crescendo faded as quickly as it had arrived.

'Thank you, Miss. Don't work too hard.'

Eleanor smiled a goodbye and started scrambling around in the cupboard below the sink. She was just looking forward to the prospect of scooping up all the tiny, hard, brown granules in her hands when she saw a dustpan and brush tucked away at the back of the cupboard, in the furthest corner possible. *Not the easiest place to get to*, Eleanor thought. *But then I'm not usually trying to juggle with the coffee.* An image came into her head. Juggling with a jar of coffee granules, a mug and a small carton of milk. In her mind she made the jar of coffee smaller than the industrial-sized tin they have in the office kitchen. *Trying to juggle with one of those would just be silly.*

~

Darryl felt guilty before the lift doors had even closed. It had been his decision to make tomorrow the deadline, not Dave's, but he couldn't explain that to Eleanor. She shouldn't have to work late for him. She had enough to deal with. Besides, he wasn't looking forward to this meeting with Rachel and he was only too well aware of the fact that he had been getting more and more jittery as the time got closer. He reached for his phone and brought up his contacts. He pressed the location marked *Rachel*. The picture he had removed long ago. This wasn't a call he was looking forward to but at least it meant he didn't have to stand in awkward silence with Pete.

'Hi Rach, it's me. I'm afraid I've got to work late ... no, please —' Darryl waited while Rachel said her piece.

'Yes, I got your text and I know—' Interrupted again, he tried to hold his temper in the silence of the lift.

'This job needs to be finished by tomorrow and I don't have much say in the matter. You're a big girl now, deal with it.'

The lift arrived at the ground floor and Darryl stepped out, annoyed with himself for losing his calm. The foyer area was noisy with people scrambling to leave even though the building didn't look big enough to accommodate so many people.

'To be perfectly honest if you just want to hassle me some more over ringing the estate agents, no I haven't done it yet and I'll do it tomorrow. Believe it or not I have a life too.'

Darryl turned away from the chattering groups of people where Sidney was trying to say goodnight to each and every one as he held the door open for them. A quieter spot laid under the stairs.

'If you have something to tell me you're just going to have to tell me over the phone or wait till it's convenient for me ... *You* may want to tell me in person but— Married? Our divorce has only just come through.'

Darryl laughed. After everything they had gone through she was ready to jump straight back in to another marriage. Someone else's strings she could pull.

'Your boyfriend? Any particular one? I seem to remember you've had several.' Darryl was still struggling to hear over the noise of footsteps pounding down the stairs above him. He put a finger in his free ear to help.

'When's it to be? Wow, that's soon. Is that why you're in such a rush to get the house sold? To pay for the next grand wedding?'

Darryl had had enough now. He wanted to move on, and he didn't want to hear any more pitiful droning from Rachel. Nothing was ever her fault. Someone else was always to blame, and it was usually him.

'Rachel, do what you want to do. You always have done. You are the mother of my children and that's where our relationship ends. If you want to get married again, go ahead. I'm not even going to try and understand your reasoning. I've given up trying to understand you.'

Darryl hung up and headed toward the lift. The doors were opening, and Gina, Marie and Miss Osbourne strode out reminiscent of a girl power film, complete with confidant hair tossing and animated laughter. He quickly turned back and headed up the stairs. Even the acute agony of his bruised limbs ascending the stairs was preferable to the alternative.

Back at the empty conference room he guessed Eleanor was still making coffee and went across to the kitchen. He found her on her knees backing out of a cupboard, surrounded by a mass of coffee granules.

'Having fun?' he asked.

'Not exactly,' she replied looking up. Her hair had started to fall out of its usual tied back state. Gravity and a stuffy cupboard taking their toll. 'Did you forget something?'

'Yes, my priorities.'

Eleanor stopped sweeping for a moment and looked at him quizzically from her knees.

'My ex wanted to see me for something. She— it doesn't matter.' The last thing he wanted right now was to discuss his ex-wife. And he certainly didn't want to burden Eleanor with his problems. 'This is my priority right now, not her. So, I rang and cancelled.'

'How very manly of you,' Eleanor smirked.

'I could reply to that with something like, "nice to see you where you belong, woman. On your hands and knees," but then I know I'd probably get thumped.'

'How quickly you've got the measure of me,' Eleanor said with a smile as she tipped the coffee granules from the dustpan into the bin. 'Did you manage to miss the lovely ladies on their way out?'

'The three cackling witches? Yes. I sneaked up the stairs and missed everyone.'

Eleanor returned the dustpan and brush to the cupboard and got back to making coffee. She now made two, and they returned to the conference room and settled back down in silence.

∼

*He's hurt her again and I can't allow this to happen. I hate to see her like this. He'll soon discover that he can't treat people this way. He will learn not to upset her. This time I will not fail.*

∼

Two hours passed. Eleanor and Darryl continued to work their way through the paperwork in the conference room. Eleanor had noticed that Darryl's pacing had slowed again once they had restarted their search with coffee in hand. Although disappointing, she guessed that there were certain older documents that he would still have found interesting, even though they weren't what he needed now. Eleanor, herself, was becoming more and more frustrated, with pages from the eighties mixed with more recent documents from the early years of the twenty-first century, in amongst references from the mid-twentieth century. Pages seemed to be missing, or more likely, still in the crate and not yet discovered. More than a few times she had to leave a sentence broken in the middle with the following page missing.

'This paperwork is ... is ...' Eleanor struggled to find an adequate description for how she felt about the mess in front of them. 'Surely everything should be in date order, or at least some kind of order. But this is like somebody dropped the crate load down the stairs and shuffled the papers together at the bottom.'

Darryl laughed at her, which riled her even more.

'Don't worry about it. I'm just glad we've got something to look through,' he said casually.

Eleanor knew he was right and laughed at herself. It was exactly the kind of thing Nick would have got himself worked up about. And her reply would have been the same as Darryl's. *Don't worry about it, at least it's all there in one place. If someone really needs it, then they can have the fun of sorting through it.* Of course, now, that someone was her. Even so, neither Eleanor nor Darryl had found anything that would even remotely help them. Callum had been right. There were no drawings or diagrams, other than those referencing the modern-day building. And, there seemed to be no reference to the actual size of the original building.

'I need cake,' Eleanor said decidedly, and she slipped on her shoes. Her feet immediately protested, and she fetched her trainers from her office. 'I'm going out to get something to eat. Do you want anything?'

'No, I'm fine, thanks. I'll just make do with a bite of yours,' Darryl answered not looking up from his page.

'Oh, will you? I'm beginning to see why your wife divorced you.'

She smiled to herself as she left the room and was surprised to discover she wasn't feeling guilty. Not about the smile, and not about the warm feeling of enjoying herself. For the first time in her life, she realised, she had begun to enjoy looking for a jigsaw piece. It was frustrating yet also exciting. The feeling that at any moment they may come across the vital piece of documentation that will complete the whole puzzle.

The lift was empty on the way down. Now that the offices were closed there was only one porter on duty, and he would be at the front door. She was surprised to see Pete emerge from the porter's room situated behind the reception desk.

'Hi Pete, I thought you had college on Thursday evenings.'

'Got a couple of weeks off,' he said unlocking the front door for her.

'I'm just popping out for something to eat. Do you want anything?'

'No, thanks. Will you be long?'

'Five minutes maybe, shouldn't be any longer.'

'I'll be waiting,' he smiled back to her.

～

Darryl took advantage of the break to stretch his legs and relieve himself in the bathroom. He was struggling to understand why there was nothing in all that paperwork about the size or layout of the building. He had found the size of the original land, but that stretched to acres and didn't reference the building at all. Newer documents with the remaining building were fastidiously accurate with their detail, but again, that was no help to what he needed now. Something it did help with though, was keeping his mind off Rachel. Though Eleanor's remark as she left meant he couldn't help but drift back to their telephone conversation. *What is she doing? I know she's impatient and insensitive, but getting married just two months after our divorce?*

Darryl returned to the conference room. The soft click of the door closing behind him was a comfort. In this building he felt there was safety behind a closed door, even if in reality everyone had left for the evening. He forced himself back to concentrating on the work in front of him, though not for long. *Two months. I guess that shows how little I meant to her.*

Suddenly, drowsiness swept over him. The smell of the gas came after.

~

Eleanor made her way to the local newsagents. During the day the narrow, unassuming shopfront was easily missed by people hurrying past, but at this time in the evening most other useful shops were closed. Cafes, bars and restaurants were open for the evening trade, but not many establishments gave the option for those essential items such as, a pint of milk, a loaf of bread, or cake. Eleanor would normally have chosen a box of individually wrapped almond slices or lemon sponges. This way she could keep the extras in her drawer to dip into during those cake-needing moments. But now she was bewildered. She didn't know if Darryl would like either of those. She spent longer than she had intended examining the contents of each variety on the shelf, which, considering the lack of options available to her, wasn't that long. She finally decided on a selection box of individual cakes. *At least he has a choice this way,* she thought.

On her walk back to the office, she realised it hadn't even occurred to her to see if she liked any of the cakes in the selection box, even though she was pretty sure she would. Cake was one thing she knew she could depend upon. But it struck her as strange that her only concern was whether they would be suitable for Darryl. She missed taking somebody else into consideration. Only thinking about herself didn't seem to come naturally anymore, especially after years of thinking about her son first and foremost. She had almost forgotten what *she* liked. Everything was about Chris. What Chris wanted; what Chris needed. He had engulfed her world and now, with both Chris and Nick gone, there was nothing. A vacuous pit in the world.

*Stop it,* she berated herself. *Why won't I let myself be happy.* Miserable thoughts always forced their way in and took over. And that was without the worry of her mother.

She arrived back at The Birds and forced herself to focus on the present moment. *Keep your mind on the job at hand. At least after cake.*

She could just make out someone through the open door of the porter's room. Two feet were crossed at the ankles and resting on the table. She knocked on the outside doors. The feet slid from view and were replaced with a book. Pete appeared through the door, swinging his large bunch of keys around a finger. He unlocked the door for Eleanor and pulled it open.

'Thanks, Pete. We'll probably only be about another hour. Is that OK?'

'Yep. Makes no difference to me. Just don't go falling asleep on the job or you'll find yourself still here in the wee small hours.'

'No worry about that. Not with the amount of caffeine I have inside me.'

Eleanor took the lift back upstairs. As she walked toward the conference room, she could see the hazy silhouette of Darryl with his head down on the table. Even though it was through frosted glass there was no mistaking the image. *Talking of falling asleep,* she smiled.

As she opened the door the smell of gas overwhelmed her. She started to choke and staggered back from the room. But Darryl was still in there. She dropped the box of cakes and her handbag and, almost subconsciously, hit the fire alarm situated in the hallway outside the conference room door. Immediately the high-pitched ringing burst into action.

She took a deep breath and returned to the conference room. She ran to the window, but the safety catch was stuck. It wouldn't open more than a crack. She tried to take another deep breath of the cool, evening air from the inch or so she had managed to expose.

She ran to Darryl and shook him, but there was no motion from him. Trying to wake him wasn't going to work.

She staggered back to the window for more deep breaths. She had to get him out of the room and away from the main source of the gas. There had been no sign of gas in the hallway, it was only after she'd opened the conference room door. It must be coming from somewhere within that room.

She held another deep breath of the cool evening air and ran back out the room. A fire extinguisher was hooked on the wall directly underneath the fire alarm. A useful wedge for the heavy fire door.

In the hall she could breathe easier, but the gas was spreading. She ran back to Darryl and tried to pull him out of the room. He was heavier than anything she could manage, even if she hadn't been beginning to feel the effects of the gas herself. The light-headedness, the weakness in her muscles. She had only succeeded in getting him to the floor and no more than two feet from his chair. Panic was starting to sink in.

A slight cool breeze drifted in through the window, created when she'd propped open the door. She decided to risk the exposure of her own lungs to the gas and screamed for help.

Still she would not give up. All the time the continual ringing of the alarm sounded. Her vision became hazy, and her knees weak, but she kept pulling and crying for help. She wasn't going to give in. Holding Darryl under the arms, she managed maybe another four or five feet. Becoming weaker every moment she was there, and every attempt to move him became more and more futile. It wouldn't be long till she was lying on the floor herself.

Suddenly, somebody was there with her. Pete took hold of one of Darryl's arms and Eleanor held the other. Together they managed to heave him out of the conference room and through to Eleanor's office a short way down the hall. Eleanor kicked the door shut behind them. Pete opened the window wide, sticking his own head out into the cool air. Eleanor collapsed to the floor. Overcome by both exhaustion and the effects of the gas. Her breathing shallow and painful. Still she placed her hand on Darryl's chest and tried to shake him.

'Darryl,' she whispered, her throat burning. 'Wake up.' The sound of sirens drifted through the open window. They weren't far.

'Is there anyone else on this floor?' Pete asked, coughing.

'No, no, everyone's left. It was just us.'

'Keep him here by the window. I'll send the paramedics up to you as soon as they arrive.' Pete took in a deep breath and hurried out the room, closing the door quickly behind him.

'Darryl, Darryl,' Eleanor struggled. She couldn't lose anybody else. The pain in her chest that she lived with every moment of every day seemed to explode and began to override any other feeling. She wanted to scream from the raw, burning ache, but her throat wouldn't let her.

The paramedics arrived in minutes and tried to lead her away.

'I'm fine,' she struggled to tell them. 'It's Darryl that needs your help,' but she wasn't sure what words she actually spoke as she could no longer hear what was going on around her. Sounds were no more than a muffled din. Her vision was blurred. She was vaguely aware of others swarming around the room, and she had the strangest feeling she was floating.

The paramedics carried her out to a waiting ambulance.

## 12

When Eleanor woke, the first thing she noticed was the headache. She felt as though her head was laid on a slab of concrete. She could feel the pounding before her eyes flickered open; before the smell of disinfectant; before the bright white of the hospital strip-lights entered her retinas, which then added to the pounding like a marching band echoing round her head as though it were an empty cavern. Pounding, just pounding.

'Good morning, Eleanor. How are you feeling?'

A nurse was standing next to Eleanor's bed, holding her arm. Eleanor found her gentle voice soothing.

'Headache,' Eleanor tried to reply. Her mouth was so dry her tongue almost stuck to the roof of her mouth.

'Headache? I bet you do. Don't worry. It's time for your next dose of painkillers. The doctors will be round to see you in just a moment, too.'

'Darryl?' she asked, the vision of his unconscious body lying on the floor flickered into her memory.

'Is that the gentleman you came in with? He's going to be fine. You'll probably be able to see him soon.'

Eleanor began sobbing. She wasn't quite sure why. Was it the pain in her head, the shock of the experience, or the relief that Darryl was still alive?

'Hey, hey,' said the nurse. 'It's OK. Everyone's fine. It's all going to be sorted.' The nurse passed Eleanor a box of tissues and sat on the edge of the bed. 'Sounds like you went through quite a lot last night.'

Eleanor wanted to ask what the nurse had heard. Did she know what had happened? Where the gas had come from? When she'd be able to see Darryl? When she'd be able to go home? So many questions, but she couldn't stop the tears and she cried herself back to sleep.

~

People were talking in the room but, for some reason, Darryl felt as though they didn't want him to hear. An argument not meant for his ears. He tried to open his eyes and blinked into the light. He was lying, facing a blank white ceiling, and the voices were coming from somewhere near his feet. There wasn't much more he could tell. As his eyes became better accustomed to the bright light, he found he was more able to focus. Only shapes at first. From his position he could only make out their heads and shoulders. Two people in dark, and one in white. He blinked again, and the men's features became clearer. The one in white was a stereotypical doctor with a stethoscope round his neck. The two men in dark suits were the two police detectives who had introduced themselves to Darryl only a couple of days earlier, trying to convince him, without alarming him, that there might be someone trying to kill him. Not your average conversation.

He was back in the hospital, that was obvious, and with the police there again it couldn't be good. He tried to move and groaned from both his aching body, and the realisation that they may have been right after all.

The groan caught their attention.

'Mr Westwood?' The older of the two detectives moved to the side of the bed, closer to Darryl's head.

'Hmm,' was the most he could reply. His mouth wouldn't open without a struggle. Never had his mouth been so dry. He was trying to remember what had happened to cause him to be back in the hospital. He was sure he would have remembered if he'd been hit by another car.

'Let him have a drink before any questions,' said the doctor. He came around to Darryl's other side and helped him to sit up. To Darryl's disappointment he needed the help. His muscles were weak and with only a little effort his arms gave way at the elbows. The doctor then passed Darryl a green plastic beaker half full of water, holding it until he was certain Darryl had hold of it. The cool liquid somehow seemed to stick as he tried to drink. Only small sips could make it through, stinging the back of his throat as it went.

'Mr Westwood?' The detective started again while the doctor hovered taking notes from the machines surrounding Darryl's bed.

'Do you remember me? Detective Inspector Selby and this is Detective Sergeant Wade.'

Darryl took another sip.

'It would seem our suspicions were right,' DI Selby went on.

'What happened?' Darryl finally managed to say.

'Do you remember anything?'

Darryl shook his head and immediately regretted it. He felt as though he had a mountain of loose rubble inside his head. He took a moment for the rubble to settle before he spoke again.

'I remember we were working late.'

'We? As in yourself and Mrs Garrett?'

'Eleanor, yes. I went to the gents, came back and then ...' he tried to remember. 'And then nothing, sorry.'

'We found a gas canister in the conference room where you were working.'

'So, it was just a gas leak?'

'No. This type of gas canister is for industrial use. It would have no reason to be in that room, or even in that type of establishment. The valve had also been tampered with and adapted to leak using some kind of remote device. We'll know more after forensics have had a closer look.'

'Somebody rigged it to leak?' Darryl said incredulously.

'Ordinarily, that size canister would create some discomfort for those in an office building of that size, but nothing lethal,' DI Selby continued. 'Whereas, in a confined space like the conference room, with the door shut, and the window safety catch purposefully jammed, it would have been fatal.'

Darryl stared at the Detective Inspector and then looked round at the other faces in the room. There was no sign that this was a joke. They were serious.

'This is now an attempted murder investigation.' DS Wade, a man in his mid-twenties and clearly new to such excitement, seemed to take delight in making this announcement.

'Thank God Eleanor had left,' Darryl sighed.

'Left?'

'Yes, she went to get cake,' he remembered with a slight smile.

DS Wade began writing in his notebook.

'So ... so how come I'm still here?' Darryl went on.

'From what we understand you have Mrs Garrett to thank for that. She alerted the authorities when she set off the fire alarm,' DI Selby said. 'We haven't managed to speak to her yet. She, too, has been recovering from the effects of the gas.'

'Eleanor?' The evening was a haze to the moment Darryl's

memory went black. He tried to recall anything. 'No, she'd left. Why would she be recovering?'

DS Wade seemed only too happy to take over the story. 'It would seem, when Mrs Garrett returned and found you, she set off the alarm, tried to open the window, and, according to ...' he flicked through his notebook excitedly, '... Peter Burrows, the porter, she pulled you almost single-handedly from the room. Mr Burrows explained how he had found Mrs Garrett almost overcome herself from the gas yet determined to get you out.' DS Wade glanced up from his notebook, smiling from excitement, until going quiet with a look from DI Selby.

'We still need to confirm these events with Mrs Garrett, but it would seem you're very lucky she found you when she did,' DI Selby continued. 'But, can I confirm that you are saying Mrs Garrett was not in the room with you at the time?' continued DI Selby brusquely.

'No, she wasn't,' Darryl said. 'She had left before I even went to the gents.'

'Sounds like the killer waited for her to leave and then when you went through to the bathroom, took advantage of the room being empty and planted the canister.'

'And jammed the safety catch on the window,' interjected DS Wade.

DI Selby threw another heated glance at him and Wade shrunk back.

'Do you remember seeing anybody else there?' asked DI Selby.

'No, it was just me and Eleanor.' Darryl's eyelids suddenly felt like lead. Overwhelmed with confusion, exhaustion seemed to overcome him suddenly. But he only thought of Eleanor. 'When can I see Eleanor? Is she alright?'

'She is fine. You'll be able to see her soon,' the doctor said reassuringly. 'I think that's enough questions for now,' he directed toward DI Selby.

Darryl fought against his tiredness. He reluctantly closed his eyes. He wanted to know more. 'Where is she? Are you sure she's alright?'

'You can see her later, Mr Westwood,' the doctor said. His voice calm and soothing. 'I can promise you she's going to be absolutely fine. You need to sleep now.'

'We'll come back later, when you're more awake,' DI Selby said.

Only murmurs rumbled until Darryl sank into darkness.

∼

The next time Eleanor woke the headache was gone and she felt like she'd slept for a week. Her body felt heavy and dull as she tried to look around her. She could just make out three others in the ward with her, all sitting quietly. The woman directly opposite her was reading a thick hard-backed book, and from the expression on her face it looked like she had reached an exciting part. The woman in the next bed along had her eyes closed and her ears plugged in. She could have been sleeping if it wasn't for those moments when her lips moved slightly with the lyrics of a song. The last woman, in the bed next to Eleanor's, was by the window and stared out into the clear blue sky, beginning to redden with the setting sun.

Eleanor tentatively sat up in her bed, forcing her muscles to waken. Waiting for the pounding to begin again. Thankfully, her head remained calm. The vision of Darryl's unconscious body refused to leave her mind. She had to find him. See for herself how he was. She turned on her bed and her legs slipped off the edge. They ached with weakness and she began to wonder if she *had* been in bed for a week. A nurse came walking into the ward with a jug of water for the patient gazing out the window. On her return, Eleanor caught her attention. A flick of her hand was all she could manage as her muscles fought against her.

'Could you tell me how long I've been here, please?'

'You came in last night so not that far off twenty-four hours ago now. You weren't in a good way. How are you feeling now?'

'Like I've been knocked out for a week.'

'I'm not surprised, but you're going to be fine. You had a lucky escape.'

'My mother,' Eleanor suddenly blurted. Aileen would know nothing of what had happened.

'Don't worry. Miss Osbourne, I think her name was, left a message for you to say that Alison, or something like that—'

'Aileen?' Eleanor suggested.

'That's it, Aileen, will stay with your mother for as long as it takes and you're not to worry.'

Eleanor smiled with relief and thanked her lucky stars once again for finding Aileen to look after her mother.

'Miss Osbourne also brought your bag in for you, we've popped it in the cupboard just here for you,' continued the nurse.

'Thank you. Could you tell me where Darryl Westwood is, please?' Eleanor asked.

'You might have trouble getting in to see him,' the nurse replied. 'I'll tell you what, I'll take you round. Come on. I'd like to see how steady you are on your feet before you go walking off anywhere on your own. It's about time you were up and about anyway.'

Eleanor hesitated. *Trouble seeing him?* she thought. *They must be restricting his visitors.* To Eleanor that could only mean he was in a bad way.

The nurse took hold of Eleanor's hands and gently held

them as Eleanor slipped off the bed and put her feet on the floor. She tentatively stood.

'Well done, you're a strong one,' the nurse said encouragingly.

The sensation of putting one foot in front of the other was strange to begin with, but even before they had left the ward Eleanor was feeling stronger. She was able to stand straight instead of holding the stoop of an old woman, and the muscles in her legs felt almost normal.

'It's not far,' the nurse said as they walked slowly together down the corridor and turned a corner to the left. Eleanor's surprise at seeing the nurse show her ID badge to a policeman standing guard at a door was nothing to her surprise when the nurse explained that Eleanor was the other victim from the gas attack.

*Attack?* thought Eleanor. *Surely not.*

The policeman let them through the door, and the nurse left again. Inside, Darryl was sat in bed. He looked a little pale, but otherwise fine. His smile brought the pain back to Eleanor's chest and she immediately wanted to leave again.

The small, crowded room didn't help ease the sense of foreboding. Large enough to fit the bed, two chairs and a myriad of machines surrounding the head of the bed. A small sink was tucked in one corner. Apart from the necessities, the room was bare. Surely not even the space to fit the troop of doctors that usually gather at the end of the bed to make their analysis. Being an internal room, there wasn't even a window to give the illusion of space and ease her feeling of the walls closing in.

'This is getting to be a habit, visiting you in hospital,' Eleanor said.

'At least it wasn't you that put me here this time,' Darryl replied with a slight ironic smile.

'And look who's Mr Special. Your own room, a guard on the

door. Is that to stop someone getting in, or you from getting out?' She tried to laugh at her own joke.

'I guess that's what happens when someone's trying to kill you.'

Darryl's nervous laughter suggested that he was feeling as uncomfortable as she was. *So, someone is trying to kill him. And has already killed Nick and my boy.* But still she didn't want to believe it. She moved closer and sat on the edge of his bed.

'The nurse said outside that it was a gas attack. Is that what this is? Someone tried to gas you?'

'It would seem so. I hear I have you to thank for saving my life.'

'Not really.' Uncomfortable with his thanks Eleanor turned away. She did no more than anybody else would have done. All she could remember was the pain in her chest. The unbearable pain. 'It was just lucky that—'

Darryl leaned forward and kissed Eleanor on the cheek.

She turned in surprise to find his face only a few inches away from hers. He moved closer again, but Eleanor jumped up quickly. The blood draining from her face.

'No,' she cried, though suddenly realised she sounded ungrateful. After all, he was only thanking her. 'There's no need to thank me,' she garbled. 'And, Pete helped too,' she added as an afterthought.

'I'm not kissing Pete,' Darryl laughed.

Eleanor forced a laugh, overwhelmed with panic as the confusion inside her swelled. At that moment Miss Osbourne came through the door escorted by a doctor, adding to Eleanor's sudden agitation.

'Eleanor, no wonder we couldn't find you in your own ward. How are you feeling?' As usual, Miss Osbourne didn't leave time for Eleanor to answer the question. 'The doctor here was looking for you, too,' she continued. 'I'll stay here and keep Mr Westwood company while you go with the doctor.'

Miss Osbourne moved to one of the chairs and made herself comfortable.

'Mrs Garrett, I would like to take one more set of tests before I let you leave,' said the doctor.

'You mean, I'll be able to go home soon?'

'I have just spoken with Nurse Daniels and she informed me how well you managed the walk here. So, as long as there are no problems with the results of these tests, you could be out in a couple of hours.'

Relieved, Eleanor glanced back toward Miss Osbourne and Darryl. She nodded her goodbye.

'Come back before you leave,' Darryl said.

'OK.' Eleanor hesitantly nodded.

'Please.'

Eleanor realised from his voice that he knew it was unlikely she would return. 'Promise,' she said quietly.

She wasn't even out the room before she could hear Miss Osbourne's patronising drawl.

'Such a sweet girl, but far too delicate for all this. She doesn't have the inner strength one needs for dealing with these kinds of traumatic experiences—'

The door closed, and Eleanor silently walked back to her own ward with the doctor, and nothing but confusion in her head.

~

The doctor took his tests and a few minutes later an elderly woman entered the ward with sandwiches. Eleanor had the choice of a ham or cheese sandwich, and decided the cheese looked slightly more appetising, or maybe it was slightly less unappealing. She tried to ring home, but her phone was out of battery. At least she knew that her mother was safe with Aileen. Finally, after nearly four hours, she was given the go ahead to leave. She thought about whether to visit Darryl again. Four hours of churning over the events from earlier had only left her with questions rather than answers. *Don't flatter yourself, woman. Or, am I being naive? Was he just thanking me for saving his life?* Again, and again she swung between defiance and self-doubt. She would rather not see Darryl again today, all she really wanted was to go home and see her mother. But she decided she couldn't risk him having the wrong impression and she needed to make it clear to him that there could never be anything between them.

## 13

'Hi Dave,' Darryl said into his phone.

He was sat on his hospital bed, thoroughly bored. He was grateful that Miss Osbourne finally left a couple of hours earlier, but he had hoped Eleanor would have returned before now.

'Mate, where were you last night?' Dave replied cheerily.

'Back in hospital. You should try it sometime,' Darryl replied sarcastically.

'Nah, not so keen on the whole sterilised ambiance. I heard about a gas leak or something at The Birds, that wasn't you was it?'

'That was me.'

Darryl held the phone away from his ear for a moment as Dave's laugh echoed loudly.

'That woman's gonna be the death of you. I thought you were seeing Rachel last night.'

'That had been the plan, but, hey, she said till death do us part, I guess plans change,' Darryl said with bitterness. He didn't want to be reminded of Rachel.

'Has Osbourne been in to see you yet?' Dave asked. 'I can't see her passing up a chance like this.'

'Yeah, for two hours. How can anyone talk about nothing for two hours? That's a skill in itself.'

'Yeah, she's really good at making the insignificant seem worthy of conversation. Well, don't worry yourself about my place, there's no big rush.'

'Just as well 'cause I don't know when I'm getting out of here. The doctors have said hopefully tomorrow, but who knows.'

The door to his room opened and DI Selby and DS Wade entered.

'I'm going to have to go,' continued Darryl as he acknowledged their arrival. 'I'll give you a call when I'm out, OK?'

'Course, I'll see you soon. But Darryl, remember, for her sake as well as yours, finish the job and get out.'

'Yeah, sure.' Darryl hung up. Confusion was seeping in deeper. He knew logically Dave was right.

'Mr Westwood, how are you feeling now? A little more awake?' asked DI Selby.

Darryl gave him a sardonic smile. 'Alive and kicking, thank you. I'd like to keep it that way.'

'So, would we. We have some more questions for you if you're up to it?'

'Sure, pull up a chair. I'm not going anywhere. Have you managed to speak with Eleanor yet? She said she'd come back before she left.'

In truth he had hoped they would know whether she had left or not, but they showed no knowledge of her whereabouts.

'That would be very helpful, thanks. But for now, how much do you remember of the conversation we had earlier?'

~

Eleanor was relieved to see Miss Osbourne had left when she entered Darryl's room. Even though it had been four hours it wouldn't have surprised her to find Miss Osbourne still there, wittering on about what a success she had made of her life. Instead the two police officers that were with him the last time he was in hospital were there at his bedside.

'Mrs Garrett,' the older of the two men stood as she walked in. 'Mr Westwood said you may be returning. I'm Detective Inspector Selby and this is Detective Sergeant Wade. If you don't mind, we have some questions for you.'

Eleanor shook the detective's hand and he sat back down.

'Of course,' she replied.

The only chairs in the room were already taken by the two detectives. Uncomfortably, she sat on the edge of Darryl's bed, almost in the same spot she had been sitting earlier.

DS Wade, the younger of the two men, briefly glanced at his notebook. 'We understand you decided to stay on and work late last night, is that correct?' he asked.

'Yes, I knew that the job needed to be done urgently and I was happy to stay.'

'With Mr Westwood?'

'Yes, well, no. Darryl wasn't going to be staying and did actually leave.'

'That's right,' Darryl said. 'I'd arranged to meet my ex-wife, but as soon as I left, I realised it was more important to stay and work. So, I rang and cancelled, and went back upstairs. It was very last minute.'

'So, very few people would have known you were there,' said DI Selby.

'I don't think anyone other than Eleanor knew.'

'Who else was around at that time?' DI Selby directed toward Eleanor.

'I think everyone had gone.' Remembering the events of the evening, Eleanor said, 'Miss Osbourne, Gina and Marie all went down in the lift just after Darryl.'

'They left,' continued Darryl. 'I saw the three of them coming out of the lift on the ground floor as I finished my call. I nipped up the stairs before they saw me.'

'Are you sure they didn't see you?' asked DI Selby.

'I suppose I can't be certain. My back was to them as I went up the stairs, but I don't think so. Even the stairs were quiet by the time I went back up. I didn't see anyone until I saw Eleanor on her hands and knees, and her head in a cupboard.'

Eleanor felt Darryl's remark deserved an explanation.

'The caretaker had made me jump when he said goodnight.' She smiled at the memory. 'Coffee had gone everywhere and I was cleaning it up. But that means he was leaving at that time, too. He already had his coat on, ready to go.'

'Could you give me the name of the caretaker, please?' DS Wade asked.

Eleanor hesitated. She suddenly felt ashamed. She had worked in the same building as him for seven months now and yet didn't even know his name.

'I'm sorry, I don't know.'

'Not to worry, we can find that out elsewhere.' DI Selby said. 'Anybody else?'

'The staff from Samson's Digital World, in the offices next to ours, they walked behind the caretaker as we were talking.'

'All of them?'

'I can't really remember. I was focusing on the coffee I'd spilt, but there was a group of them. They all usually go for a drink together after work.'

'Thanks, we'll verify that. Who else would have been in the building?'

'There would be the porters, Pete Burrows and Sidney Cooper. Although Sidney would have finished about an hour after, and only Pete was there for the evening. I was surprised to see him actually because he's usually at college on a Thursday. He goes to evening classes.'

'Which college?' Inspector Selby asked.

'I don't know. I don't even know what it is he's studying.' Again, Eleanor felt ashamed that she didn't know this simple piece of information. Had she really been so wrapped up in herself that she hadn't bothered to ask other people about their lives? 'He told me he has a couple of weeks off.'

DI Selby turned to look at his Sergeant. 'Is it the holidays at the moment?'

'No, sir. Not for at least another couple of weeks. At least not at my kid's school.'

'Thank you, Miss. We can look into that. Carry on.'

'Pete unlocked the door for me when I went out and then let me back in again as soon as I got back,' Eleanor said thoughtfully.

'How long would you say that took?'

'Probably just five minutes, ten at the most. Everyone is usually out by that time.'

'Where was Mr Burrows when you returned?'

'In the porter's room behind reception. I could see his feet up on the table through the door. He was reading.'

'He would have known I was upstairs,' Darryl interrupted. 'I made my call in the lift on the way down and said that I was staying to work late. Pete would have known I was there.'

'So, Pete knew you were returning to the office when he heard you on the phone to another woman,' DI Selby clarified.

DS Wade jotted it down in his notebook with a knowing look from DI Selby.

'Anybody else you can think of?' he turned back to Eleanor.

'Maybe Callum.'

'Callum?'

'Callum Matthews, the archivist. I didn't see him at all, but I guess he may have been there. I know he's doing a lot of reorganising in the archives at the moment and I believe he often stays late. Pete and Sidney would be the best ones to check with on that. And, I don't know about the offices on the other floors. Surely you don't think it was someone from the office.'

'We have explained to Mr Westwood previously, there have been a number of deaths and disappearances all connected with that building.'

'Yes, Darryl has explained to me. One of which was my husband,' Eleanor said firmly with an air of don't-you-think-this-should-have-been-mentioned-to-me-before?

'Yes, we appreciate that,' DI Selby said apologetically. 'You understand, we couldn't say anything at the time as it appeared to be an innocent accident, and there was nothing to say otherwise.'

'But, even if it is true, no one at the office would want to kill Darryl. They wouldn't have even known him before Tuesday.'

'It doesn't take long for strong emotions to take hold as I have found out in my time in the police force. Also, from what you have told us this couldn't have been planned.' DI Selby turned back to Darryl. 'You didn't even know yourself you were going to be there, Mr Westwood, so how could the killer know? I believe it must have been someone close by. Someone from that building. They saw you return upstairs and took their chance. If we're right, and there is a serial killer here, this is the first time they have slipped up. With all the other occurrences he or she has managed to make them look like nothing more than accidents. This was definitely attempted murder.'

DI Selby turned his attention back to Eleanor.

'In light of this new attempt on Mr Westwood's life, as we have explained to Mr Westwood, we will also be looking in more detail into the car incident that happened on Wednesday. Mrs Garrett, we understand that you believe someone pushed you.'

Eleanor sighed, relieved that somebody was going to take her seriously.

'Yes, they pushed me, and I knocked into Darryl, which then led to him ...' She couldn't bring herself to say it. She couldn't even bring herself to look at him.

'We understand you were very upset at the time. Highly distressed? Maybe a little uncoordinated?'

Eleanor's anger began to rise at his insinuation.

'Somebody pushed me. It was a definite push,' she said firmly.

After a short pause DI Selby sighed and said, 'I believe you, but I needed to check your conviction. You are certain you were pushed?'

Eleanor nodded vigorously.

'We have seen this domino effect used before. One person is pushed with the specific intention of knocking into somebody else who is the real target. Can either of you remember who was around at that time?'

'All I remember is I knew I had to get to Eleanor,' said Darryl. 'There were people everywhere, but I've no idea who.'

'And I was, as you said, highly distressed at the time.' Eleanor shook her head. There was no way she would have been able to remember who she had seen.

'What about immediately after the incident? Mrs Garrett, what happened then?'

'I remember I tried to get to Darryl but ...' Eleanor said, uncomfortable with all the memories of that moment being brought back into focus. 'Callum, yes it was Callum, he was holding me back.'

'Callum Matthews?' DS Wade began scribbling in his notebook.

'Yes. He must have seen what happened and came out to help me.'

'He is the archivist, yes? Shouldn't he have been down in the archives at that time?' DI Selby asked curiously.

'I guess, I don't know ...' Eleanor's words drifted off with confusion.

'Not to worry, we can check on that,' he continued with a nod to DS Wade. 'What happened next?'

'Then Pete was there, too. They both helped me back to the offices.'

'Pete Burrows?'

'Yes.'

DS Wade scribbled in his notebook again.

'Unfortunately, I wasn't making it easy for them.' Eleanor tried to laugh light-heartedly, embarrassed by the commotion she had caused. 'I remember we fell against a van as they were trying to move me away.'

'What van?'

'There was a van parked at the side of the road.' Eleanor was surprised by the Inspector's serious tone.

'By the crossing? They shouldn't be parked there.'

'They always pull up there when there are deliveries for the offices. They're not there long.'

'Still, that would have cut down on visibility,' said the Inspector. 'This is a regular thing, you say?'

'Yes. I don't know what the company is, but it's a large green van that comes every week.'

'That shouldn't be too difficult to find out. Now, you say both these men were with you directly after the incident?'

'Shortly after,' she corrected him. 'I couldn't really say how soon.'

'Carry on, what else do you remember?'

The small room was stifling. The air had suddenly become warm and close. Eleanor tried to push the image of Darryl lying in the road out of her head and move on.

'The porter, Sidney, and the caretaker were inside when we reached the entrance hall. A few minutes later, after Darryl was put in the ambulance, Miss Osbourne, Gina and Marie all came in from outside.'

'So, they were outside too at the time of the incident?'

'I don't know about at the time. I just know they came in after the ambulance had left. They could have gone out at any time before that, I suppose.'

DS Wade looked as though he couldn't keep up with all the notes he was frantically scribbling in his notebook. A thin smear of sweat appeared on his forehead.

'Anything else you can remember about that day?' asked DI Selby.

She glanced briefly at Darryl. She could remember it was later that evening that she had been dancing in the town square. Waltzing in the arms of a man somebody seemed intent on killing.

'No,' she said quietly.

'Well, thank you both,' DI Selby said standing, ready to leave. 'I think that will keep us busy for a while. We'll be in touch again soon. Please contact us if there is anything more you remember, or anything you think may help.' He handed Eleanor a business card with his contact details.

Eleanor managed a smile in reply as they left. She turned to Darryl, keeping her head low, avoiding his eyes.

'I'm leaving for home now,' she said abruptly. 'I'm assuming you've spoken with Mr Saunders and he's not expecting your report just yet.'

'I have, yes. The doctors think I'll be out tomorrow, and Dave's said I can have a couple more days next week. Eleanor,' he continued gently. 'I'm sorry if I—'

'Good, then I'll see you on Monday morning,' Eleanor interrupted. 'If the doctor's change their minds and decide to keep you here longer, just ring the office and leave a message.' Eleanor made to leave.

'Eleanor, wait,' he pleaded.

'Have a good weekend and I hope you don't have to stay in here too much longer.'

'Eleanor—'

'No.' Eleanor finally faced him. She didn't want to hear anything he had to say. 'Please don't.'

She left the room as quickly as she could.

∽

It was gone ten o'clock by the time Eleanor reached home. Being so late at night, she had decided to get a taxi home direct from the hospital. She was smothered with attention from Aileen as soon as she walked through the door.

'Och, hen, I'm just grateful it was nothing worse,' she said when Eleanor tried to apologise for not returning home. 'Have you had a wee drop of scotch?'

'No,' Eleanor laughed. She knew that Aileen's answer to everything was a wee drop of scotch. 'The doctors here aren't as well educated as those from your home town and don't prescribe scotch.'

'Aye, progress isn't always a great thing. Let me get you some now.' Aileen hurried off to the kitchen.

Scotch wasn't something Eleanor kept in the house until Aileen began working there. Since then it had become a kitchen cupboard staple.

'Thank you again for taking such good care of Mother. Honestly, Aileen, I don't know what I'd do without you.' Eleanor took the glass from Aileen. 'I understand if you want to stay in the spare room tonight as it's so late, but I also know you like to be home. So, why don't you go home and put your feet up. I understand the true meaning now of someone being worth their weight in gold, and more.'

'I'm not leaving you like this, lassie. The spare room will do me just fine.'

'You've been too good to me already. Go on home.'

Eleanor could see the hesitation in Aileen's face as she fought with her nurturing instincts. Instincts that were clearly telling her she should stay.

'Only if you're sure. I really didn't mind staying. That lovely old woman's no trouble at all.'

'Go. Go and do something special for yourself tomorrow. You're just too good, I don't deserve you.'

'You make sure you have a quiet weekend too, and I'm only at the end of the phone if you need me. Take it easy, hen. What you've been through would be a horrific shock for anyone.'

'I will, I promise.'

Aileen collected her bag, said goodbye to Margaret with a kiss on her forehead, and left. Eleanor was left in a quiet house. Quiet that is apart from the television at volume thirty-six for her mother to be able to hear it. She was determined not to think about work at all until Monday morning. No work, no buildings, and certainly no Darryl.

## 14

Darryl sat at his dining table. His lunch no more than a sandwich bought from the hospital's shop as he was leaving. The room was empty except for the dining table and chairs, and some almost empty shelves on the wall. Almost empty as the remaining items had been packed away years before. Even if they had been on display Rachel wouldn't have been interested in taking the three archaeological finds. A Saxon brooch, a World War I bullet and an indistinct something or other.

'Do we really have to have this ... lump on display?' Rachel had said looking at it, picking it up as though it was a smelly sock discovered under the bed after several years of hibernation.

'Careful with it. It's delicate,' he'd said, gently taking it from her.

'What is it?'

'It's a stone Tudor rose and at least 400 years old. And, yes it does need to be on display. Just as much as your ... cushions.'

'At least you can see what my cushions are,' Rachel had replied.

'But how many cushions does a person need? We don't even use them. They just get thrown on the floor every time I want to sit down. OK, OK,' Darryl conceded after receiving a derogatory look from Rachel. He'd carefully wrapped it in some tissue paper and stored it away in a box. That was the first of his finds that ended up in that box. *It's OK if she doesn't understand the significance,* he'd thought at the time.

The day she'd left he had brought the box down from the loft and put the three items on display. That conversation had only been three years into their marriage. At the time he'd thought, *Why are we arguing over such a small thing? Surely, it's not worth it.* Now he was beginning to wonder if maybe he should have argued back. Maybe he would have been less of a walk-over. Maybe she would have thought twice about having an affair if he'd ... If he'd what? Was there really anything he could have done differently?

He finished off his mouthful of chicken sandwich and picked up his phone. He'd been putting off making this call, but now he felt ready to move on.

'Hi, I need to put my house on the market. Would someone be able to come and assess the damage? ... No, I mean come and give me a valuation.' *No sense of humour there, then,* Darryl thought. 'Monday would be great, thanks.'

Darryl answered a few basic questions for the estate agent with some details of his house; three bed semi-detached, off-street parking, one bathroom, downstairs cloakroom, and gave his address. He listened wearily to the estate agent's spiel about a desirable area, good schools, people already on their books looking for such a place. *Yeah, yeah, I wonder how many of your new clients you don't say that to.*

'See you nine o'clock, Monday. Thanks again,' Darryl said ending the call as quickly as politeness would allow.

The doorbell rang as he hung up the phone. He took another bite of his sandwich and went to open the front door.

Darryl was surprised to see DI Selby, a thick file tucked under his arm.

'Don't you guys at least get the weekend off?' Darryl asked.

'There has been a development in the case, and weekends are kind of insignificant when dealing with a serial killer. I hope you don't mind, but I have some photographs I'd like to show you.'

'Sure, as long as you don't mind me finishing my lunch.'

Darryl led the detective back to the dining room. There was only one seat in the lounge, and that wasn't comfortable, so no good for guests. At least the dining table still had four chairs.

'Are you moving?'

Darryl guessed DI Selby must have noticed the sparsity of furniture as they walked through the house.

'Soon, I guess, but most of the furniture went with the ex.'

'Ah,' said DI Selby in a manner that told Darryl he had been in a similar position himself.

'What are the photographs?' Darryl asked.

'I know this may not be very pleasant for you, but I was hoping to show you some photographs of other victims from the last eighteen months or so, to see if we can find any other connection, other than that building. We've never been in the position before where we know who the next victim is— who the next intended victim is,' the detective corrected himself at a glance from Darryl.

'Sure, let's have a look.'

Darryl relaxed into his chair and started again on his sandwich. There were only a couple of bites left to go. DI Selby opened his file and placed a photograph of a man Darryl had never seen before on the table. A happy man in his late twenties or early thirties, dark hair. The photograph had clearly been cropped and a woman's hand could be seen around his waist. A couple posing for a happy memento.

'Who is he?' Darryl asked.

'The latest victim. His name was Douglas Armstrong. He was a porter at The Birds Building and disappeared almost two weeks ago.'

'Eleanor told me about him. He just didn't turn up for work one day.'

'His body was found last night in the river. It is believed to have been there almost two weeks. Nothing but an accident so it would seem. We're pretty certain it wasn't suicide. This photograph was taken a month before he disappeared. As you can see, he's a happy man. He'd just proposed to his girlfriend and life looked rosy. You're sure you don't recognise him?'

Darryl looked again at the photograph. He had known the facts of the case. People killed in accidents or disappearing, but the word 'people' meant nothing. It didn't tell the story of this man's life. Happy, everything to look forward to. A life cut short and his loved ones left behind to carry on without him.

'I've never seen him before,' Darryl said finally.

The detective placed another photograph on the table.

'How about this man?'

The next photograph showed a man in his sixties relaxing at a garden barbecue, beer in hand. A pastime enjoyed by so many, including Darryl himself.

'No, who is he?'

'Charles Walker, another porter who disappeared about a month ago. We haven't found him yet. How about this one?' Another photograph on the table.

Darryl recognised this man. He had seen him before, dancing with Eleanor. On his shoulders was a small boy of about four or five years old.

'This is Nick and Chris,' he said automatically, picking up the photograph for a closer look.

'You know them,' DI Selby said almost excitedly.

'No, I had seen Nick with Eleanor at a class I go to, but I never spoke to either of them.'

'Still, it's a connection. What class is this?' DI Selby took out his notebook ready to write down the details.

Darryl's embarrassment caused him to hesitate. 'It's Francesca's Dance Academy in North Brooke town centre. I really don't know him, though, I only know it's him because I recognised Eleanor from the classes.'

While DI Selby wrote down the details Darryl couldn't help but feel a little of Eleanor's loss. Seeing their smiling faces, it was hard to imagine that they were no longer around. What made it worse was that Darryl could see that the photograph had been taken at the ruin in the park. Nick's surprise birthday picnic, which meant Eleanor had probably taken the photo. Those smiles in the picture were for her. Darryl remembered their time at the ruin. He had been so engrossed in the find he hadn't noticed her fade into her thoughts. And, now he understood why she had. He hadn't realised the consequences of taking her there until it was too late. He had tried to distract her, moving on into the town. Drawing her attention away from that moment in the photograph, from that memory. How inept it all felt now.

'We believe the son was just in the wrong place at the wrong time,' DI Selby continued. He finished writing in his notebook and put another photograph on the table. 'How about this one?'

Darryl drew his eyes away from Nick and Chris and placed the photograph back on the table. He pushed it toward the detective. He didn't want to see it anymore. He focused on the new photograph. A curly haired blond in his late teens, early twenties. He was wearing a tuxedo and looked very proud of himself. It brought to Darryl's mind a graduation photo or similar celebration. He had one much the same of himself at his own graduation hidden away in one of those boxes in the loft.

'No, I don't know him.'

'You're sure?'

'I'm sure. Who is he?' Darryl was beginning to find he was struggling to breathe. The air seemed thick and suffocating.

'Zachariah Thompson, a designer from Crevice Edge Designers on the ground floor. He died from a combination of binge drinking and first-time drug use with some old university mates about a year ago.'

Darryl simply shook his head and DI Selby placed another photograph on the table. This man was older, maybe in his fifties.

'How about Thomas Whittaker, the caretaker. Died in a gas explosion in his caravan. In light of the gas incident on Thursday we will be taking another look into this one, as much as we can.'

Darryl could no longer speak. He simply shook his head.

Another photograph.

'Russell Simpson, a porter—'

Darryl felt sick. He pushed his chair back and walked away from the table taking deep breaths.

'How many ... how many more are there?' he asked in short gasps.

'I'm sorry, Mr Westwood. I understand this must be difficult for you. There are only two more. A job applicant, Ryan Walker, and a solicitor from Dolby and Patterson's, Ian Wright.'

Darryl's head was spinning.

'I thought you meant two or three people, not ... not ... how many is it?'

'Eight.'

'Eight?' Darryl exclaimed. 'Eight people have been killed in that building?'

'No, never *in* the building until—'

'Oh, well, that makes all the difference,' Darryl replied sarcastically.

'Please, Mr Westwood. Try to stay calm.'

Darryl was pacing the room. Forcefully blowing out each breath. The reality had now hit him. Eight people had either died or disappeared, probably dead, and someone was trying to make him number nine. All these eight, nine including Chris, happy, smiling, normal people were now no longer alive, they no longer breathed, no longer laughed, no longer existed.

'Please, sir. Come and sit back down. You must remember that we can now investigate. We only had suspicions before, and our hands were tied. All the deaths looked like accidents, no matter how hard we searched for evidence to the contrary. We had nothing. Now, we have proof that there is a killer. Thursday's gas incident was the first time an attempt has be made within the building itself. This gives us a definite link with The Birds Building and he or she is either becoming careless or complacent, which puts us at an advantage. We have forensics working on the gas canister and the conference room. We have a list of suspects, which thanks to you and Mrs Garrett shows only a few people had the opportunity to have placed and set off that gas canister.'

'And you have me as live bait.' Darryl finally landed heavily back in his chair. 'Let me see the last two photos. I want to get this over with.'

∼

Monday morning had seemed like a long time away when Eleanor had left the hospital on Friday evening. When it arrived it had been no time at all. She had had a pleasant weekend with her mother. There had been moments of recollection, but Eleanor didn't force the issue. The only times she had been really concerned were those times when her mother would try to walk for herself. She was so unsteady on her feet, but she did insist on trying, or she would simply forget that she wasn't supposed to try.

Eleanor now sat in her office as the conference room was still cordoned off. The paperwork had been cleared from the conference room and left on Eleanor's desk so, as Darryl had not yet arrived, Eleanor started without him. She hoped that she would be able to either find what he wanted or definitively say it was not there when he arrived.

She jumped at every ping of the lift bell, inadvertently glancing up. Expecting, and at the same time dreading to see his face. By ten o'clock he still hadn't arrived, but when the lift bell sounded this time the doors opened, and DI Selby and DS Wade strolled out and made their way across the hallway toward Eleanor's office. Immediately Eleanor's stomach tightened. She scrutinised their faces as they walked toward her for any indication of the reason for their visit. Had something happened to Darryl? Was that why he hadn't yet turned up?

'Good morning, Mrs Garrett. We're looking for Gina Pickering,' DI Selby said.

Eleanor gave out a huge sigh. She hadn't realised that she had been holding her breath since the moment she first saw the two policemen approaching. 'She's just through the door propped open there.' She pointed through the door to the right of the detectives.

'Thanks,' he replied, and they went through.

'Good morning ladies,' Eleanor heard him say when he entered the office. 'We're looking for Gina Pickering.'

Although not usually one for listening at keyholes, Eleanor couldn't help but hear the conversation between Gina and the detectives.

'Yes, that's me. How can I help you?' Gina replied.

'I'm Detective Inspector Selby and this is Detective Sergeant Wade. We'd just like to ask you a few quick questions.'

'Regarding?'

Eleanor could tell by the incredulous tone of his voice that the detective couldn't quite believe she had asked that question.

'Regarding the attempted murder that took place here on Thursday evening.'

'No, don't be silly,' Gina giggled. 'It was just a gas leak.'

'No, Miss Pickering. It most definitely was not a gas leak.'

'You're kidding. Oh. How can I help you then, officers?'

'Is there somewhere we can talk more privately, Miss?'

'Oh, don't worry about Marie. We tell each other everything. Ask away.'

'We understand that Mr Westwood upset you on Thursday.'

'Did he? I can't remember.'

'The porter, Peter Burrows, stated that you were very upset when Mr Westwood ...' DI Selby said.

Eleanor could hear the flicking of pages of a notebook. '"He shut the lift doors on her,"' continued DS Wade. '"Snubbed her like she was nothing. As if he's Mr High and Mighty, and she's not worthy of his greatness. I could see she was really upset by it."' His monotone words were constant and plodding. He was unmistakably reading.

'He did do that,' she admitted, 'and it really was very rude of him, but I wouldn't kill him over it.'

Eleanor heard the lift ping again and watched as Darryl exited. He headed for Eleanor's office. Her mind on the conversation next door, she was distracted from any other thoughts.

'It wasn't the only time he was rude to you,' interjected Marie. 'The first day he arrived I knew he was going to be trouble, and I told you to steer clear of him.'

Darryl was closer to her office now and about to speak. Eleanor put her finger to her lips to stop him. Then he too heard the voices coming from the office next door.

'You sound like you're not very keen on the man, Miss ...?'

'My name is Marie Appleton, and no I'm not. He's been nothing but rude since he arrived. He slouches over the furniture like he was brought up in a pigsty and it wouldn't surprise me if he eats from a horse trough. And, furthermore, he doesn't appreciate an offer of help even though he doesn't deserve it.'

Eleanor guessed that the two detectives standing in the doorway had blocked the view of Darryl arriving.

'Was he rude to you, Miss Appleton?' DI Selby continued.

'Not directly, but then I wasn't falling at his boot clad feet, like certain others. But still, there is no excuse for rudeness.'

Eleanor couldn't believe what she was hearing. Darryl had been squirming at Marie's opinion of him, but Eleanor was now quickly counting in her head all the times Marie had been rude to her. Immediately, the image of Oliver Hardy came into her head, playing self-consciously with his bowtie. *Oh, but that was just a little bit of fun. That's not rudeness. Where's your sense of humour, Eleanor?*

'Sounds like you're very protective over your friend, Miss Appleton,' DI Selby went on.

'And why shouldn't I be?' replied Marie indignantly. 'She is a very good friend. Wouldn't you feel the same if someone was so blatantly rude to a good friend of yours?'

'Yes, I would, but would I act on it?' replied DI Selby. 'You see, there are some who quietly seethe internally, others who make their feelings known openly, and then there are those who you'd find butter wouldn't melt in their mouths, even while they're stabbing the knife in your back. Which one are you, Miss Appleton?' There was only a moment's pause before DI Selby continued. 'Maybe you're jealous of someone moving in and breaking up that friendship; maybe you'd like a bit more than friendship?'

'Don't patronise me, Inspector, I'm not an idiot. Just because I'm beautiful doesn't make me stupid. In fact, quite the reverse. I like to take advantage of *all* my assets. Whatever you may think, I wouldn't waste my time on a man like Mr Westwood. For my sake or Gina's. And, what if I do have feelings for Gina? I think you'll find that's no longer a crime.'

Eleanor heard Gina give a small gasp followed by one of her giggles.

'You say it was Pete that told you,' Marie continued. 'Well that doesn't surprise me. If you're looking for someone with jealousy as a motive, you may want to talk again to Pete.'

'Why? What do you mean?' said Gina curiously.

'Pete has been ogling you like a lovesick puppy ever since he started working here. Don't tell me you hadn't noticed.'

'Don't be silly,' Gina giggled.

'You're saying,' Inspector Selby interrupted, 'that Mr Burrows is in love with Miss Pickering?'

Gina giggled again.

'I'm not saying anything as strong as that, but he would certainly like to find out. Ask him.'

'We will be speaking with Mr Burrows again once we have completed our enquiries here. Where were you both on Thursday evening about seven o'clock?'

'Thursday,' Gina said thoughtfully.

'Red's bar,' said Marie with certainty. 'Cecilia— Miss Osbourne, was with us too. We all left together at five and spent the rest of the evening at Red's. We didn't leave till about ten.'

'Did either of you see Mr Westwood return back to the office?'

'No,' they both replied.

'That will be all for now, thank you ladies.'

The detectives left Gina and Marie's office and turned into Eleanor's.

'Good morning, Mr Westwood,' said DI Selby.

Eleanor could see he was uncomfortable about the fact that Darryl had overheard his previous conversation.

'As you probably heard we're continuing our preliminary enquiries. We spoke with a few people from the office block over the weekend, since I saw you on Saturday. Mainly those from the other floors, and we're double-checking alibis to be able to eliminate them from our enquiries. So far, it would seem that everyone other than yourself, Mrs Garrett and Mr Burrows had left the building. We've heard from forensics that the remote used to initiate the leak only had a ten-metre range. That cuts down possible suspects dramatically. It had to be someone within the building, and within ten metres of the canister. We'll be in touch as soon as we have anything else. Are you sure you should really be here?'

Darryl looked dumbfounded, as though he couldn't speak. 'I'm fine,' he managed to murmur. 'From what you told me, I'm probably safer here than outside.'

'Well, it's your decision,' replied DI Selby with a frown.

As the detectives walked toward the lift Pete exited with the morning's post.

'Mr Burrows, may we have another word with you?'

Eleanor could see that Darryl was just as interested as she was to know what Pete had to say to the detectives. Pete, DI Selby and DS Wade came together in the middle of the hallway. The two detectives had their backs to Eleanor, and she couldn't quite make out what they were saying. Darryl was clearly in the same position as he moved quietly closer, behind the detectives. Eleanor got up from her desk and followed Darryl out into the hallway.

'We have checked with your college and apparently your course is still running for the next couple of weeks, contrary to what you told Mrs Garrett on Thursday. In fact, they were wondering where you were as you didn't turn up for class when they expected you.'

'So? I just didn't fancy going. That's not a crime.'

'Did you hear Mr Westwood on the phone making arrangements to stay late Thursday evening?'

'Yeah, I heard him. Didn't care though,' Pete replied beginning to sound defensive.

'Did you then make your own arrangements to work late so that you could be here at the appropriate time, ready to gas him as soon as he was on his own?'

'Of course not. I was down in reception all night.'

'Once Mrs Garrett had left the building it wouldn't have taken long for you to have nipped up the stairs to find the conference room empty and plant the gas canister. The leak was done by remote. You could have done that while sitting in the porter's room with your feet up.'

'Why? Why would I?'

'We understand you are fond of Miss Gina Pickering. Just how fond are you, Mr Burrows?'

'You think I would risk everything for a girl who doesn't even know I exist?'

'No,' said Darryl joining the interrogation. 'There is something more. You've shown nothing but contempt toward me since I walked in, and I'm sure that's not on your job description.'

'How would you know what job I'm capable of?' he growled at Darryl. 'I know your type. Come swaggering in here with such good looks, you forgot you need a personality.'

Eleanor was aware of Miss Osbourne, Gina and Marie joining them in the hall.

'What have I done to annoy you so much?' Darryl asked. 'I'm not interested in your girl in there. If she doesn't know you exist that's your fault, not mine.'

Pete's reaction was fast. He lifted his fist ready to throw a punch at Darryl, but the sergeant was faster and intervened. He grabbed Pete's arm in mid-thrust and twisted it round his back in a well-practised sweeping motion. Envelopes and parcels flew from Pete's hands and scattered themselves across the floor.

'Let's finish this conversation down the station, shall we?' said DS Wade, looking pleased with himself.

'I didn't try to kill him if that's what you're thinking. I'd just like to put my fist in his face.'

'I'm sure many people would,' said the Inspector, 'but it's just not the kind of thing we can go around doing.'

The two officers took Pete back to the lift and they disappeared behind the sliding doors.

'Doesn't surprise me,' Miss Osbourne said with her usual air of self-assurance. 'Have you seen how he treats the caretaker? He teases him terribly.'

Eleanor was shocked at her audacity. The endless amount of times Miss Osbourne had done a lot worse than tease him. And, with Pete, it was just teasing. There was no malice in Pete. Not until Darryl came along, anyway.

The commotion had brought everyone from their rooms further down the hallway too. Gossiping murmurs coming from them as they returned. Eleanor began collecting together all the post that was now strewn across the floor.

'I knew he gave me the creeps,' Darryl said.

'But it makes no sense. Pete helped rescue you on Thursday. Why would he do that if he was the one trying to kill you?' Eleanor said walking back to her office. 'And, why would he want to kill Nick? He's always been so kind to me.'

'Maybe he was so kind to you because of what he had done. But then again, who knows how crazy people think.'

Darryl's arrogance clouded Eleanor's thoughts like a storm. Dark and agitated. She didn't care what he or the police thought.

Pete was not a killer. She dumped the post on her desk with a loud thud. She sat back down, and immediately started back to work without another glance toward Darryl.

'I didn't expect to see you started already,' said Darryl ignoring her protest.

'We're behind,' she said abruptly. 'I just want to get it done.'

Eleanor continued reading and purposefully didn't turn to face him.

'Eleanor, can we talk?' Darryl said closing her office door behind him.

'I'd rather get on. Like you said, this will all be finished in a few days, and then we'll never see each other again.' She finally plucked up the courage to look him in the eye. 'It's better that way.'

'It's better to be safe than sorry then, is that it?'

Eleanor didn't answer. She looked back down at the document in front of her and pretended to continue reading.

'You won't get involved with anybody else ever again, just in case?'

Eleanor's eyes were full of tears. She couldn't see the writing on the page anymore, but she was determined not to get involved in this conversation. Darryl forcibly pulled up a chair and snatched a handful of the paperwork. She knew he wasn't happy with her, but it was for the best. They worked in silence.

∽

It was almost one o'clock before either of them spoke again.

'Shall we go and get some lunch?' Darryl asked.

Eleanor could tell from his voice that he was making an effort to sound casual, as though their previous conversation hadn't happened.

'I have a sandwich with me. I'll just carry on here,' she replied, not looking up.

Darryl was silent for a moment. Eleanor could feel he was watching her.

'Eleanor, I'd like to ask you something,' he said quietly.

'Am I going to want to hear it?'

'Probably not, but I'm going to ask anyway because I think you need to hear it.' Darryl paused. 'Do you regret the time you spent with Nick?'

Eleanor looked up at him, astounded. 'Of course not,' she replied. 'What a thing to ask.'

'And what about your son? Do you regret having your son?'

Eleanor was now furious. So furious she couldn't even speak.

'If you could have that time again, but this time knowing what was going to happen, would you do it?'

'I wouldn't be without that time for anything.' Her throat so tight her voice was no more than a whisper.

'Then why deny yourself the possibility of having some kind of happiness again?'

At that moment Miss Osbourne gently opened Eleanor's door.

'Eleanor,' she said quietly.

Eleanor tore her eyes away from Darryl's face. Her anger vanished the moment she laid eyes on Miss Osbourne. She had the same remorseful expression that Eleanor had seen on the officers' faces the day they came to tell her about the accident.

'Aileen has just called. She didn't want to tell you over the phone, so she asked if I could tell you ...'

Eleanor's throat tightened further till she could hardly breathe.

'I'm afraid your mother has had a stroke. A fatal stroke. I'll take you home.'

## 15

Darryl had arrived at the pub before Dave tonight. He was sat staring thoughtfully at his pint when Dave arrived.

'What have you done now?' Dave said as he joined him at the booth.

'What makes you think I've done anything?' Darryl switched back to present time with a jolt. He raised his glass with enthusiasm though he didn't drink. Dave only raised his eyebrows. Darryl's pretence clearly hadn't fooled him.

Darryl hadn't been able to focus properly all afternoon. Thoughts of Eleanor kept drifting into his mind no matter how hard he had tried to keep them out. He didn't want to upset her further, but who else did she have that was going to help her? She needed to hear it. He hadn't lost anyone in the manner she had, and it was hard to comprehend, but surely things should be improving for her by now. He had almost convinced himself that he had done the right thing when the image of Eleanor's face had drifted into his mind. Her angry, pale face that he wouldn't have believed could have become any paler, until Miss Osbourne had entered the room.

After Eleanor had left, he had struggled to work his way

through the paperwork. So far, he still hadn't found anything there to help him, but that was irrelevant. Eleanor seemed to be the only thing he could focus on. Maybe he should have moved from her office, but with the conference room still unavailable he hadn't had much choice. Every now and again he would glance up expecting to see her at her desk. And, every time he did, he would try to convince himself again that he had done the right thing. *Finish the job and get out*, he kept reminding himself. *Even if this is an entire crate of nothing, at least I'd have finished my job here and can leave.*

He had finally given up working in Eleanor's office when Miss Osbourne had returned from taking her home. She'd perched herself on the edge of Eleanor's desk, leaning conveniently forward to enquire just exactly what it was he was studying so intently. He'd known she had only done it for effect as her blouse fell forward and, glancing up at that moment, he'd had no choice but to catch a glimpse of her cleavage. It had been at that point that he'd decided even the sticky, dark, and oppressing pub was better than staying at the office. He'd collected together what was left of the paperwork, thankfully not too much, the water-colour print and the diaries. Sitting in the pub now, he subconsciously rubbed his arm at the memory of leaving the office. He had bumped into the caretaker, simultaneously tripping over his mop as he'd turned out of the office. His arm had caught on the caretaker's large bunch of keys, which scratched at his skin. *Is everyone out to get me?* he'd thought.

That was two hours ago, and he was still sat with the same pint in front of him.

'I know that look, mate. You've really got it bad, haven't you?' Dave said.

Darryl didn't reply. He returned to staring into the depths of his beer.

'Or, you've really fucked up?' Dave took a large gulp of his lager. 'Or, both.'

*That's the one,* Darryl thought.

'I told you to leave her alone. Come on, talk. What have you done?'

Darryl hesitated. Would his old friend really understand?

'I tried to explain—' he started.

'In other words, you told her,' Dave corrected him.

Darryl knew he was right. To Eleanor it would have seemed like he was lecturing her. What right did he have to make assumptions on how she should be feeling?

'I tried to explain,' he repeated, 'that she can't keep thinking in the past all the time. She should think about her future.'

'I've said it before, and I'll say it again. Darryl, you're an arse.'

'I believe it needed to be said.'

'Maybe so, but not by some hot shot who wants to get into her knickers.'

'That's not how it is.' Darryl wondered why he felt he needed to defend himself. 'I care about her. I care that she's not living her life, she's just living their death.'

The anguished expression on Dave's face revealed that he wasn't making a convincing case. Darryl sat back with a heavy sigh, not knowing how else he could explain.

'I bet she was furious.' Dave gave a derogatory laugh.

'That wasn't the worst of it,' Darryl continued.

Dave sat forward, leaning over the table. A grin appeared on his face. 'What did she do?'

'It's not what *she* did. At that point Osbourne came in and ...' Darryl still couldn't believe what had happened, '... she came to tell Eleanor that her mother had died from a stroke.'

Dave's grin disappeared. 'Shit, I can't laugh at that.'

'I didn't intend to upset her.'

'Do you want my advice?' Dave asked.

Darryl knew Dave's advice was not going to be what he wanted to hear, but he also knew Dave was going to give it whether he wanted it or not. 'Go on,' he said.

'Finish the job and get out.'

Just as Darryl had expected.

'She'll be fine,' Dave continued. 'She'll grieve for a while longer yet, but that's her choice. Get out of her way and let her.'

'Even when I can see she's in so much torment?'

'Especially because she's in so much bloody torment. She's not ready to move on.'

Darryl wasn't sure what to say to that. 'This is profound stuff coming from you,' he said.

'And you're just a sucker for a hard luck story.'

Darryl stared at his old friend across the table. He had almost been convinced by Dave's reasoning. Almost.

'I can't do it,' he said as he stood and pulled his bag out from under the table. 'I may be a sucker for a hard luck story, but at least it means I care. And, maybe that's what she needs right now.'

'What are you going to do?'

'Go and apologise. It's the least I can do.' Darryl paused and considered what Dave had said. 'If she wants me to leave, I'll leave. I promise. Then I'll finish the job and get out. But I can't leave it like this.'

He left, leaving his untouched beer still on the table.

∽

That evening Eleanor sat on the sofa with nothing in her head. The numbness seeped into every synaptic nerve, every vein, every pore. She had done everything that needed to be done on autopilot; papers were signed, arrangements had been made, and now she just wanted to stop. Stop thinking, stop moving, stop doing. Stop.

Aileen entered the lounge with a hot cup of coffee and placed it on the small table beside the sofa. 'Here, get this down you, lassie, and I've made you a sandwich for a bit later. Make sure you eat it.'

'Thank you, Aileen, but I'm not at all hungry.'

'Och, I don't care if you're hungry, you just make sure you eat.' Aileen knelt down in front of Eleanor. 'I'd recommend an early night, hen. You've had an exhausting day and it's time to look after you now.'

Eleanor let the words drift over her.

'I'll be off now, but I'll be here tomorrow to help with things.'

'No, it's fine. You take a few days off. Maybe come back next Monday and we'll see what more needs to be done.'

'OK. You take a few days for yourself but call me if you need me before then. Promise?'

Eleanor nodded.

'Say it, lassie.'

'I promise,' said Eleanor.

'Aye, that's better. See you next Monday if not before.'

Aileen kissed the top of Eleanor's head as she stood up, and then she left.

'Evening,' Eleanor heard Aileen's voice from the front door. 'She's in the lounge, go on through.'

She heard the front door close. The last person she wanted to see stopped and stood at the lounge door. She couldn't even bring herself to be polite and she looked away.

'I can't tell you how sorry I am,' Darryl said.

'Sorry for what?' she replied. 'Just sorry in general, sorry that my mother has died, sorry for insulting me, sorry for being an arrogant pig? Shall I carry on?'

'What I said I believe needed to be said, but it was shit

timing. I would never have said it if I knew what had happened to your mother.'

'That would have been OK, would it? It would have been OK to tell me I should just forget about my husband and my son if my mother hadn't inconveniently died at the same time.' Eleanor was furious now. Her hands were shaking, her throat tight.

'I can only imagine what it must be like to lose someone like that—'

'No, you can't,' she screamed back. 'If you tried you would be sad, miserable, maybe even distraught for a while. But then you can stop. You can stop imagining and everything is alright again. I can't stop. It's always there. I have a constant pain in my heart that makes sure I can't forget. It's a physical pain. Can you understand that?'

The tears she had been holding in all afternoon finally came. She hid her face in her hands and let them come. Darryl moved quietly next to her and sat down.

'I'm not saying you should forget them. I'm saying you should remember the good times instead of focusing on the pain. It's obvious to see that you had several wonderful years with them, but it seems to me that all you can remember is the day they died.'

Eleanor wanted to scream at him to get out, but her throat felt so raw she couldn't get the words out.

'Don't ever forget them.' Darryl went on. 'The reason you hurt so much is because they were, and still are, such a large part of you. Everyone at work has been trying to protect you, which is great – although, I don't always think it was for your benefit, but for their own – but all the time they are protecting you, they are also holding you back. I understand that you need time to grieve and I am sorry about your mother. But, remember the good times too, not just the pain.'

There was a moment's silence before he stood and started to leave.

'I ... I can't bear the thought of another death because of me,' she choked.

'Because of you?'

'Nick and Chris—'

She couldn't stop herself. She sobbed so hard she shook. She knew the truth. She knew she must be such an awful person to have deserved this. Darryl sat back down beside her and held her, letting her cry as hard as she needed.

'What happened to your husband and your son was a horrific thing to happen and nobody should have to go through it,' Darryl said quietly to her. 'But it wasn't your fault. Stop punishing yourself.'

Eleanor sat and cried for quite some time. She found it a relief to finally let the tears come. She had tried to hold them back for a long time, too long. She had moved into her mother's house only a week after the car crash and immediately turned her attention to looking after her mother. She needed to be strong, she could not show her weakness. At work she was always hiding away from her emotions, believing that it would not be professional to show her true feelings. But maybe Aileen was right. Perhaps it was time to start thinking about herself. Finally, she felt as though she had no more tears left inside her.

She silently pulled herself away from Darryl's arms and went through to the bathroom to compose herself. She washed her face, taking time to enjoy the freshness of the cold water against her skin, washing away the salty residue of her tears. After a few moments she felt mildly respectable again and went back to the lounge.

'Would you like a coffee?' she asked as naturally as she could, now feeling embarrassed by her outpour.

'Please.'

She moved through to the kitchen and put the kettle on.

'How are you feeling now?' came Darryl's voice from behind her. He had left the lounge and followed her through to the kitchen.

'Much better, thank you,' Eleanor replied, but didn't turn to face him. She was afraid her face would give away how she truly felt. She knew this wouldn't be the end of it. She would still cry, still miss them, still have moments when life felt hollow without them. But for the first time she felt as though maybe life wasn't as worthless as she had thought. Instead she busied herself with making the coffees.

'No, how are you feeling now?' he repeated. 'I want an answer from the real Eleanor, not the putting-on-a-strong-act Eleanor.'

He was now right behind her. She could feel his breath wafting her hair against her neck as he spoke.

'Why are you here?' she asked through a sudden panic.

She still didn't dare turn around to look at him.

'I came to apologise, I told you. Now, don't avoid the question. How are you feeling now? The truth this time.'

His voice was soft in her ear. His breath warm on her neck. Her emotions were already in turmoil and she suddenly felt scared. Scared of her own feelings. Maybe that's why she had often found herself so angry with him. She didn't want to accept the truth of her feelings.

'Lonely,' she whispered though hoping he wouldn't hear. But it was only a moment before she felt his fingers sweeping her hair aside and his lips touched her neck.

'You should stop this,' she said. His hands now on her waist.

'Tell me to stop and I will.' He kissed her again.

'*I* should stop this,' she whispered.

He turned her round gently to face him.

'Then why don't you?' he asked.

She could almost feel his eyes boring deep into hers.

'Because I don't want to.'

He placed his hand on the side of her face and wiped away one last tear. He kissed her gently on her mouth. This time she didn't resist.

# 16

When Eleanor woke the following morning her conscience was in turmoil. She rose from her bed, taking every care not to wake Darryl. She needed time alone. Time to think; to consider what to do next. She showered, dressed, and out of nervous habit, made coffees. Darryl stirred as she entered the bedroom. The coffee almost spilled in her shaking hands. Trembling from nerves or embarrassment? She wasn't sure. She knew there would be feelings of guilt, but she also felt as though she needed to apologise, for she had been weak.

'I've brought you a coffee,' she said without looking directly at him. Afraid that focusing on him there, lying in her bed, would only send her mind into further chaos.

'Thanks,' he said as he sat up blinking from the small patch of light that shone through the gap in the curtains. 'I like the service here. I'll come again.'

Eleanor didn't laugh. Her own thoughts dominated.

'I'm sorry,' she said, still not able to look him in the eye. 'I took advantage of your kindness last night. It won't happen again.'

'Jesus, Eleanor. Anybody else would be accusing me of taking advantage.'

Eleanor was taken aback by his exasperated tone.

'You don't get it, do you?' he continued. 'You're not a conquest, or just for passing the time. I want to be here with you.'

Eleanor's mind went blank. All she could do was shake her head. This was not something she could comprehend.

'I understand if you're not ready for that,' Darryl went on, 'and we can take things one step at a time. But I want you to know that I'm here for you. If you say you never want to see me again, I'll accept that. I won't be very happy about it, but I'll accept it. Just give me a chance before you make any final decisions.'

Eleanor still could not find any words to say. Of all the scenarios she had played over in her head that morning, this was not one of them. She turned and started to leave the room.

'I guess I'd better go and leave you to it,' Darryl said. 'You'll have lots to do today.'

His voice sounded despondent. It didn't have the usual cheery tone Eleanor was getting used to. She stopped in the doorway. She suddenly felt cold and uneasy. She didn't want to be left alone. Alone with her thoughts, her memories.

'Are you going back to the office?' she asked without looking back.

'No, I finished reading through all the paperwork after you left yesterday. I was going to take the print and the diaries back to the County archives. They are no good to me now.'

'You know you could just leave them with Callum. He said he'd take them back for us.'

'I know, but I don't like to take advantage of people.'

Eleanor could tell he was trying to be humorous, but she couldn't bring herself to smile.

'Besides,' he went on, 'for some strange reason I don't particularly want to go back to that building. I'm finished there. There was nothing in all that paperwork. My job is done.'

'May I come with you?' Eleanor asked quickly, before she could give herself time to change her mind. 'I don't want to be on my own today.'

Eleanor was surprised at Darryl's enthusiasm.

'Of course,' he said.

She quickly left the room.

~

They sat in silence in Darryl's old Land Rover. Eleanor had changed from her jeans and casual shirt to a trouser suit while Darryl had showered. The change wasn't necessary as she wasn't going in to work, but it helped her feel more human. Though, just to be on the safe side, she had popped her trainers into her large handbag, and they left together for the County archives. It hadn't been until now that Eleanor started to wonder about Pete.

'Did Pete come back to the office yesterday?' she asked.

'No, not that I saw. I can only guess the police still have him for questioning.'

'I just can't see Pete being a killer.'

'Can you actually see anyone at the office being a killer?' Darryl asked.

'No, not really. Maybe the police are wrong about that.'

'Who else could have had the opportunity to plant that gas canister? If Pete's as dopey over Gina as Marie makes out, I guess he could see me as a threat.'

'And you were rude to her.'

'She shouldn't keep throwing herself at me. It's not my fault if she can't take a hint.'

Eleanor laughed and turned to look at Darryl for the first time that morning. It strangely felt as though it was for the first time since they had met. This time she really noticed him. He was handsome. And yet, she noted, he was the opposite of Nick. Nick was always smart and well organised. Darryl was unpolished to say the least. Methodical was the word she would use to describe him, rather than organised. But he certainly had a way of irritating people. Her thoughts drifted back to Pete again.

'I just can't see it being Pete. Did you annoy him in any other way?'

'Not that I can think of, apart from pressing his stupid lift buttons. And, can I just say for the record, I don't go around annoying people on purpose,' Darryl laughed.

'Of course not, I didn't mean ...' Eleanor floundered. She stopped herself and bit her lip anxiously. 'Why would Pete kill Nick? They were friends,' she went on quickly. 'He used to tell me how interested Pete was in the archives and that he was going to college one day a week studying for something or other. No, it just doesn't fit.'

'OK, Sherlock, are you ready to get out? We're here.'

Eleanor hadn't noticed Darryl parking up outside a large modern building that stood out for all the wrong reasons. Darryl especially found the County Offices offensive to the eye, especially in amongst such a historic town. They walked up to the entrance together and Darryl led the way to the desk. If he didn't like the outside of the building, the inside was worse. The large entrance hall didn't give the feeling of spaciousness that Darryl assumed they were trying for, more the feeling of bleakness.

They approached the large streamlined counter that swamped the boy sat behind it.

'Morning, can I help you?' he asked meekly.

'We've come to return some items to the archives,' Darryl replied.

'You'll need Mrs Hamilton; I'll call her for you.'

The young boy, thin and gangly, who looked no more than a teenager, disappeared through a door to the left. Two minutes later he was back with a severe looking woman in her sixties. A large ledger under her arm. She came over to the desk and opened the ledger without a glance at either Darryl or Eleanor.

'Receipt number?' she said bluntly.

'We don't have a receipt number, sorry,' Darryl replied.

The woman looked up from the ledger and glared at Darryl. 'You would have been given a receipt number when you took the items out.'

'Well, that will be where the problem is then, because we didn't take the items out.'

'When were they taken?' she asked, with a sharp tone.

She looked back at the large book with numerous columns down the pages. The stark lighting accentuated the frown lines on her forehead as she peered down the columns.

'It was last Wednesday. A print of a watercolour and two diaries.'

'I can't find it. Wednesday you say?' she said with an accusational tone.

'Yes, Wednesday morning.' Darryl felt the uncomfortable need to lighten the atmosphere. Something to lessen the air of austerity surrounding the woman. 'That's a great old ledger. I haven't seen one of those for years,' he said cheerily.

Mrs Hamilton looked up at him with the same unnerving glare as before, as though her face was made of stone. 'I'll be glad when we finally have our systems back up and running. Even old people like me feel there's a time and place for technology. And right now, is one of them.'

'The fire, huh?' Darryl's cheeriness fading behind a false smile.

'Mmm,' was her only acknowledgement and she returned to her search.

Darryl now felt the uncomfortable need to help speed up her search. 'They were taken out by Callum ...,' he hesitated, not remembering Callum's surname and looked toward Eleanor for help.

'Matthews,' Eleanor added.

'Callum Matthews,' repeated Darryl.

'Here it is,' Mrs Hamilton said. A watercolour print, and three diaries.

'Three diaries?' interjected Eleanor. 'No, we only have two.'

'I'm sorry, but you can see here that it was *three* diaries taken out Tuesday evening, and you can see Mr Matthews' signature here.'

Mrs Hamilton pointed to the final two columns in the ledger where one was a print of Callum's name, and then his signature. In the column headed *Items Borrowed*, it clearly stated three diaries.

'OK,' said Darryl, now becoming curious. He had also noticed that there had been no recognition of Callum's name from Mrs Hamilton, and he wanted to test a theory. 'We'll go back to Callum. He's obviously forgotten to pass one on to us. You know how he is.'

'No, I don't know how he is,' she replied harshly. 'Will you be returning the items you do have?'

'Didn't he used to work here?' Darryl kept a close hold of the items.

'No, he didn't. I do now remember him taking out these items on Tuesday evening because it's our one day a week when we stay open late to the public, and he seemed very ...' she paused for a moment to think, 'excitable. He was flicking through the pages of the diaries before he'd even left the building. He promised me he would take good care of them, and there he was dropping crumbs from a cookie all over them.' She spat out the word cookie as though it was a swear word. 'You can tell your friend from me that that is not how we expect our items to be treated.'

'You are the archivist here?' Darryl asked hesitantly.

'For the last twelve years. What of it?'

'My mistake,' Darryl said. 'I think we may hold on to these a bit longer if that's OK. And I promise I'll take great care of them.'

Darryl took Eleanor's hand and almost dragged her from the building.

'So, Mr Can't-do-enough-for-you-Eleanor has been lying to us,' he said as they made their way back to his car.

'I'm sure it's a simple mistake.'

'A simple mistake?' Darryl repeated incredulously. 'He only gave us two of the diaries. He told us he used to work here, which he obviously didn't. He came out to get the items on Wednesday morning, and yet according to their records it was Tuesday evening. With all that in mind it's no wonder he wanted us to let him bring the documents back, then we'd be none the wiser.'

'But why would he do all that?'

'I think he found something and has been keeping it from us. Does Callum tend to go out for lunch?'

'I think so.'

'I think we've just found trench number five,' said Darryl excitedly.

'Where?'

'I think he's hiding something in the archives. Are you OK to go back to The Birds?'

'Shouldn't we tell the police?'

'And tell them what? Your archivist is hiding a diary? No, come on. Let's see what we can find out before we take it any further.'

## Neither Safe nor Sorry

∽

Darryl and Eleanor arrived at The Birds Building just after eleven thirty and took a seat in the coffee shop across the road with a direct view of the front doors.

'He's been one step ahead the whole time,' said Darryl sipping at his hot coffee. 'Think about it. On Tuesday afternoon, while we were searching room four, I bet he searched, and found, all the paperwork in room two. Something in those documents sent him to the County archives Tuesday evening where he picked up the print and the three diaries. When he told us he was going to that monstrosity of a building on Wednesday morning he was actually taking the time to finish reading through the diaries.'

'That's what he would have been doing when we saw him in the coffee shop. And, why he didn't want us to go to the County archives ourselves,' said Eleanor. Her eyes fixed on the entrance to The Birds. Her coffee almost untouched.

'Otherwise we would have found out his secret back then. There must be something in that third diary that he doesn't want us to see,' Darryl added thoughtfully.

'But what did he find in our archives that would have sent him there so soon? He must have taken out whatever it was before he copied it all.'

'That's why he'd managed to get all that paperwork copied in one morning,' said Darryl with a smug tone. 'Because he'd actually been doing it since Tuesday afternoon. Going through it bit by bit to make sure he didn't give us anything of significance.' He couldn't help but feel a sense of satisfaction in finding Callum out.

'But why? What is it he could be hiding?' asked Eleanor.

'That's what we're going to find out.'

Darryl had always loved mysteries. From examining the

wrapped presents under the Christmas tree to treasure hunts in the garden with his father. Following clues to lead him to the prize. He had always planned to simulate those treasure hunts with his own children. Longing to create the happy memories he'd had with his own father. The reality never materialised though. He was often away on a job, or simply too tired when at home. Life just seemed to get in the way.

At twelve twenty Darryl's thoughts were brought back to the present when Callum exited The Birds and strolled further into town. Eleanor and Darryl took their chance and trotted quickly over to the office. As they approached, they saw Sidney entering the lift with a client. There was no sign of Pete, he didn't seem to be back yet, so they were able to get through the front doors and down the stairs without being seen. The door to Callum's office was locked.

'You said before that the archives were never locked,' said Darryl.

'No, I'm certain. There wasn't even a lock on the door. Callum must have had it put on.'

Darryl put his shoulder to the door and shoved. It may have been locked but it wasn't a strong one. The door fell open into the dark room. Eleanor turned on the light and they both started searching silently. Darryl started with the shelves to the left. Eleanor went to the desk and started looking through the drawers.

'This one's locked,' she said when she reached the bottom right drawer.

Darryl came over to the desk.

'I never understood why people hide things in locked drawers,' he said as he scanned the desktop and found a pair of scissors. 'If you're looking for something and you come across somewhere that's locked,' he continued as he used the scissors to jimmy the drawer open, 'it's the first place you're going to look.' The drawer jumped open from the force. 'And a stupid little lock isn't going to stop you.'

Inside the drawer was a pile of papers, similar in font and style to some of the title deeds and other documents they had spent the last few days examining. And a third diary. Copied and bound just like the others. Eleanor picked up the diary.

'There are pages marked,' she said indicating several fluorescent green sticky markers projecting out the side of the diary at various intervals. She turned to the first marked entry and started reading.

Darryl was inspecting the paperwork. 'There are plans here of the original building. This is exactly what we were looking for. Why would he hide these from us?'

'Listen to this,' Eleanor said. 'The servants did well tonight. Everyone did their duty, and both the priest and the altar furniture were hidden safe from the priest hunters, though I am not sure how long we can continue like this. It has been suggested to me that we create a space for the purpose of hiding. This could be the answer to our prayers during these treacherous times. I admit I am keen on this plan and work will begin as soon as arrangements can be made.'

'Let me see,' Darryl said excitedly.

Eleanor handed him the diary. 'It's dated later than the other two diaries,' he said, and he turned to the next marked entry, which was penned three weeks later.

He read aloud, 'The priest hunters came again tonight. Each visit their frustration increases. Without the priest hole we would not be able to hide our treasures, both human and tangible. I thank the Lord every night for their safe-keeping.'

Darryl's mind was racing. 'A priest hole? There was never any mention of a priest hole in the records of Thornewick Manor.' He read the next marked entry.

'The servants did well again last night. They all did as

required when the priest hunters came. I would not be surprised if they come again tonight. I am sure they are suspicious and continue to arrive at times of great inconvenience. Tonight, I discovered some of our silverware had been taken during the search. Thankfully, we have a place well-hidden that is large enough to keep these other treasures too.'

He skipped to the final marker.

'We have made the decision that our most beloved wares and treasures will remain hidden until such time as it is safe to remove them. Last night the priest hunters arrived when the entire household was sleeping, and a silver candlestick was taken during the search. We have been targeted by thieves, not just soldiers. The only way we can trust ourselves to be ready is to keep everything hidden. I'm sure these times will pass, but until that day we will do what we can to protect what we have,' he read aloud, and turned the page over. 'That's the last entry in the diary. If they were hiding the household's silver and other treasures in the priest hole, this entry could mean that it is still there.'

'Why?' asked Eleanor.

'Lady Rose has made the decision to keep everything hidden because they're expecting the priest hunters again. So, tell me, why hasn't she written anymore?' he asked Eleanor.

'Because ... she couldn't for some reason,' Eleanor guessed.

'But for what reason?' Darryl was becoming more and more excited and was enjoying seeing Eleanor struggle for ideas.

'What if the priest hunters did come?' he said after a few impatient moments. 'What if they came and either took the household away, imprisoned them, or even killed them, as they sometimes did during that time?'

'So, then there wouldn't be anyone left to take the silver out again after the priest hunters had gone.'

'Exactly.'

'Do you think Callum's looking for treasure?' Eleanor asked.

'It certainly looks that way.' Darryl turned back to the paperwork they had found with the diary. 'Look, the original Manor was a lot bigger than was thought. It would have been a very wealthy family that lived there. And here, he's got a tracing that fits over the building with these two corners circled.' Darryl indicated the two far corners at the front of the building. 'He's no archivist, he's just a common, vulgar treasure hunter.'

The high-pitched single tone of the lift bell seemed to punctuate the end of Darryl's sentence. The door to the office was only a couple of metres away from the lift doors. There was no way they could try and escape without being seen, and there was nowhere for them to hide. But Darryl didn't want to hide. Two seconds later and Callum was standing in the open doorway with a pre-packed sandwich and tall cardboard coffee cup in hand. His face turned pale when he saw Eleanor holding the open diary and Darryl with the house plans. The sandwich and coffee landed heavily on the floor as Callum turned and ran.

Darryl, only held back by the large desk in front of him, set off after Callum. He couldn't let him get away. He knew that Callum could be the killer, but he felt in control now. No hiding in basements. It was all out in the open.

'No,' he could hear Eleanor scream after him.

He realised that she must have worked it out too.

Callum headed straight for the stairs and ran up two at a time. Darryl's muscles were still feeling stiff after the car incident last week, but he was determined not to let that hold him back as he ran toward the stairs, toward the man that had caused so much pain for so many people.

## 17

Eleanor knew everyone had been wrong about Pete. He was no killer. She was still hoping Darryl was wrong about Callum, but then why did he run? Why had he lied to them?

She reached the top of the stairs just in time to see Darryl leap at Callum. His arms wrapped around Callum's waist and they fell heavily to the floor. Callum's face hit the hard, wooden floor with a clear audible smack. Darryl landed on top of him. A few people were around, but nobody interfered. Nobody until Sidney. He ran toward them and tried to pull the two men apart as they fought on the floor. Darryl pulled back to make a punch. His elbow striking Sidney in the face. Sidney staggered backwards. Darryl's fist then thrust its way into Callum's face. Sidney removed his radio from his belt and radioed for assistance, blood trickling from his nose. At least the police would be on their way now.

Sidney returned to his attempt at parting the two men with his focus seemingly on Darryl as he was the one doing the attacking. Callum was only trying to escape his fury. Sidney succeeded in pulling Darryl away from Callum for just a moment, but that was all that was needed. Callum took advantage of the reprise and scrambled backwards up and on to his feet. Eleanor hesitantly tried to get Sidney's attention to explain the truth of what was going on, but Darryl was struggling wildly in Sidney's grip. She was almost hit herself as Darryl broke free and charged again at Callum. Eleanor squealed, staggering backwards out the way. Terrified of being caught up in the conflict and struck by a flailing arm or leg. Callum was almost at the door when Darryl hit him from behind and they both crashed into the door. There was the crack of a bone breaking. Callum yelled out in pain. Sidney was back with them again when Eleanor became aware of the first sound of sirens nearing the building. Sidney had managed to grab Darryl's arms from behind and this time his restraint was successful.

'Get off me,' Darryl growled.

Sidney's grip only became tighter. No matter how much Darryl struggled this time, he wasn't getting away. Callum took his chance and ran out the door, cradling his left arm.

'Calm down, sir,' bawled Sidney.

Darryl continued to struggle, understandably furious that Callum had managed to escape.

'Leave him,' Eleanor cried, relieved that nothing worse had happened than just a few cuts and bruises, and maybe a broken bone in Callum's case. 'Let the police handle it.'

'But he'll be long gone now he knows we're on to him.'

'"On to him,"' repeated Sidney. 'What do you mean "on to him?" Are you saying Callum's the ... the one ...' Sidney's face turned pale. His grip on Darryl released suddenly as his body went limp, and Darryl fell forward from his own momentum.

Concerned Sidney was about to faint, Eleanor led him over to the porter's room for a chair.

'But I let him go,' Sidney stammered.

~

Sirens wailed outside and police rushed in, including Detective Inspector Selby and Detective Sergeant Wade.

Eleanor was tending to Darryl, now sat at the reception desk, holding a blood-soaked wad of tissues on a cut above his right eye. She was used to tending to grazed knees, but she'd never even seen a fight before, let alone clean the wounds from one. Darryl was still clearly furious from Callum's escape when a paramedic arrived and took over dressing the cut.

Sidney, holding tissues to his bleeding nose, stepped forward to speak with the detectives as though bravely stepping up to a hangman's noose.

'I called you,' he announced. 'And oh, I'm so sorry. I let him get away. I'm so, so sorry. But I didn't know.' Sidney welled up. His large, muscular body shook from trying to hold in the tears.

'Is there somewhere you can sit down?' DI Selby said to him sympathetically. 'DS Wade here will take your statement.' He made a gesture to his sergeant as if to say *All yours*. 'I need to speak with Mr Westwood.'

DS Wade disappeared into the porter's room with Sidney.

'Mr Westwood,' DI Selby said. 'Looks like you've found your enemy.'

'I found him you can catch him.' Darryl winced. The paramedic had finished administering the steri-strips and had given Darryl a cold compress to hold to his swelling eye.

'Any idea why he wanted to kill you?' DI Selby asked.

Eleanor was more than happy to let Darryl deal with the detective. She listened quietly while he explained that they had found information in Callum's office that he had hidden from them. Specific information that Darryl had asked for. He didn't mention anything about breaking down the door or forcing the drawer open.

'So, you think,' said DI Selby, 'that he may be some kind of treasure hunter and he was trying to do away with you because you were sniffing around too close to his mark?'

'I've heard of these kind of treasure hunters before, though never encountered one. I've never heard of one going to such extreme measures either. I don't know what he expects to find there. Thornewick Manor has been thoroughly searched and every inch examined over the years, according to all the paperwork we've been wading through.'

'It could explain the break-in,' Sergeant Wade said who had re-joined the group a few moments before.

'What break-in?' Darryl asked.

Eleanor could understand why Darryl's interest had been piqued, as had her own. Could this have been Callum too?

DI Selby paused a moment as though trying to decide whether it would be appropriate to speak about it.

'There was a break-in at Thornewick Manor last night, while the owners were away,' DI Selby finally said. 'Floorboards were pulled up in two rooms, but nothing seems to have been taken. No reason for the break-in was apparent. But, back to the matter in hand. Could you show me just exactly what it is you and Mrs Garrett found in this man's office?'

'Sure, no problem. But what about Callum? He's getting away.'

'A search is already underway for him,' DI Selby said reassuringly. 'We'll get him soon enough.'

Eleanor and Darryl led the detective down to the archives. Darryl motioned to the Inspector to enter Callum's office first. As Eleanor passed Darryl, he gently pulled her back slightly.

Putting his finger to his lips he whispered, 'Open your bag.'

She was curious to know what he had in mind but didn't dare ask. The glint in his eyes was enough to tell her it wasn't up for discussion, let alone the whisper. She did as he asked as secretively as possible. Her confusion continued in the room when Darryl led DI Selby to the shelves at the back of the room, behind the desk. She was certain he hadn't even gone to those shelves during his search. Then, she saw him pointing to the diary behind his back. It was still lying on the desk where she had dropped it earlier. It didn't take long to realise what Darryl wanted. She moved to the desk and, while Darryl was explaining how they had been searching through the files on the shelf, she silently slipped the diary in her handbag. She gave a little cough to signify the job was done.

'In between these files were a couple of sheets,' Darryl told the detective and he turned around to the desk.

'These sheets here.' Darryl picked up the two top sheets of paper and pushed the others aside as though making space to sit down. He sat on the desk hiding these other sheets from view in the process. The documents on the table were in such disarray from earlier, it wasn't hard to do. Darryl had practically thrown them back onto the desk in his attempt to catch Callum. 'These are what we found, and they are exactly what I asked him to look for a week ago,' Darryl continued.

Eleanor got the idea and moved round the desk to slip the rest of the sheets behind her back. She rolled them till they too were easy to slip into her bag. She then surreptitiously moved other sheets from nearby into their place. The desk was already cluttered, it took only seconds to fill the hole.

'This is it?' said the detective. 'Just these two bits of paper?'

'It may not seem like much to you, Inspector, but to me this will change the outcome of my whole report.' One of the bits of paper was Callum's tracing. 'And look at this,' he pointed to the two circles Callum had drawn. 'I bet those two circles correspond to the two rooms where the floorboards were pulled up during the break-in.'

'Well, that's not my case, but do you know, it could well be,' DI Selby said thoughtfully. 'But that's something I'll need to check,' he added quickly as though he had given away too much information already.

'I can take these can't I?' Darryl asked reaching for the two sheets he had passed to the detective.

'I'm afraid they're evidence now. You'll be able to have them once this is all over.'

'But they're crucial to my whole project.'

'I'm sorry, Mr Westwood, but that's how it goes. I'm afraid a murder investigation takes precedence over a house project,' he said in a derogatory tone. 'They'll be returned in due course.'

DI Selby purposefully held the two sheets close to his chest as though hiding their information.

Eleanor caught Darryl's wink as he feigned disappointment.

'Can we go then?' he asked.

'Yes, you can go. You've been very helpful. I'm sure it won't be long till we have this man, Callum Matthews. Then we'll see what he has to say for himself.'

Eleanor only now remembered Pete as they were walking out. 'So, does this mean you'll be letting Pete go?'

'Pete? Oh yes, Peter Burrows. We let him go yesterday. Turns out Mr Westwood here took a job he was hoping for.'

'What do you mean?' asked Darryl.

'Apparently, he'd decided to stop going to college as there didn't seem any point. He was just a little disillusioned, that's all, when he found out you had been given a job he was hoping for just because you are an old friend from college. He's been studying part-time for the last couple of years and was hoping to get a job as a researcher in a local architect's company, D. Saunders and Co.'

Eleanor turned to look at Darryl. Darryl turned to look at Eleanor with an expression that told her that he too was thinking that this could have been a good reason for Pete being annoyed with him.

'Yes, he had high hopes of impressing Miss Pickering,' the Inspector continued, 'by returning to the offices with a proper job, as he called it. It made him a bit annoyed, but not really enough to kill over. But this Callum Matthews sounds much more promising. This could even be a good motive for knocking off the old archivist too, in a bid to get closer to the information in the archives.'

The impact of everything that had happened over the last hour or so suddenly hit Eleanor. The loss of her husband and son were down to the man who had always been so friendly, so kind to her. A man that she had even pitied for being in the position of taking her dead husband's job. The blood drained from her face. The detective must have noticed and realised what he had said.

'Oh, sorry, Mrs Garrett. I forgot for a moment that he was your husband.'

'But, it's true,' she said in a daze. 'My husband was murdered, and my son is dead because of some greedy treasure hunter.'

'Unfortunately, I have seen people killed for less.'

'Come on, let's go and sit down,' Darryl said quietly to her.

He put his arm around her shoulders, but she pushed him away. His touch made her skin crawl and a nauseous feeling came over her. They left the offices in silence. The activity, even the excitement, of the past couple of hours slipped away in just a few moments. She was now left with her usual feeling of numbness. They returned to the cafe where they had been sitting that morning, but this time further toward the back, away from the glances of passers-by.

'I can't believe it,' said Eleanor cupping her mug of coffee as though trying to warm her hands. 'He was always so kind. I don't understand.'

'Drink your coffee, Eleanor,' Darryl said reassuringly. 'Get something warm inside you and you'll start to feel better.'

For the next hour they sat in silence. Darryl could see the colour slowly returning to Eleanor's face as the minutes went by. Her eyes were darting side to side without seeing. He knew whatever was in her vision appeared only in her head. She needed time for it all to sink in. Darryl himself was feeling relieved. Though Callum hadn't yet been caught, it was surely only a matter of time. There would be no more deaths because of him; no more families destroyed because of one man's obsession.

Darryl sat patiently, waiting for her to recover, although he desperately wanted to see the paperwork and diary Eleanor had sneaked into her bag. His patience was rewarded as an hour, a caramel shortbread for Darryl, half a lemon drizzle slice for Eleanor, and two coffees later, Eleanor picked up her bag and started to pull out the new items.

'Shall we have a look at these while we're here?' she said. 'I can't just sit here.'

'Of course,' replied Darryl sympathetically. 'If it's what you want.' His conscience was eased.

'I want to know what all the killing has been for.'

Darryl noted a new determination in her voice. He pored over the maps and plans, while Eleanor continued reading the labeled pages in the diary. Although Darryl had let the Inspector take a couple of pages there was still enough to help him see that Dave's building was indeed once part of the original Thornewick Manor.

'Listen to this,' Eleanor would interject every now and again with another excerpt from the diary. 'The priest hunters came again tonight. I am beginning to think it would be better to leave our most treasured possessions in the priest hole and only remove them when needed. It was a frantic evening as we were caught quite off guard and more of our silver disappeared during the search.'

'Then it's probably more than likely that there could be artifacts left in the priest hole on that last night's entry.'

'How big is a priest hole?' Eleanor asked. 'I always had the image that it was just a space for the priest to fit behind a wall or something like that.'

'Sometimes it is,' Darryl replied. 'Some are literally a hole big enough for the priest to hide in for a short while until the priest hunters or soldiers disappeared. They could be under the floor, behind panelling, concealed behind stairs or chimneys. In fact, they were so cleverly hidden that the search parties would go to great lengths to find them. Or, they would sometimes pretend to leave so they could wait for the priest to come out of hiding.' Darryl loved having a willing listener and continued eagerly. 'Sometimes the priest could be stuck there for days. From the size of the original Manor, this was a wealthy family. They would have had a lot to hide. If they are keeping items in it as well as space needed for the priest, who knows. It could be that this is one of the ones that lead through to an entire other room. Some even have a tunnel leading right away from the building as an escape route. If the priests were caught, they were often killed, and really quite gruesomely too. The family of the house would be killed or imprisoned—'

'OK, I get the idea. You can stop now.' Eleanor laughed at Darryl's enthusiasm.

'Stop laughing at me. It's fascinating.' Darryl reigned himself in. 'Look, I have enough here to complete my report for Dave, but I have to admit it would be something special to find that priest hole.'

'So, what's stopping us?' said Eleanor.

'Don't you need to go home? I thought there would be things you need to do,' asked Darryl.

'There are things I should be doing,' Eleanor said thoughtfully. 'But, like you said, I need to start thinking about what I want. And right now, I want to help you find this priest hole, and I want to know what my husband and son died for.'

'I'll need some of the other paperwork that's in your office,' Darryl said tentatively. He wasn't sure she'd be so happy with that. 'I do still need to change my report.'

'OK, let's go.'

To Darryl's surprise Eleanor did not even hesitate. She had put all the items back in her handbag and was out the door before Darryl had time to get out of his chair.

## 18

'Mrs Garrett, back again?' said Sidney as he held the main entrance door open for Eleanor and Darryl. A large white plaster stuck across the bridge of his nose. 'I didn't expect to see you back at all, not until next week at least. I didn't get to say earlier, my condolences, Miss.'

'Thank you, Sidney,' Eleanor said. 'I feel I need to keep busy right now. How's your nose?'

'Not broken, just a bit sore. I am sorry for the misunderstanding,' Sidney said.

'No harm done. Don't worry about the lift, we'll see ourselves up.'

'I am a little short-handed as we're now three porters down. I'm beginning to think this job is jinxed.'

The lift doors closed on his last words.

'"No harm done." Really? He let a killer get away,' Darryl said incredulously.

'It's just an expression. OK, so maybe it wasn't the right thing to say but I didn't want him to feel bad. It did look like you were the one doing the attacking. And, Callum did look a little overwhelmed.'

'For a killer,' Darryl said with sarcasm.

They both smiled at the memory.

'Ready for the onslaught?' Darryl asked as the doors opened on the first floor.

'Ready,' Eleanor said, and she prepared herself for her colleagues' questions, sympathy and the one thing she'd had enough of, pity.

As they walked across the hallway, she noticed the police tape had gone from the conference room. She hoped they could collect the pile of work Darryl needed and make it to the conference room before being seen.

Unfortunately, Miss Osbourne's voice drifted through the door, 'Eleanor, you're still here.'

Eleanor turned just in time to see Miss Osbourne enter her office with cat-like agility. 'Yes, Miss Osbourne,' she replied.

'How are you? You shouldn't be here. Go home.'

'I'd rather carry on working actually. There's nothing at home that's urgent and I'd like to keep my mind busy on other things.' Eleanor was determined to stay strong.

'And Mr Westwood, I see, is looking after you.'

'He's been very kind.' Eleanor suddenly saw a jealousy in Miss Osbourne's face that she'd never noticed before. It made her feel ashamed. What gave her the right to receive Darryl's attentions? She began to flounder. 'He won't be back after today. We're just finishing off now, in fact, and then he'll be gone,' Eleanor said, her eyes lowering with almost every word. *I must stay strong,* she tried to tell herself.

'Mr Westwood, I see you didn't escape completely unharmed from your earlier dealings with Callum.' She ran her fingertips across his forehead brushing the edges of the steri-strips.

Eleanor noted he didn't flinch. She turned her back to them and began the walk to the conference room. She could still hear

Miss Osbourne speaking to Darryl, in supposed subdued tones, but it was quite clear to hear.

'Remember, Mr Westwood, when she breaks, I'll still be here.'

*Because she's right,* Eleanor thought. *I will break.* As she removed the items from her handbag and placed them on the table, she noticed her hands shaking from the effort of holding in her emotions. She kept her back to the door in the hope that nobody else would see. She heard the conference room door open and close behind her.

'She has no right to treat you like that,' Darryl said. He placed a comforting hand on her shoulder.

'It's fine,' Eleanor whispered in reply. The sound of his voice behind her, the touch of his hand, brought back the memory of last night's weakness. And the guilt came flooding in.

'It's not fine—'

'I need the bathroom,' Eleanor quickly interrupted and left, crossing the hallway almost at a run.

She entered the bathroom and before she reached the corner that led round to the cubicles and basins, she could hear Gina and Marie laughing. Eleanor immediately froze. The knot that had appeared in her stomach from Miss Osbourne's remark grew tighter. She knew they were laughing at her. Not just Gina and Marie, but everyone. Everyone in the building. Laughing at her for being weak. She couldn't let Gina and Marie find her here. She crept back out the toilets and stood by the door, leaning against the wall. Her legs couldn't take her any further as she gasped for breath.

She realised Darryl must have seen her reappear through the frosted glass as he had opened the conference room door. Concern on his face, he began to speak. The bathroom door started to open cutting him short. Marie's over-enthusiastic laugh howled through the open door. Eleanor's body became rigid.

'I don't understand how a man that good-looking would want anything to do with her,' said Gina.

'I know, it's not as though she has anything to recommend her. She's just plain and ordinary in every way,' said Marie.

At this point they became aware of Eleanor leaning against the wall by the door, and Darryl further along the hallway, still at the conference room door. They both looked from side to side between Eleanor and Darryl, before staring at each other. They barely attempted to stifle their laughter as they continued past.

Eleanor's skin crawled with disgust. She retched and threw up in the hallway, then returned to the bathroom. Darryl was calling her, coming closer, but she ignored him. Besides, she could feel a second bout on its way.

Crouched in a cubicle, waiting for that burning sensation to rise again, she could hear Darryl calling from the door.

'Go away,' she cried followed by the second bout that had been promised.

∽

Darryl's confusion only grew. Not only could he not understand why Eleanor let Gina and Marie treat her in such a way, but he was also concerned that *he* had somehow upset her. It hurt that she had told him to go away. The term walking on eggshells came to mind. Did she still not understand that he wants to help? *Take it slow,* he told himself. *She's been left to deal with things on her own for so long, she's probably finding it difficult to allow someone to help. But why did she run out in the first place?* Darryl's only option was to leave her. *Let her calm down and sort herself out. She'll explain when she gets back.* He returned to the conference room and picked up the papers he had been reading.

He continually glanced up to look for any sign of Eleanor coming back; the papers in his hand were for show only. He knew she wouldn't appreciate him pacing the hallway, waiting for her. The frosted glass made him suspect every movement. An image appeared from the far end of the hallway. It moved closer, walking toward the lift. It was a man's walk, a man's stance waiting for the lift. Staff or a client from Samson's Digital World's offices. Not Eleanor. The unmistakable image of the caretaker carrying a mop and bucket arrived to clean up. But no Eleanor. It was only ten minutes or so until he saw Eleanor's form emerge from the toilets, though it felt much longer. His impatience grew as he furtively watched her talking to the caretaker. Eventually, he was pleased to see her returning.

∼

Eleanor had left the bathroom after washing her face with cold water in the inadequately sized basin. *Why am I always making such a fool of myself?* she'd thought as she had stared at her dripping face in the mirror. *They're right. Why would anyone want anything to do with me?*

Just outside the doorway the caretaker had been cleaning up her vomit.

'I'm so sorry. Let me help,' she'd implored.

'No, Miss. There's no need. It's all part of the job. I'm good at cleaning up people's messes,' he'd replied with a smile.

Eleanor now realised how wrong she had been all this time. Here was this man cleaning up after her, never asking for thanks. And yet, people she thought had cared for her; given her work; protected her from those outsiders who didn't understand her situation, none of them really cared for her at all. They all had their own motives. What Eleanor had thought was ignorance and pure misunderstanding from Gina and Marie, was spitefulness and self-indulgence. Miss Osbourne gained a feeling of generosity for those that needed to be pitied. It bolstered her own self-importance. Callum, who she had always considered to be so kind to her, turned out to be her husband and son's murderer. *How could I be so wrong about everyone?* Then she saw the blurry image of Darryl through the frosted glass in the conference room's door. Sat back at the table, absorbed in his work. *And what about Darryl? Is he really as kind and thoughtful as he seems, or does he have his own motives too?* A thick, stifling fog had enveloped her since the car accident, over eight months ago. But the fog was lifting. She was beginning to trust her own instincts again. She had welcomed the numbness that had surrounded her, used it like a comforting blanket, as a means of protection. Now she could see it was a barrier. She could no longer keep her feelings, her emotions, her *self* hidden.

She strode into the conference room and without so much as a glance toward Darryl she asked, 'What needs to be done first?'

'Are you OK?' he asked eagerly.

'I'm fine,' she replied doggedly. 'Let's get on.'

Eleanor picked up the third diary and started to flick through it. She wasn't going to give him any more than that.

Darryl hesitated. She could only guess what must have been going through his mind. Ten minutes ago, she was throwing up and having, what probably looked to him like, a panic attack. Now she says she's fine? More like she's crazy.

'We need all references of the priest hole,' Darryl began, tentatively. 'Or anything that may be referring to it. We don't have the tracing that Callum made, where he had circled two specific areas, but they weren't that specific. The two far corners in the front of the building. He must have found the information for those areas in that diary. If you could start with that, and I'll finish off this report. Is that OK?'

Eleanor didn't reply. She sat down and started to work

systematically through the diary. They sat and worked in silence for over an hour. She was aware of Darryl glancing up toward her now and then, but she purposefully avoided his looks.

∼

It was clear to Darryl that Eleanor had no intentions of explaining herself or of what had upset her, so he worked on the report for Dave. Even though the plans they had found clearly showed Dave's building was part of the original Manor, Darryl was too distracted to focus and the job was taking a lot longer than necessary. He hoped he could catch Eleanor's eye as they worked in silence. He was no psychologist, but he could be a willing listener, if only she would talk. He wouldn't be able to make her, he had tried that before with disastrous consequences. *She'll open up when she's ready*, he kept reminding himself.

Finally, Darryl slammed his report closed and announced it complete. He hadn't managed to catch her attention any other way. He needed a more direct approach.

'How are you getting on with the priest hole?' he asked, ignoring the events of earlier.

'I've found a particular entry where ...' Eleanor flicked through the pages to one of Callum's markers and read aloud. 'Without knowledge of the priest hole's existence, the priest hunters will not have a chance of finding it. Even I have trouble locating the knot hole required to open it. I only wish, sometimes, it was located further from the main entrance, but if we can persuade the priest hunters toward the kitchen and away from the front parlour—'

Darryl smiled at her enthusiasm. She seemed as excited at the prospect of finding the priest hole as he was.

'That's great,' he interrupted, relieved that she had returned to the familiar Eleanor. He hoped it meant he hadn't upset her, but then, what had? He pulled out a plan of the entire original building. The plan showed a large square building with a central courtyard. 'So,' he continued, studying the plan. 'It's not far from the entrance. Here's the main entrance so I would say it must be somewhere within this block.' He indicated the whole front elevation of the building.

'If they want the hunters to move away from the parlour, that suggests it's probably in the parlour, or close by.' said Eleanor. 'But do you know which way the parlour would have been from the front door?'

'No, there's nothing in these plans that give any indication as to the layout of specific rooms. Did you find anything else that might be helpful?'

'I was wondering about where Lady Rose mentions the knot hole. That's obviously from something wooden, and probably explains why the floorboards were pulled up during the break-in at the Manor.'

'That would make sense, although it could be wooden panelling around the walls,' Darryl suggested.

'I thought about that, but there's another excerpt later where she mentions that one of the servants fell in the hole when they were rushing to hide everything.'

'Then it must be under the floor.'

'And,' she continued excitedly, 'what if Callum got it wrong? The inspector said that floorboards at both ends of the building had been pulled up, but there was obviously nothing underneath. If the priest hole was under there, I'm sure he would have said something, but he just said nothing was taken and there seemed to be no reason for the break-in. But Callum may have thought that the part of the Manor still standing *was* the front, like we did to begin with. So, what if, it is the side of the building, just as you theorised, and the front was down the main road here ...' Eleanor indicated the road leading past the front of their office building.'

'He was looking in the wrong place,' Darryl said. 'I told you it was all about the research and he didn't do his. Although,' Darryl went on thoughtfully, 'if the building is turned ninety degrees it means he has searched the left side of the Manor's entrance hall, but not the right.'

'But the right side doesn't exist anymore,' Eleanor said.

'The building doesn't, but if the priest hole was under the floor and underground, there could be a possibility that it is still there. Come on.' Darryl grabbed his jacket and left.

Eleanor quickly chased after him. 'Where are we going?' she called.

'To take some measurements,' he said heading toward the stairs.

'Can't we take the lift?'

'I have no patience for lifts,' he replied from six steps down and continued bouncing down the stairs.

Eleanor stopped at the top of the stairs and looked at her shoes. *Well, you can damn well learn some patience and wait for me.* She quietly and calmly made her way back to the lift.

When she reached the ground floor Darryl was hopping impatiently from one foot to another just outside the main doors. Eleanor walked nonchalantly from the lift and made a point of thanking Sidney who held the door open for her.

Once outside Darryl was already striding up the road toward Thornewick Manor. Eleanor followed on but at a more feet friendly pace. She hoped they weren't going to be wandering around the town again, and she wished she'd put her trainers on. She was pleased she had picked up her coat on the way out, though; the sun had lowered behind the rooftops and a chill was in the air.

When she reached the corner of Thornewick Manor Darryl

was walking toward her. He was now striding out and counting his steps from one end of the Manor to the other. Eleanor tried to stifle a giggle. Not only because of how ridiculous he looked, or the funny looks he was getting from passers-by, but also by his complete disregard to the fact that he was receiving those funny looks.

'What are you doing?' she asked.

'Measuring,' he said as if walking down the road in Neanderthal strides was the most natural thing to do. He stopped at the corner of the building. 'According to the plan the Manor was originally square, or thereabouts. As we have one side we can work out where the other corner of the front facade is. The watercolour print shows that the windows layout of the front was the same as for this side, so it's a safe bet that the room layout inside is going to be pretty much the same, or thereabouts.'

Eleanor laughed. They both knew he was theorising again, but she had to admit it did sound plausible.

'So, now you're going to walk like that down the main street?'

A huge grin came to Darryl's face, 'Yeah.' He strode off counting, 'One, two, three ...'

Eleanor followed him back down the road she had just come along, although now she had a different reason for hanging back, never mind her shoes.

Darryl was standing in front of The Birds Building, a few metres past the entrance when Eleanor finally caught up with him.

'This is the far-right corner of the front facade. What room is that?' Darryl pointed toward a window on the ground floor.

Eleanor looked around at the windows surrounding it, working out what room was where.

'This window, with the security bars, is the store for hazardous chemicals, directly beneath my office.' Eleanor indicated the window immediately to the left of the one Darryl had pointed out. 'Which means this one is the caretaker's storeroom for all his other equipment.'

'Great, come on then, let's go open trench six,' Darryl said energetically and dashed off toward the entrance of the building.

'Wait,' called Eleanor. 'If we're opening trenches, I'm changing my shoes.' A feeling of rebellion came over her. She had spent the last few months trying to stay out of people's way, hiding from the world, but now, she wanted to be part of that world again.

'We don't have time for you to change your shoes, just take them off.'

Eleanor didn't need to reply; it was clear that Darryl understood from the look she gave him that that was not an option.

'OK,' he submitted. 'I'll wait in the corridor. Just hurry up.'

'There is no rush. If it is still there after all these years, then I'm sure it will still be there in five minutes time.' Eleanor strolled past him. Darryl followed behind sulking like a petulant child.

'Don't go in there without me,' she called to him as the lift doors closed between them.

Eleanor made her way back to the conference room, removed her coat, and changed into her trainers. Although she had a certain sense of satisfaction from making Darryl wait, she was secretly just as eager to go on the hunt for the priest hole and, once she had tied up her laces, she trotted down the stairs.

~

Darryl jittered from one foot to another while thinking how ironic it would be if the priest hole that Callum had been trying so hard to find was in his own place of work, just a few metres away.

He nodded an awkward acknowledgement to Sidney while he waited in the hallway, just off the entrance hall. Seeing the large plaster across Sidney's nose gave Darryl a small pang of guilt as he remembered the thud of his elbow colliding with Sidney's nose. He watched as Sidney disappeared into the lift taking clients to their respective floors. All the time becoming more and more impatient. During one of these times he poked his head through the door to the caretaker's rooms. Behind the door was a small dark corridor. The same dimensions as the small corridor directly outside Eleanor's office that led to Miss Osbourne's office to the left, and Gina and Marie's office to the right. Here, there was no door to the right as on the ground floor that space was part of the large entrance hallway. The door straight ahead of Darryl was solid wood with fluorescent yellow hazardous and red warning stickers. *She was right,* he thought. *Her room is a cupboard.* The lift bell sounded and, thinking it might be Eleanor, Darryl came back out to the hallway again. Sidney stepped out of the lift on his own and greeted another client entering the building. Back into the lift again. Still no Eleanor.

Darryl only saw a glimpse of the green cloth as it approached from behind and smothered his face.

## 19

Eleanor reached the bottom of the stairs only to find Darryl was not there. The spacious emptiness of the entrance hall meant there was nowhere he could be hidden.

'Sidney, did you see where Mr Westwood went?' Eleanor asked with a touch of annoyance.

'No, Miss. I saw him a few minutes ago, standing over there, but I'm afraid I haven't been here for the last couple of minutes as I've been taking clients up to offices.'

*He didn't wait,* she thought. *He's worse than a child. At least Chris had an excuse for not listening to me.*

She strode over to the caretaker's room, where Sidney had indicated, and entered. Even though the layout was the same as the entrance to her office, the offices had windows between the rooms and plenty of light. Here all the walls and doors were solid making the small corridor grim and austere. She knew the door straight ahead of her would be locked, but still, she tried it. She tried the handle to the door corresponding to Miss Osbourne's door and found it opened easily. Inside was another dark space. The room felt drab and claustrophobic. Items were stacked in front of the only window, blocking out most of the light. Eleanor shivered from a confined feeling, as though the walls were closing in. She flicked the light switch. Directly ahead of her were shelves filled with boxes of paper towels and hand soap. She walked around the crammed but well-arranged room, dotted with shelves of various boxes containing nothing more than Eleanor would expect in a cleaner's storeroom. Toilet paper, cleaning cloths, bin liners. Larger items, such as the floor polisher and at least four mops and buckets were tucked in gaps between the shelving units. Everything as it should be. But no Darryl. She walked back out to the main entrance hall blinking at the bright light. Still no Darryl. She went back into the relative darkness and began pacing the length of the short corridor.

Options were running through her head. *The bathroom? Surely, he would have been back by now. Gone to get a coffee? Not when he's so excited about a new trench. Gone to check more measurements?* She marched outside and searched up and down the street, but there was no sign of him. Something was wrong. Her heart began to thump faster, and the knot appeared in her stomach. She went back inside.

'Sidney, I'm sorry to ask, but could you check the gents for me?' she pleaded.

'Of course, Miss. You still not found him?'

She smiled in reply. A frustrated kind of smile.

Sidney disappeared into the toilets, but it didn't take long before he came out shaking his head. 'No one's in there, Miss.'

Eleanor went back to the cleaner's rooms to check he hadn't slipped past her while she was outside. Frustration was beginning to get the better of her. The door to the main storeroom wedged open behind her as she pushed it with more force this time. She was beginning to lose her patience, or was it concern she was feeling? She began pacing again. *He wouldn't disappear off somewhere when he's so close to finding an unknown priest hole.* The priest hole. With an overwhelming fear she remembered

Darryl explaining how sometimes they had tunnels. Tunnels that left the building completely and exited elsewhere. What if Callum *had* found the priest hole and had returned to the offices through it? The knot in her stomach tightened further and the fog in her head began to seep its way in. If Callum had managed to return, there was no telling what he would do. Eleanor's lungs constricted; her breaths became shallow gasps. She paced quicker up and down the small corridor. Not focusing on her steps, she almost walked into the shelves of paper towels directly opposite the larger room's door. That was the moment the fog lifted, and she realised something wasn't right. She walked back to the door of the hazard store and started counting her steps. One, two, three, four, five from the door to the shelves. If she was right the shelves in the storeroom should directly correspond to Miss Osbourne's filing cabinets that sat against the same wall, but it didn't feel far enough. She had walked those steps from her office to the filing cabinets many times, but she needed to make sure. She burst out of the cleaner's storeroom and ran up the stairs. From her office door she counted, one, two, three, four, five, six, seven. Now she was standing in front of the filing cabinet with Miss Osbourne staring at her from her desk.

'Eleanor, you're still here,' she said, surprised by the interruption. 'What are you doing?'

Eleanor ignored her, turned and ran. She didn't understand what was going on, but she was sure her fears were now justified. Darryl was in danger.

∼

Darryl tried to lift his head, but it felt like solid lead. He tried to open his eyes, but he could see nothing but a thick grey mist across a darkened room. He wanted to rub his sore eyes but found he couldn't move his arms from behind him. His entire body felt heavy and weak. The memory of a green cloth came back to him. A strong smell of ... he didn't know what it was. Something he had never smelt before. He assumed it must have been some kind of drug smothering his face, and then nothing.

Now he was trapped in a chair, weakened by the toxin. A slight movement sounded behind him.

'Hello, is someone there?' he tried to say, but his mouth felt numb and only an indistinct noise came out.

*Callum.* His eyes closed again from exhaustion.

∽

Eleanor reached the caretaker's room and counted her steps again, just to make certain that she had done it right. There was no doubt. It wasn't the darkness that made the room feel smaller, it was smaller. Eleanor reached through the shelving and knocked on the wall. The sound was the low thump of a partition, not the higher tap of a brick wall as it should be. She began looking around for something that may make sense of the dimensions. Approximately two metres along the partition an arch shaped abrasion led from the wall out into the room as though something slid across the floor. On closer inspection she noticed the shelving was different too. All around the room, the shelving units were free standing. In just this one spot the shelving units had been attached to the wall. She pulled on the shelving, but it didn't take much to discover they were too insubstantial for the effort needed to pull open a door. She immediately started to check the wall behind and soon found a small hole that had been hidden by boxes on the shelf. She could just fit two of her fingers through. She pulled and there was a slight movement. Her heart beat faster as she pulled with every muscle. Her head completely clear of any fog, only determination remained.

'Eleanor?'

Eleanor jumped at the sound of Miss Osbourne's voice behind her.

'What are you doing?'

'Help me pull this door open,' Eleanor pleaded.

'This is the caretaker's room; you shouldn't be in here.'

'I think Darryl's in danger. Please, help me get this open.'

Miss Osbourne hesitated. The door had now opened far enough for Eleanor to get her fingers behind the door itself and pull. The attached shelves moved with the door but didn't make her attempt any easier. A dull light seeped through from behind.

'Where does this go?' Miss Osbourne asked as she approached and squeezed her fingers through the crack too.

'I think it goes to an old priest hole, and I believe Darryl has been taken down there.'

They both pulled together, and the false door opened more easily. Eleanor rushed through the doorway first, but then stopped in the gloomy light. To her right was an open trap door in the floor leading down into darkness.

*They're called trenches, are they? This one is definitely a hole.*

A high-pitched gasp came from behind her. Miss Osbourne had followed her through the doorway and turned left behind Eleanor. She was standing in front of a collage of torn out pictures on the wall. A collage of faces lit by a bare bulb hanging from a hook screwed crudely into the wall. Eleanor was immediately drawn to a picture of Nick.

'That's the old caretaker,' Miss Osbourne said. 'And there's one of the porters that went missing.'

The sight of Nick on this wall, in amongst at least a dozen other faces sent Eleanor into a whirlwind of confusion. Her heart swelled with pain once again.

'That's the other applicant,' continued Miss Osbourne.

Eleanor thought about what the police had said. Deaths and

disappearances going on for ... 'How long has this been going on?' she wondered out loud.

Miss Osbourne turned away from the photographs and looked at Eleanor. Her face pale with fear.

A distant groaning sound drifted through the air, emanating through the trap door. Eleanor's focus turned back to Darryl. She couldn't go through losing someone again. It just couldn't happen. Eleanor moved across to the open trap door and looked down. The ground wasn't visible through the darkness, but at least there was a ladder. Eleanor didn't hesitate. She began the climb down.

'What are you doing?' said Miss Osbourne. The high-pitched ring of shock in her voice.

'Stay here if you want to, but I can't leave him.'

Eleanor climbed down the rusty, metal ladder attached to the side of the wall. Down into the darkness, leaving Miss Osbourne behind. The walls seemed to be a mixture of cut away stone and solid, hard earth. Large boulders created the majority of the surface. It must have been less than two metres before she reached the ground, just far enough to create a tunnel she could walk through at a stoop. The ground was uneven, also made of the same earth and stone mixture, though it was nothing but blackness to see. The eerie groaning came again, echoing through the tunnel. She felt her way around the wall and seemed to be following a passage. She moved around a corner and the darkness enveloped her like a thick, black, velvet shroud. Its presence almost physical as it smothered her, her lungs restricting from its coldness. She could not even see the wall that was only inches in front of her. The rough stone tore at her fingers, but she ignored the scratches. The groaning became louder as she moved closer; the only indication that there may be an end to this blackness.

She passed through the tunnel as quickly as she dared

following the noise through the darkness. Finally, just ahead, she could make out a faint light coming from around another corner, highlighting the roughness of the bare wall. The passage turned and widened into an area similar in size to Miss Osbourne's office with two make-shift electric lights hooked on to the uneven walls. Identical to the one above the collage of photographs. The walls were constructed of the same stone and earth mixture as the tunnel; the space resembled a cave more than a room.

Darryl was sitting in one of two worn, wooden chairs in the middle of the room. His arms tied behind him. His head hanging down on to his chest. He looked as though he was struggling to waken, quietly groaning, but Eleanor didn't dare go to him. She stopped at the entrance to the room. A figure was hunched by the wall on the opposite side of the room, almost as though he was trying to blend into the wall itself. Quiet and unassuming. A large solid metal knife held loosely. The silver-coloured ten-inch steel blade glinted in the light with each subtle turn in his hand. The figure's subdued presence was enough to make her falter.

~

Darryl heard his name. Faint and muffled, but Eleanor's voice. He struggled to lift his head, groaning at the effort. 'Eleanor? What's going on?' His mouth still felt numb. He could just make out a figure standing only a few metres in front of him. He blinked slowly, screwing his eyes tight each time. Was it Eleanor? Had he just imagined her voice because it was what he wanted to hear?

'I wondered how long it would take you,' a voice came from behind him. A man's voice this time, but not Callum's.

'Why are you doing this?' asked the first voice again.

Now he was certain it was Eleanor. Relieved, but also afraid, to hear her voice. She too was now in danger.

'I don't understand,' Eleanor went on. 'Were you waiting for me?'

'Waiting for you? Yes, I was waiting for you,' came the voice from behind.

'Why?'

'Who is it?' Darryl interrupted. 'Eleanor? Tell me, who's there?' The man's voice was one he recognised, but he couldn't place it. The din in his head muffling every sound didn't help.

Eleanor hadn't moved since she had entered the dark room, standing rigid. Something had scared her from moving any further forward. He shook his head. None of his senses seemed to be working properly.

There was no reply to his question. He tried again, 'Eleanor, who is it?'

'The caretaker,' Eleanor replied.

'What?' Confusion added to Darryl's panic. What had he done to the caretaker? Why would he be trying to kill him?

~

'Those photos,' Eleanor murmured. The image of Nick's photograph kept pushing its way into her mind. Now, face to face with the murderer of her husband and son, she couldn't think of anything more to say. It was the thought of all those photographs that paralyzed her.

'You saw my garden,' the caretaker said with pride.

'Garden?'

'Don't you think all those faces look like a garden of flowers? So beautiful.'

There was a familiarity about those words that reminded Eleanor of something she had heard before.

'Beautiful as a flower,' she whispered.

'That's right, Miss,' said the caretaker with a gentle smile.

'You told me the other day that I was as beautiful as a flower, when you gave me my beads.'

'Yes, unfortunately you were becoming too friendly with Mr Westwood and I couldn't let that happen. You needed to be reminded of what you'd lost. I knew the sight of the beads would bring you back to your despair. A necessity, I'm afraid, but you'll make a lovely addition to my garden.'

Eleanor quietly gasped with shock. His matter-of-fact tone sent shockwaves up her spine. It only took a moment for what he had said to sink in.

'You want to kill us both, why?'

'Oh no, no. I don't want to kill Mr Westwood. I want to save him.'

Eleanor's head started to spin. *Why would Darryl be drugged and tied to a chair in order to save him?*

'I want to save him from you, Miss,' the caretaker answered as though reading her thoughts. 'From the very first day when the two of you left together, I knew I'd need to keep an eye on you. And then my suspicions were confirmed when you returned together the following morning.'

'Then why have you been trying to kill him?' Eleanor asked incredulously.

'I was trying to kill you, Miss,' he said. Never wavering from his pragmatic tone, yet also somehow childlike. 'It was you I pushed into the road.'

'The delivery van,' Eleanor exclaimed. 'You were there. You would have been dealing with the delivery from the van parked at the crossing.'

'That's right. You very conveniently almost ran into the road yourself while I was taking in the delivery. You only needed a little push, but Mr Westwood got in the way.'

'What about the gas leak? The police would have checked that you had already left the building.'

'Of course, I left, but it's so easy to sneak back in.' For the first time the caretaker lost his pragmatic tone and took delight in his actions. 'I have done it many times. Have you seen how many people are trying to get out of this place at the end of the day?'

'You didn't know Darryl had returned,' Eleanor said thoughtfully.

'No, I thought you were working alone. Later, I saw you leave and sneaked in with the gas cannister. When I heard the conference room door close again, I assumed it was you returning. I guess anyone can make a mistake.'

'Make a mistake? You nearly killed him.' Eleanor said incredulously.

'I know. It's a good job the cannister didn't explode like the first one, otherwise he would have been lost.'

'You mean, you've done it before?'

'Oh, yes. It took me a while to work out how to adapt the valve. Unfortunately, the first one exploded, but the second one worked perfectly.'

'But why? What have I done? Why are you doing all this?' Eleanor implored.

'Because he is my brother,' came Miss Osbourne's voice, though not her usual brash self. Quiet and subdued.

Eleanor spun round, surprised to see her there. There had been no sign of her following through the tunnel.

'Cissy, what are you doing here? You're not supposed to be here,' he replied, panic rising in his voice.

'I had to find out for myself if— Please tell me you didn't kill all those people.'

He shook his head, bewildered. 'I ... but I did it for you.'

'For me? I didn't want those people to die.'

'But I had to help you. You've done so much for me. You cared for me when I was pushed out by everyone else.'

'Cared for you?' Eleanor said astounded. She remembered the way she had seen Miss Osbourne treat the caretaker in the past. 'She's shouted at you, humiliated you, how is that caring?'

'And she was right to. I understand that she cannot risk her reputation by being associated with me.'

'All those people,' Miss Osbourne whispered. 'Jake is my half-brother,' she managed to say through a strangled voice. 'The result of one of my father's affairs.'

Jake's demeanour suddenly stiffened at her words.

'I try to take care of him as best I can,' she continued. 'I managed to get him the job as caretaker here when the old one was killed in ... in an accident.' She paused for a moment and looked questioningly at her brother.

'It was easier to help you once I was working here,' Jake said. 'I could keep a closer eye on you.'

Miss Osbourne quietly gasped at his inference, before continuing, 'He's ... not well, shall we say. One too many knocks about the head from our father.' She gave a small, forced laugh.

'Stop it.' Jake's anger exploded. His face contorted in torment. 'He cannot hurt us now. Don't speak about—' Jake stopped himself and suddenly became soft and loving. 'You know I'd do anything for you.'

Silence seemed to echo round the space. Eleanor daren't move. Rigid with fear.

'Eleanor,' called Darryl tentatively. 'What's going on?'

'Are you OK?' she stammered.

'Where are we? What's going on?'

His eyes were glazed as he blinked and shook his head. At least his speech had improved since the last time he spoke. The effects of whatever drug Jake had given him seemed to be wearing off quickly.

'You did it,' Eleanor replied with a slight nervous laugh. 'You found the priest hole.'

Miss Osbourne appeared to have been stunned into silence, but now she stepped forward. 'Jake, I have to know. Our father, did you ...'

Jake's face softened as he looked at his sister. 'You were so happy after he died.'

'But did you kill him?' Miss Osbourne persisted.

'Of course, and he deserved it. I would no longer let him or anybody else hurt you.'

'No,' she pleaded. 'Jake, you can't do this.'

'You deserve to have everything you want.'

'Not like this,' Miss Osbourne pleaded.

As they spoke things started to slip into place for Eleanor. The obsessive protection of the personnel files in case someone found out the connection. His subtle manipulation with her beads. If he killed all those in his so-called garden, then that must mean—

'What about Nick and Chris?' Eleanor interrupted. She needed to hear it. Fury was beginning to rise inside her. 'Did you kill them? Did you kill my husband and son?'

'They were regrettable,' Jake said sadly. 'Mr Garrett came into my store needing a mop and I had left the door open. He found my garden and so he had to die. I didn't intend for your son to be in the car too, but I couldn't let Mr Garrett live. He would have ruined Cissy's life.'

'How would he have ruined *her* life by finding out *your* secret?' Eleanor cried as the pain in her heart overwhelmed her once again.

'Because I handle everything.'

'Everything?' Miss Osbourne repeated. 'This job?'

'You were overjoyed when you got this job.' A smile appeared on his face from the memory.

'No, *I* got this job,' Miss Osbourne said defiantly.

'Because the other final applicant didn't turn up,' Eleanor whispered.

'That's not true,' Miss Osbourne snapped at her. 'That's a nasty rumour. I got the job on my own merit.'

'You saw his photograph on the wall,' Eleanor gently reminded her.

The room went quiet.

'On my own merit,' Miss Osbourne repeated quietly.

'Of course, you did. I only helped,' Jake said.

'You killed him?' she gasped. 'What about the porter, Doug? Did you kill him, too?'

'He was rude to you.'

'But that doesn't give you the right to kill him,' Miss Osbourne barked at him. 'All of them?' She shook her head in disbelief. 'You killed all of them.'

Eleanor turned to look at Darryl. He was still quietly shaking his head, blinking the mist from his eyes. The glaze she had noticed earlier was now clearing when he turned to face her. For one quiet moment they stared at each other. A calmness came over Eleanor and she knew what she had to do.

'Do you promise to let them go?' Eleanor said calmly. Jake was serious about what he was doing. He could see the logic in it, though to everyone else it was insanity.

'What?' exclaimed Darryl. 'No.'

'Do you promise to let them go?' Eleanor repeated turning back to Jake. She couldn't bear to look at Darryl's face any longer. Her heart couldn't cope with anymore.

'No, Eleanor. You can't do this,' Darryl roared.

'Please,' she replied calmly though not turning to face him. 'I'll be fine.'

'How will you be fine? He wants to kill you.'

'I know, and then the pain in my heart will finally end.'

'No, no, don't do this.'

'It's better this way. I'll be with Nick and Chris again.'

'What if they're not there,' Darryl yelled at her. 'What if there is no after-life and they are not waiting for you. No, I won't let you do this.' He struggled with the ropes that tied him to the chair.

Eleanor still could not face him. The thought of going through it all again repulsed her.

'I have nothing here to live for now and if it means he'll let you go, then—'

'You can't do this.'

'Please,' Eleanor implored. 'I want to.'

She could understand that he was angry, and she knew there was no way she could make him understand why she had to do this.

Darryl continued to struggle but it was useless. 'I won't let you do this; I won't let you.'

He couldn't break free from the ropes binding his wrists and so tried to break the chair he was sitting on instead. He slammed it against the floor. It would not break. Still weak from the drug, his efforts were futile.

The caretaker stepped forward and presented Eleanor the second chair.

'This is the way it should be,' she said.

Eleanor sat in the chair and moved her hands behind her back as though waiting for them to be tied, though first she faltered.

'You must give me your word that you won't hurt him,' she said.

'If it's what Cissy wants,' Jake agreed.

Eleanor relaxed with relief; her arms hung loosely by her side.

The last few months had been relentless for Eleanor. The

initial numbness that came from the news. The denial that it had happened; there must have been a mistake and it wasn't *her* husband and son who had been killed. Then the anger. Anger that they had gone. Anger that they had left her. Left her alone. Next came the guilt. It must be her fault. She was being punished and she deserved such a life.

Then came the hardest of all. The acceptance. Not the accepting that they had died, that was, in comparison, the easy part. It was accepting that they weren't coming back. They weren't going to walk through that door; she was never going to hear their voices again; never going to see their faces again except in unfeeling, cold photographs. That acceptance was something quite different.

The prospect of what was about to happen didn't fill her with dread. If she was honest with herself, she would say she welcomed it.

## 20

'I KNEW YOU WOULD COME,' THE CARETAKER SAID GENTLY.

'I don't want to hear anymore,' Eleanor replied, repulsed by the sound of his thin reedy voice. 'I just want the pain to end. All I ask is that you do it quickly. Would you do that for me?'

'Under any other circumstances I would've done anything for you, Miss. You've been very kind to me. Most people don't even notice I'm there, or they tease me thinking I am no better than the rats that scrabble at their bins.'

Eleanor sat quietly, waiting for the end to come. Jake's words meant nothing to her. He was wrong. She had shown no particular kindness toward him.

'Unfortunately for you,' Jake went on, 'your kindness is your weakness. I knew that by bringing Mr Westwood here you'd follow. You'd not be able to walk away from someone in danger. Especially someone you care about.'

*Someone you care about.* Those words resonated through her. Eleanor had not wanted to admit to herself that she did care about Darryl. It was something else to feel guilty about. Enjoying the company of another man; looking forward to seeing him again no matter how much she told herself it wasn't true. Hearing it out loud somehow made it more real. But she found there was no shame there. The guilt she had expected to feel from admitting it didn't come.

'Eleanor, please don't do this,' Darryl begged, plainly still struggling from the effects of the drug.

'Once you are gone,' Jake continued, 'it will leave Mr Westwood free to fall in love with my sister. I've been around enough to know that that is what she wants.'

Eleanor looked into Miss Osbourne's face. She had backed herself into a corner like a terrified puppy. Eyes wide with shock. Darryl, to her side, continued to blink and shake his head. Sudden bouts of anger raged in him, but he was so weak they came to nothing. Until now there had been a certain logic to Jake's actions. But, as Eleanor was only too well aware, there was no logic when it came to emotions.

'You can't make him fall in love with her,' she said quietly, almost to herself.

'I'll do whatever it takes to make my Cissy happy and he'll learn not to upset her.' Jake had returned to his matter-of-fact tone. 'He'll pay for making her suffer. Like now, the pain of losing you will teach him he needs to be more respectful toward my sister. He will learn.'

'That's not love. That's coercion ... blackmail.'

'Whatever it takes,' Jake repeated.

Only now Eleanor began to truly believe that her husband and son's death were *not* her fault. She wasn't being punished as her mind had convinced her over the last few months. *She* didn't kill them. It was Jake. The helpful caretaker. Timid and humble. It was him who had destroyed her life. He had taken the lives of those she loved most without a thought as to the consequences, as to the pain it would leave those left behind.

Once more the fog in her brain began to lift. This wasn't going to be over with her death. Darryl would still be in danger for there was no way he would agree to be with Miss Osbourne after this. And then after Darryl, who would be next? Who else would be killed just to make Miss Osbourne happy?

'I'll always be there to help her and to make sure things go her way. I'll keep her safe,' Jake continued, pacing to and fro, always keeping behind her. Out of sight. 'After all, it's better to be safe than sorry.'

~

Darryl turned to look at Eleanor. He had said those same words to her only yesterday. Had she understood anything of what he had been trying to say? He willed her to understand.

'Is it?' Eleanor asked quietly, turning to look at Darryl.

'What?' asked Jake, clearly not expecting to be argued with.

'Is it better to be safe than sorry?'

Darryl almost laughed with relief. Maybe she did now understand. Jake had said that she cared about him. Was it true? Did she care about him? Or was it just loneliness? He knew how powerful loneliness could be. He had learnt that lesson at the cost of his marriage. He searched her face, looking for some indication that she did care. Her features were still bleary, and she gave nothing away, though she was sat no more than two feet away. She stared calmly back.

'If I'd been safe, I would never have enjoyed those years with Nick and Chris.'

'But look at where it's brought you,' sneered Jake. His anger rising. 'In so much pain that you're willing to give your own life to save others.'

'Don't do this, this is crazy,' Darryl implored.

'The decision isn't yours,' Jake snarled from behind.

Darryl jolted at the hard thump on the back of his head.

Eleanor yelped with shock as Jake swung his arm round and struck Darryl on the head with the hilt of his knife. Darryl slumped in his chair, unconscious. She couldn't bear it, not again. The knot in her stomach appeared again, but this time, instead of crippling her, it enraged her. Eleanor stood and stepped away from the chair, turning to face the caretaker.

'Not being safe didn't bring me this point. You did.'

She had decided that she *didn't* want this anymore. She *didn't* want her life to come to an end. Maybe she will see Nick and Chris again one day, but they would not want to see her like this. Giving in? Weak? No, she wanted to live.

'Jake,' came a soft nervous voice from behind Eleanor.

Miss Osbourne had stepped away from the corner of the room where she had been cowering and had walked forward, toward Jake.

'Jake, you need to stop now,' she said tentatively.

'But you want him. This is the only way—'

'No,' she spoke softly as though to a child. 'He doesn't want me.'

Jake paused for the slightest of moments.

'Then he needs to die too,' he replied simply. 'You deserve to have what you want. That is what's important.'

'Is it? So, if I want you to stop, you'll do that for me?' She stepped closer.

'Of course, if that's what you want,' Jake said.

Eleanor was already tense from both anger and fear. Even so, each muscle tightened further with every step Miss Osbourne took toward him.

'Yes, that is what I want.' Miss Osbourne held out her hands toward him.

Eleanor watched as the knife in his hand became loose.

They needed to keep him talking for any chance of overcoming him. She believed, or rather hoped, that Miss Osbourne had the same idea as she continued the conversation with her brother.

'Tell me, Jake, how did you find this place?' Miss Osbourne went on.

'I didn't find it, it found me. The building itself was telling me that I should be helping you. This room just appeared one day.'

'It's a priest hole,' Eleanor explained gently, attempting to keep her trembling voice in the same soft tones as Miss Osbourne. 'It's been here for many years.'

'No, you don't understand,' Jake said anxiously, turning on her angrily. 'It appeared from nowhere.'

Eleanor's breath seemed to have been snatched from her body, and she once again froze with fear.

'What do you mean, Jake?' said Miss Osbourne quickly, taking Jake's attention back to her. 'How can it just appear?'

'I knocked over one of my buckets one day, and the water was pouring through the floor. I pulled up the floorboards and found this space. The floor led me to this room.' Jake gave a small laugh. He genuinely believed everything had appeared just for him. 'It was proof that everything I did for you was the right thing to do.'

Eleanor took this time to breathe. Jake's explanation was short and to the point, but animated. It was clear he was enjoying the telling of his story. If she could reach him during a time when his grip wasn't fully focused on the knife, she may be able to get it from him.

'Is that when you built the partition wall?' Eleanor tried again, almost as a whisper. Fear keeping hold of her voice.

'Yes, I made it during the nights when not many people were about. Usually just the porters.'

Eleanor was relieved Jake continued with his explanation just as animatedly, and even with excitement.

'Now and again one of them would find me,' he went on, 'and then they would have to die.'

Miss Osbourne gave a short, sudden gasp as though she struggled to breathe. Jake turned his attention back to his sister.

'Don't be upset. It was all meant to make you happy.'

'Jake,' she whispered gently to him. Her face full of pity. She reached out to hold his hands.

For that short moment, Jake's focus was on nothing but his sister. It could have been that there was nobody else in the room. Eleanor took this as her chance. She lurched forward and made a bid for the hand holding the blade. She brought her knee round and hit him hard, causing him to double up in pain, but he did not let go of the knife. She tried to grab it from him, but he had already tightened his grip. He turned toward her. There was no doubt now that he would never let her go.

'No Jake,' Miss Osbourne cried. 'Stop, please stop.'

Eleanor and Jake stood staring at each other. She had only succeeded in making him angrier and more determined. The blade now threateningly pointing toward her. His focus fully on his original intention. Eleanor had to die.

'If Cissy wants me to stop, then that is what I'll do. But I must protect my garden,' he snarled as he stepped purposefully toward Eleanor. 'If he won't love her, both you and Mr Westwood will die and then I'll stop.'

'No, Jake. Stop now,' Miss Osbourne cried from behind him. 'If you continue, I will not be able to help you.'

'They must die to protect us both.' Jake did not move his eyes away from Eleanor.

He lunged at her; the knife shone in the light as he raised it. Eleanor managed to lift her arms in time to push it away from her body, but it sliced into her arm and she was thrust across the room from the impact of his body. Miss Osbourne threw herself at her brother in an attempt to retrieve the knife. Eleanor clutched her arm tight to her, recoiling in pain. She could only watch as brother and sister fought on the floor. Her arm bleeding profusely.

She struggled to her feet, still grasping her arm, trying to stop the blood that was running free from her wound, trying to ignore the pain. She looked around for something else in the room to use as a weapon, but there was nothing. The room was bare except for the two chairs. Darryl, still unconscious, was slumped in one. She picked up the other and lifted it through the pain in her arm. She hit Jake over the head with it as he scrambled up from the ground. The chair broke, but Jake only shook his head and then turned to face Eleanor again.

Miss Osbourne struggled to get up behind him. Her clothes torn; her feet bare. Jake moved toward Eleanor again. The rage on his face somehow brought her an element of satisfaction. It wasn't the same rage, but maybe at least he could feel a little of what she'd had to endure through her grief. He had lost his sister's respect and her love. He now had to deal with the grief that brought him.

As he came closer Eleanor desperately looked around her again for something that might help her. She had lost so much blood that she didn't know how she could cope with another full assault from him. But still, a full assault came as he threw himself at her again. Eleanor focused on the blade. She couldn't hope to avoid him completely, but she may be able to avoid the knife. Suddenly, Miss Osbourne was between them. The blade entered her body. Jake's momentum caused both he and Miss Osbourne to fall against Eleanor, and all three landed on the hard, bare ground together.

'Cissy,' Jake cried. 'My beautiful Cissy.'

Miss Osbourne's body went limp in Jake's arms. All the air

seemed to evaporate from Eleanor's lungs in a single moment. As she watched, Eleanor began to feel overwhelmed with exhaustion. She felt so weak she doubted she could manage the long walk back through the tunnel and up the ladder if she tried to escape. It would also mean leaving Darryl and Miss Osbourne behind. And yet, she knew there would be no cavalry coming to save the day. The police were looking for the wrong man. It was down to her.

Jake continued to cradle Miss Osbourne's body. Whimpering over her. Whatever Eleanor was going to do, she needed to do it now. She reached out to her side to help her stand. Her hand fell against one of Miss Osbourne's shoes lying on its side next to her. One of those high heeled shoes. She couldn't do anything for Miss Osbourne now, but she still may be able to save Darryl. Eleanor grabbed the shoe and, with the last ounce of effort left in her body, she threw herself at Jake aiming for the neck, and pushed. The heel, she had only weeks before considered to be a lethal weapon, punctured his neck. His body went rigid. He staggered for a moment before falling to the floor, next to the motionless body of his sister. Eleanor took the knife from his limp hand and dragged herself over to Darryl. Her vision was nothing but a blur; she could hardly walk from loss of blood. Only determination kept her going.

'Darryl,' she rasped. 'Darryl.' She tried to wake him while cutting through the ropes tying him to the chair. There was the slightest of movement from him. Then there was darkness as she hit the floor.

## 21

'Dave, it's me,' Darryl said into his phone. He stared blankly out the first-floor window at the park opposite.

'Mate, I've been trying to get hold of you the last couple of nights. I'm taking that as a sign you got your wicked way,' Dave laughed. 'Either that or you're in the bloody hospital again.'

'Well, actually ...'

'Do not tell me you're back in—'

'Not for me this time. The doctors have given me the all clear.'

'What's going on then, mate?'

'It's Eleanor. There was a bit of an incident at the offices on Tuesday. She's unconscious, lost a lot of blood. They keep saying she's going to wake up, but we just don't know when.'

'I would ask you to come round, mate, but—'

'No, no.' Darryl interrupted quickly. 'I want to stay here in case she does wake up. I thought I'd better let you know that I've finished the report you need. If you want to go into the offices sometime, they'll give it to you. It's on the desk in the conference room if it hasn't been moved.' Darryl's eyes followed two joggers running along the park path without seeing them. An innate reaction to the movement.

'You mean, I've still got to go in and see Osbourne?' Dave asked in a defeated tone.

'No, Cecilia's in the room next door.'

'Cecilia? When did she become Cecilia? And why is she in the hospital?'

'It seems she helped save our lives, almost at the cost of her own. I think she's earned the right to be called Cecilia.'

'Shit. Look, we'll have to meet up one night and you can fill me in on all the details.'

'Yeah, sure. Can I ask before you go, those interviews you were holding, do you remember Pete Burrows?' Darryl was hoping he might be able to do at least one good deed, an attempt at an apology. Pete had clearly shown the job meant a lot to him.

'Pete Burrows. Yeah, he seemed good, but he hadn't even finished college. Doing evening classes, I think it was.'

'That's him. I was wondering if you could take another look. You're going to need somebody. I'm not planning on sticking around. This was always just a one off, done as a favour.'

'Well, he was certainly enthusiastic about the job, but I've found someone now. I suppose I could take him on as a kind of apprentice or work experience.'

'I'd appreciate it.'

'I've gotta go now, mate,' Dave said.

Darryl could hear a female voice in the background.

'Where are you,' he said. 'That doesn't sound like the pub.'

'I'm at Alicia's place.'

'Who's Alicia?'

'Have I not told you about Alicia? She's ... my new researcher.'

Darryl could hear Alicia giggling briefly.

'Some things never change,' Darryl said and hung up.

Just one more call he needed to make before he returned to the chair he had spent most of the last twenty-four hours sat in. The doctors had given him the all clear. DI Selby and DS Wade took what statement they could from him, which wasn't much considering he was unconscious for the majority of the time. And then he waited. Even Miss Osbourne, who had been admitted for an emergency operation on her arrival at the hospital, was awake before Eleanor. She had explained to Darryl how Eleanor had fought back, how she herself had tried to stop her brother. And now Darryl waited some more.

He took a business card out from his wallet and rang the number.

'Hi, this is Darryl Westwood. I have an appointment with someone to view my house this afternoon at three o'clock, but I'm not going to able to get there.'

'That's no problem, Mr Westwood,' came the man's voice at the other end of the line. 'Would you like us to rearrange it, although if you want to sell—'

'No, I'm happy for someone else to take them round as you have a key. I had thought I was going to be there, but I can't make it now.'

'No problem, we'll organise that for you.'

'Thanks,' and Darryl hung up.

He turned from the window and looked back at Eleanor lying dormant in the hospital bed. The sight of her unconscious body was more than he could cope with and he tore his eyes away. She had been unconscious for more than thirty-six hours. The doctors had been clear about her chances when she first arrived. They weren't going to give him any false hopes. But later, as long as she woke, they didn't see any problems with her making a full recovery. *As long as she woke.* As each hour had passed Darryl began to truly understand some of the torment

Eleanor had been going through over the last few months. He hadn't eaten for hours. Just the thought of food made him nauseous. His petty life now seemed empty and devoid of all feeling except for a constant dull ache across his chest. He returned to the chair by her bed. Placed his phone, together with the business card, on the bedside cabinet, and, though determined to be there for her the moment she woke, he nodded into sleep.

∼

Eleanor woke, blinking in the bright lights of the nearby striplights. Mechanical bleeps sounded intermittently behind her. She knew immediately what they were. She had heard that sound before. She recognised the lights; she recognised the smell. She moved her eyes left toward the window. *At least I have a room of my own this time.* She turned her head right toward the door and could just see, in her peripheral vision, someone slumped in the chair in the corner beside her. She tried to turn to see better but winced from pain.

'Eleanor?' came Darryl's voice.

The sound of her flinch had woken him. He rose from the chair and moved to sit on the bed, taking hold of her hand. The relief in his eyes spoke more than any words could have done.

'I thought ...,' he said. The lump in his throat prevented him from saying any more.

'Where's Miss Osbourne?' Eleanor asked, almost as a whisper. Dreading the answer. 'Is she ... dead?'

Darryl shook his head and tried to speak but seemed to be having difficulty. He took a deep breath and began again.

'Cecilia's in the room next door. They needed to operate on her but she's going to be fine,' he managed to say in short gasps.

'What happened?' she asked. 'I think I blacked out.'

Darryl nodded. 'I woke as you hit the floor. I managed to get you back through the tunnel and Sidney called for an ambulance. You— you—'

Darryl couldn't continue. After a few moments of silence, he said, 'Those detectives have been in to see you. Remind me not to get on your bad side.' His laugh was forced, but the change of subject seemed to make him stronger. 'It's pretty safe to say that nobody's going to be pressing charges.'

'It was self-defence,' she said quickly.

The memory of what she had done suddenly came back to her, and it horrified her. A wave of nausea ran over her.

'It's OK, Cecilia told me what happened, and she explained everything to the detectives.'

*Cecilia again.*

'They also said they had caught Callum. So, it turned out that he wasn't a killer after all, but he has caused a lot of trouble. Once he realised he was the prime suspect for attempted murder he soon started talking. And we were right about him being the one who broke in to Thornewick Manor. Smarmy git.'

Eleanor smiled at Darryl's cynicism. He was clearly pleased that Callum had still been arrested for something. She noted a nervous energy about the way he spoke. His eyes darted around the room, never lingering too long on Eleanor herself. *What is it that he's not telling me?*

'All that effort he went to, though, was pointless,' Darryl went on. 'There was no treasure in the priest hole. No sign of it. Nothing but a mad man.'

While he spoke, Eleanor realised how much her body ached. She felt as though she had been drained and beaten. It was an effort to try and move any single part of her body. Instead she laid quietly and listened to him talk.

'He, as it turns out, was the cause of the fire at the County archives,' Darryl continued. 'He had broken in on one of his treasure hunts and was disturbed by a security guard. They said he'd told them he only set a small fire as a distraction for him to escape, but, with all that paper about, it got a bit out of hand.' Darryl laughed. 'You'd have thought he'd know better, being a supposed archivist. They lost a major part of their collection thanks to him.'

Darryl stopped his commentary and looked back down at Eleanor. 'I'm sorry, you must be tired.' Darryl kissed her hand, and held it enclosed in both his.

Eleanor, feeling exhausted but safe, fell asleep.

∼

Darryl watched as Eleanor drifted back to sleep. Her hand in his fell limp as her muscles relaxed. He gently stood, being careful not to wake her, and returned to the chair.

He had managed to distract himself talking to Eleanor, but now he had no such distraction. He sat and wept with relief. The tension in his shoulders melted away and he fell into a deep sleep. His subconscious finally allowing him to relax.

∼

A couple of hours later Darryl was still on the chair by Eleanor's bed, deep in sleep. A nurse had been in and had helped Eleanor turn onto her side. With the next dose of painkillers inside her, she felt much more comfortable. She watched Darryl's gentle breathing as he slept. The nurse had told her how he had barely left her side once the doctors had finished with him, and he hadn't slept except for a few moments here and there when his eyes just couldn't stay open any longer. Eleanor didn't know what her future was going to bring, but she felt better able to cope with it now. More to the point, she felt she wanted to cope with it now. As she laid there watching him, she felt that she would be happy if Darryl was there to share it with her, but she was unsure of what would happen now. The sound of Darryl using the name Cecilia kept coming back to her. She couldn't help but wonder what had happened over the last thirty-six hours or so for him to have changed his attitude toward her so drastically that he now called her by her first name. She knew that Miss Osbourne had helped fight back against her own brother, but was there something else? Also, her eyes kept drifting to the cabinet by her bed. She could see Darryl's mobile and a business card, lying underneath. Half hidden but there was no mistaking the logo of a stylised house. The logo of *Winterbourne's*, a local estate agency they often had business with in the office. Was he selling and moving away?

The door opened and the sound woke him. She watched him rub the back of his neck where his head had dropped forward and ached from the stretch. A nurse had entered the room with Gina and Marie following close behind carrying flowers and a bag of grapes.

The nurse helped Eleanor to sit up in her bed.

'Thank you,' Eleanor said to the nurse, but it was Gina and Marie that answered.

'You're welcome,' they said, though they didn't look comfortable being there.

'Thank you for being so original,' Eleanor remarked satirically as they handed her the flowers and grapes.

Darryl quietly sniggered.

Gina and Marie stammered a nonsensical reply and seemed almost apologetic. Eleanor felt no regard for these two ladies and felt no need to show them any courtesy.

'It's OK,' she said to them both. 'I know you're only here because you came to see Miss Osbourne. In fact, I wouldn't be surprised if she sent you in here. She's probably feeling very guilty right now.'

Eleanor knew that even though Miss Osbourne had helped defend them, she would still feel guilty that, in the end, it was her own brother that had brought all of this about, and all for her benefit.

Gina and Marie started to stammer a reply, but Eleanor cut them off.

'I wouldn't expect you to come and see me. After all, I'm not going to help you get on in the world, not with my fashion sense.'

They were both stunned into silence.

'Sorry for taking up your time,' said Marie finally, feigning strength but clearly flustered.

They both turned and were walking out the room when Eleanor called after them, 'By the way ladies, if you think my trainers are ugly, you wait till you see the bunions you're going to get from always wearing those high heels.'

They left in disgust with an attempt at slamming the door behind them, but with the soft close system the effect was lost.

'I know,' Eleanor said as she saw Darryl laughing at her. 'I'm not good at insults.'

'I think that was just fine. You know, Cecilia really does feel guilty. Apparently, her brother had been doing it for years, even before she started working at The Birds. She had no idea that he was the one behind all of this, and what he did to you.'

'And what he did to you,' Eleanor continued. She began to see that Darryl was feeling pity for Miss Osbourne. Maybe even regret. *It's amazing how your opinion of someone can change once the entire picture is seen.* Even though Darryl had been at *her* bedside, and not Miss Osbourne's; it was *her* hand he kissed when she woke. She still felt she needed to know where things stood between them but was unable to ask him directly.

'What are your plans now?' she asked tentatively. 'Your report is finished, the job's done. What's next for Darryl Westwood?'

'I think a change of scene is needed,' he said.

Eleanor couldn't be certain, but it seemed to her that he purposely didn't look her in the eye at this statement. She was right. She knew that this would be the end for them. Her throat began to tighten.

'You're leaving town?'

'Yes,' he replied. 'My ex is keen to sell the house as soon as possible, and then I'll be moving on.' He looked up at her, 'Will you come with me?'

Eleanor was stunned by the question. It took a moment before her brain caught up with the sentence and she realised what he was asking.

'May I borrow your phone?' she asked.

She knew the number; she didn't need the card. She had rung it many times over the last few months in the course of her job. Darryl reached for his phone and passed it to her curiously. She rang the number and waited for a voice at the other end.

'Hi,' she said cheerfully to the man's voice. 'I'm looking to put my house on the market.'

She turned and looked at Darryl, a smile on her face. A smile that reached her eyes. A true smile.

Thanks for reading! If you enjoyed *Neither Safe Nor Sorry* stay tuned to find out more about the next book in the series, *Never Out of Mind*

**A quaint village in England. Who would suspect the gruesome horrors that lie beneath the soil?**

Eleanor Garrett is desperate to rebuild her shattered world. Still struggling to find her way after the tragic loss of her husband and son, she's hoping renovating a four-century-old house with her new partner is a metaphor for her return to a better life. But her plans for normality descend into a nightmare when she uncovers human remains buried under the rustic building's patio...

Haunted by ghosts, both past and present, Eleanor seeks the truth. But when she pushes for clues in the tight-knit community and an arsonist targets her home, she fears the killer wants to bury some fresher bones in the pretty English garden.

Can Eleanor prevent a murderer from striking again before she's the next one pushing up daisies?

Printed in Great Britain
by Amazon